Kiss Between My Lines

I've been compared to lots of women – mostly ex-girlfriends, renowned high school sluts and the occasional overweight actress – but never to a classic erotic character. I didn't know how to take Steffen's compliment, with spice or salt or both?

'What are you thinking?' Steffen lowered his voice to ask the question, and I suddenly imagined him saying that to me in bed, as we lay together in a post-coital fog. I love a man who cares about what I'm thinking. I love it even more when he takes the trouble to ask.

'I was just thinking how much ordinary people hide. I'd never have guessed that you have an erotica collection at home. Or that the women you work with like to be tied up naked in the janitor's closet.'

'Very few people are ordinary once you get to know them,' Steffen said. 'And which one of my colleagues likes to be tied up naked in the janitor's closet? That's a bit of gossip that hasn't gotten around to me yet.'

'You should hang out in the ladies' restroom once in a while.'

'I'm not quite that much of a pervert, I'm afraid.'

'Oh, I don't know. I'd imagine you lead a fairly twisted life, when you're not sitting behind the reference desk.'

'Ah, but the life of a reference librarian isn't half as tame as you'd think. Nor is the librarian himself.'

By the same author:

Head-on Heart
Lying in Mid-Air
Possession
Taming Jeremy

Kiss Between My Lines

Anne Tourney

This edition published in 2008 by
Cheek
Thames Wharf Studios
Rainville Rd
London W6 9HA

Copyright © Anne Tourney 2008

The right of Anne Tourney to be identified as the Author of the Work has been
asserted in accordance with the Copyright, Designs and Patents Act 1988.

A catalogue record for this book is available from the British Library.

www.cheek-books.com

Typeset by Palimpsest Book Production Ltd, Grangemouth, Stirlingshire
Printed and bound in the USA

Distributed in the USA by Macmillan, 175 Fifth Avenue, New York, NY 10010,
USA

ISBN 978 0 352 34181 5

1 3 5 7 9 10 8 6 4 2

Chapter One

Dana: Disowned

Darling Deviant

I'm going to let you in.

Let's dive in deep, through all those pink caves and tunnels, straight to the juicy peach pit of my sexiest body part. Nothing's more erotic than the brain, right? You'll find all kinds of dreams and worries and factoids swimming around in there, but mostly you'll find me obsessing over love: where to find it, how to snag it, when and where to shed it.

That's how I ended up in love junkie rehab. Yes, they do have love junkie rehabilitation programs for chronically infatuated rich girls. Three months before my dad kicked me out of the penthouse, he sent me to one of those sex sanitariums in a last-ditch effort to recover my virginity. The Center for Psychosexual Awareness is housed in a rambling redwood building, nestled among gold-and-green vineyards (good thing we were all love addicts, not alcoholics). I'm not sure what possessed the founding therapists to choose this setting: how could anyone look at those sun-kissed rolling hills and *not* think about a sweet, languid, Sunday picnic fuck?

Fortunately we spent most of the three-week program locked inside the bunker, lounging around on sofas, sipping skinny lattes and mochas prepared by the CPA's on-site baristo, who happened to be as skillful at pumping his hips as he was at pumping flavor shots (hazelnut, cinnamon, frankincense, myrrh, whatever the obscenely wealthy brats wanted) into our coffee.

Not that I fucked the baristo during my incarceration; I just heard about him from a couple of my fellow inmates. I was sworn to celibacy by Dad. 'Just for three weeks,' he pleaded, holding my platinum credit cards in one hand and a pair of shears in the other. 'Twenty-one days. You can stay away from men for twenty-one days, can't you?'

Sure I could, especially since there were no men on the cloistered ground of the Center, except for the baristo, and the gardener, and the chef, and a couple of neighboring vintners, and a band of golfers who kept mysteriously losing their balls on the Center's grounds.

(No, not *those* balls. We girls were a bunch of crazy little lust-monkeys, but we weren't savage enough to castrate anyone with our fingernails, not with our French manicures at stake.)

So I kept my platinum cards, packed three weeks' worth of baggy T-shirts and shorts in neutral shades of beige and white, and set off to the Center to be saved.

I knew I was in deep trouble the first day, when the therapist who led our opening session told us that we were going to have to surrender our hyperactive libidos to a higher power.

'It doesn't matter what or who it is,' said the therapist, 'as long as it's a power greater than yourself.' A blonde with a faded Valentine of a face and a truly tragic boob job, she looked like she'd rolled around in more than one motel bed herself. She suggested Jesus. Buddha. Or if we

2

weren't religious, we could turn to the power of the universe, or to the stillness within.

'What about Kali?' I suggested. 'I can relate to her.'

I'd always loved those images of the Hindu goddess waving her octopus arms, holding one of her toned ebony thighs aloft as her foot rested on the body of Shiva, her lover-god. The therapist looked pained. The six other girls sitting around the table looked confused.

'Goddesses of sex and destruction aren't appropriate in this program,' said the therapist.

'Why not?' I asked. 'Kali is a strong female deity with a rich and complex erotic history. What's wrong with that?'

The therapist's lips squeezed into a lipsticked knot. 'You wouldn't recommend Bacchus as a higher power for an alcoholic, would you?'

I crossed my arms over my chest, pouted, and dug the heels of my Italian sandals into the floor. I'd already lowered myself about a hundred notches by saying *My name is Dana, and I'm a love and sex addict.* I wasn't going to cheapen myself any further by choosing a higher power of someone else's understanding.

'OK, then. Lingerie,' I announced. 'My higher power is lingerie. Thongs, teddies, corsets, the whole shebang. Take it or leave it.'

The other girls perked up. Maybe there was hope for all of us. Maybe we wouldn't have to totally abandon the addictions that made us the cherished, gleaming, gorgeous young animals that we were.

The therapist sighed. 'Your higher power cannot be your underwear, Dana.'

'You said it could be anything we wanted,' objected Belinda, a straw-thin blonde. 'If she can have lingerie as her higher power, I want shoes as mine.' Belinda narrowed her eyes at my Rubenesque figure. 'Where do you buy thongs in a size twenty, anyway?'

'I happen to be a size *sixteen*,' I corrected her, though her dig didn't bother me. To a neo-Barbie like Belinda, anyone who wears a size above two looks like a hippo. Besides, one of my lovers once told me a secret about chubby girls: we're way more fun than banging a bone-bag.

'Ladies, listen to me! You won't recover from your addiction unless you find something significantly large to fill your inner void.'

Katie, an ex-cheerleader with a history of romancing her way through entire football teams, exploded into giggles at the thought of filling her void with something large, and soon the whole room was rocking with hah-hahs. We couldn't stop laughing. We were all wound up like cheap watches, and this was the closest thing to an orgasm – at least the non-solitary kind – that any of us had had in twenty-four hours.

The therapist sent an email to my dad that day – or maybe it was an instant message, since she was pretty alarmed – warning him that I didn't have much hope of achieving a healthy level of psychosexual awareness, and that I should probably go home before my cynical attitude infected the young ladies who were trying to make an 'earnest effort'. My father called me that night and begged me to take my recovery seriously.

'Please, Dana. We can't go on living like this. I can't have you seducing everyone from the chauffeur to my CEO. It's just . . . killing me. I'm going to have a stroke at this rate. Can't you consider abstinence for once?'

I could picture the way his shoulders were drooping as he spoke, his gray head sinking into his hands. My greedy horny little heart expanded like a Sea-Monkey in water, and for the first time in recent memory, I felt something real and warm melting through my rib cage. But how could I promise to be the princess that he wanted? His vision of the perfect daughter, or even the not-necessarily-perfect-but-at-least-not-a-slut daughter, just isn't who I am.

'I'm sorry, Dad. But "abstinence" is someone else's gig. Not mine.'

'Dana, I never wanted to have to say this, but you're not giving me much room here. If you can't successfully complete this program, you're going to have to move out and find your own place to live.'

'Really? That's it?'

Moving out wouldn't be so bad. I could rent a trendy downtown loft and decorate it however I wanted, primarily with a never-ending chorus line of lovers in all shapes, sizes, and colors. I'd have shy younger emo guys with sharp hip bones; and distinguished fifty-something attorneys with silver-threaded hair; and surly existentialist poets; and a few lovely bisexual girlfriends to help me try out my new sex toys. Daddy would send me a check every month to cover living expenses and the occasional trip to my favorite weight loss spa in Palm Springs when 'living' included too many champagne brunches and four-star dinners. Even if he slashed one or two of my credit cards, I could still lead a hip, happy, sexy little life in the heart of the city. He'd probably confiscate my beloved cream-colored Jeep Wrangler, too, but that would be OK. I've never had sex on public transportation before.

Dad cleared his throat. 'And you'd be cut off. Financially. No more money, Dana. I'm not going to support you in a self-destructive lifestyle that's damaging to your future, and to the family's reputation.' He cleared his throat again, as if something was stuck in it. 'Besides. You're twenty-four. You should be making your own way in the world.'

I swallowed a wail. In less than a day at the Center, my pride had been stomped wafer-thin, and I wasn't going to blubber for Daddy.

'Fine. I'll stay. I'll stay and . . . I'll succeed,' I said, feeling like Barbara Stanwyck in one of those old black-and-white movies that my father used to love to watch with me, before he started compulsively marrying bimbos and spending all his free time with them. Sometimes I wonder which one of us has the real problem, me or Dad.

We ended the conversation with telephonic kisses and hugs, and I walked off to my afternoon therapy session. We reconvened in the lounge where we'd had the disastrous higher power discussion, cracked open cans of Diet Coke and bags of peanut M&M's, and dug in for another brain-picking session. This time we were supposed to talk about the fairy-tale hero we'd swooned over when our brand new eyes had just opened onto the world of males.

Three of the love junkies chose Prince Charming from *Cinderella*. Three chose the prince from *Sleeping Beauty*. But we ended up with a hung jury, because my pick was Bluebeard. I've always had a thing for older, dominant, obscenely wealthy men. I never minded the thought of playing princess to a blue-bearded sugar daddy, as long as I could have the run of the castle, and its male staff. And, like the heroine in that fairy tale, doomed by her curiosity about the castle's mysteriously locked room, I've always been way too snoopy for my own good.

So are you. That's why you're reading this, isn't it? After all, you could be lying under your own lover right now, rutting away, swapping vows of love and sharing sloppy kisses, instead of trying to sneak a peek into *my* life.

Well, I'm flattered. Not just flattered – I'm honoured. But I have to warn you, Dear Deviant, before I give you any false hopes for a feel-good ending, that I didn't end up rising to a higher plane of psychosexual awareness at the Center. I gritted my teeth through the rest of the program, went home, and resumed my place in the penthouse. Three nights later, at a cocktail party for my father's clients, I fell hard for one of his accountants, a thirty-something bean-counter with a mask of mute panic glazed across his Clark Kent face.

The moment I saw Blake, hiding on the edge of the crowd, fishing around in his martini glass for giant olives, I felt my usual symptoms come on – the palpitations, the itchy palms, the little glitch in my breathing – and all my hopes of serenity and self-control flew away like pigeons scattering at the roar of an oncoming train. His clumsiness, as he let one of the olives slide through his fingers onto the carpet, then dropped his glass in a scramble to pick it up, made me moist around the edges.

When he crouched down to dab up the spilled Beefeater with the edge of his jacket, and his cheeks turned brick red in despair as he realised he was only spreading the wetness into a wider arc, I melted all the way. I love an awkward man. I love a confident man, too, and a cocky man, and a completely incompetent man, but there's something about those shy average Joes that brings out the predator in me.

I might have had the strength to leave Blake alone, with his missing olive and the puddle of gin he'd spilled on my father's cranberry rug, if his eyes hadn't locked with mine as he was rising into an upright position. He recognised me right away as the boss's lusty oversexed daughter (God, I'd be sick of that rep, if it hadn't served me up so many yummy males), and before his features settled into a sociable smile, I saw a pilot light of electric blue lust flare behind his glasses.

I used every ounce of junk in my trunk to turn that pilot light into a bonfire as I sashayed over to the bar. I bent over at a deep angle to swipe a bottle of Beefeater and a jar of olives from the back of the forest of liquor, then I straightened, pivoted on one stiletto heel and headed straight for my target. Doing my best catwalk stroll, one fleshy thigh crossing the other with each step (if you haven't clued in by now, I'm not a skinny girl), I plowed through the crowd of faceless suits, eyes dead set on my target. I came close enough to my father's accountant to let him catch a lungful of my scent – no perfume for Dana, just a heady blend of pheromones and baby oil – then passed him by. As his head swiveled to follow me, I shot four whispered words toward his squeaky clean ear.

'Next drink's on me.'

Like most number-crunching nerds, Blake was a bit slow on the uptake when it came to blatant come-ons like mine. On my way out of the door, I glanced back to see him standing frozen in the middle of the room, staring after me with a mix of longing and skepticism, as if he thought I might be leading him into the jaws of some fraternity prank. I held up a hand, the one holding the gin, and beckoned to him. He scanned the room with terror in his eyes, probably trying to locate my father, then he took one zombie step toward paradise.

I led him down the hallway to the bedroom that my father shares with his third surgically enhanced wife, Chastity (yes, the irony of that kills me, too). While he was still six or seven paces behind me, I stepped into the room and closed the door. I made him wait for a few mortified seconds, then I opened the door again, just wide enough that he could see my lips moving through the crack.

'Give me three minutes to get ready,' I told him. 'Three, exactly. Count them on your watch.'

'Sure,' he said. I saw a sliver of his Adam's apple bobbing as he swallowed. I knew he'd take my order literally. He'd be counting seconds with the zeal of a Boy Scout until it was time to come in and claim his prize.

I switched on the lamp beside the king-sized bed, wriggled out of my panties, and stripped off my dress. I left my garter belt and stilettos on, for effect, and lay down on the satin comforter to mix my guest a martini unlike any he'd had before. Jar of olives in hand, I parted my thighs and inserted three of the little green orbs between my lips – the lips that shall never speak a word – then cracked open the Beefeater and called out for Blake to enter.

The door opened slowly. One masculine hand and the toe of a wingtipped leather shoe appeared in the doorway, then Blake peeked in.

'I hope you like your Martinis dry, Blake. I forgot to bring the vermouth.'

The accountant watched me, dumbstruck, as I dribbled gin down the slope of my belly, letting the clear liquid flood the pink crevice between my legs. I wasn't thinking about the wet spot that the liquor would leave on Chastity's blue satin; Blake and I would be generating plenty of wetness of our own as the night went on. I just wanted him to appreciate the vision in front of him: a voluptuous young nympho with a blaze of red pubic hair. From the heart of that fiery bush, between pouting pink lips, protruded a cluster of glistening green olives.

'Go ahead. I saw you gobbling these earlier,' I said. 'Now you can eat to your heart's content.'

And he did. The shy, awkward, cocktail-spilling accountant turned out to be a fiercely passionate lover. As soon as he stripped off his three-piece suit and kicked off his polished wingtips, Blake turned into a primal love machine, alternately tender and aggressive as he lapped the gin from my belly, then nipped and bit at my pussy folds before dislodging the olives with his tongue.

'Don't you want to take off your glasses?' I asked him, as his head was disappearing between my raised legs.

He looked up at me, grinning. 'No way I'm missing this,' he said. 'I want to see every inch of you.'

I couldn't argue with that. I lay back, took a swig from the gin bottle, and let him lick me inside and out. His tongue turned my giggles into deep laughter, and my laughter into moans. He moaned himself as he tasted the olives soaked in my special recipe. As soon as he'd eaten the last one, he promptly filled me with two fingers, swirling them inside my wetness as his tongue teased my clit.

'Stirred, not shaken,' I murmured. 'You already know me so well.'

I'd had a feeling, when I saw Blake, that he'd be an oral type of guy. I'd seen a soft neediness about his mouth that promised a craving to suckle, nibble, gulp, bite. That night, as I sipped my Beefeater, Blake's mouth made hungry contact with every one of my pink parts; he couldn't seem to get enough of my pussy lips, my clit, my nipples, my mouth. He was also gifted at straight-up kissing, lapping gin out of my open mouth until I groaned for breath. Maybe it was the liquor, but I don't clearly remember any of my orgasms that night. The two or three or six hours that we spent on that bed were a dazzling range of peaks and valleys; the pleasure never ended, it simply rose and fell and rose again. Blake hadn't brought a rubber (the wedding ring on his finger warned me that he'd be unarmed), so I wrapped his cock between my breasts while he plunged back and forth in the creamy crevice. He climaxed on my chin, shouting as he clung to the bed frame, banging my great-grandmother's ornate cherry headboard against the wall.

It was either the shout or the banging that brought Chastity, my dad, the staff, and most of the guests storming into the bedroom, while Blake and I were still shuddering back to reality.

I really don't want to describe the horrors that unfolded in the next moments. Picture this ugly montage: a naked girl being inadequately shielded by a naked accountant; a bottle spilling the rest of its contents on the expensive bedspread; a shrieking stepmother; a general roar of amusement and shock.

It could have been worse. I've had lovers who cried out with such orgasmic agony that they prompted calls to 911. At least there weren't any paramedics crashing this party.

The next morning I woke up in my bed, a headache the size of the Empire State Building pushing its way through my skull. I opened my sticky eyes to an ominous silence: no whirring of the coffee grinder, no technobounce from one of Chastity's workout DVDs, only the echo of unoccupied rooms met my ears. In the middle of my room, where my thick white fake fur rug used to be, sat a pyramid of boxes. Taped to the top of the pyramid was a sheet of my father's stationery, the official stuff, with his company logo on it.

I'm sorry, Dana. I never wanted to resort to such drastic measures, but I'm afraid 'drastic' is the only way to get through to you. Estella packed your things early this morning. I've had the locks changed. Chastity and

I will be spending the rest of the weekend at the cabin. Please accept our wishes, darling. We love you, but we can't have you with us if you're not willing to change. By Monday morning we expect to find you established elsewhere.

My eyes, still blurry from last night's Martinis, bugged. Elsewhere? Where was *that*?

Clearly it was my new address. As soon as I left the penthouse, I'd be homeless. Penniless. Credit cards gone, Jeep Wrangler gone. The cabin in the mountains and the house at the beach were already turning into memories. Where do you go when you have no money, no shelter and no car to sleep in? Not to the accountant's bed. Blake's wife wouldn't be thrilled about waking up to find a nympho-maniac wrapped around her hubby's body like a naked pretzel. What about a friend's place? You cut off most of your girlfriends when they started looking too much like sexual competition, and you don't want your three or four remaining shopping buddies to know that you're two steps from a homeless shelter.

That's how you end up in the only place in the city where a girl with no money and no reliable way to groom herself can find halfway decent architecture, a clean water supply, an unlimited supply of toilet paper, free internet access, and wholesome entertainment.

Yes, Darling Deviant, your suddenly homeless love junkie crammed her favorite clothes and shoes and lacy bras and panties into a duffel bag, packed a hair dryer, a bag of cosmetics, and her favorite vibrator, stole a few boxes of her stepmother's Lunar bars, and became an undocumented resident of the public library.

Chapter Two

Jordi: Disconnected

The chick with the stringy black hair and the stripper sashay approaches the scruffy guy wearing an orange road-crew vest. Jordi half hopes they'll fall into each other's arms. What a doomed love connection that would be! In the middle of the sidewalk, with midday traffic rushing by, they join hands, but instead of leaning close for a kiss, they execute the classic clasp-pump-release of a professional handshake. Then they pivot in opposite directions and stride off to separate destinations.

Jordi watches the black-haired girl's skinny hips swing in her faded jeans. A pair of cheap black sunglasses hides her face, except for an angry puff of a mouth. Fire-engine red panties peek through the shredded pocket over her left butt cheek. She wears the kind of clothes that Jordi, with her adamantly pear-shaped hips, can never hope to fit into, and she moves with the feline confidence of a woman who's used to committing daylight crimes.

Watching, Jordi feels that clutch in her belly that she always gets when she's found an especially attractive specimen. The city is filled with spectacular specimens, swift and shiny, darting in a thousand different directions. The human network is too big and dazzling for Jordi's brain to hold. That's where her splendid, sexy, ultraloaded laptop comes in.

Jordi's eyes follow the black-haired girl down the street. She doesn't want to stalk the girl through actual physical space – Jordi's too comfy, sitting on the patio of Café Wifi with her cappuccino and her computer – but she can follow the sexy little skank online. With a few swift moves of her fingers, Jordi captures data on urban drug use in the city, conviction rates among women in their 20s, relapse statistics among female addicts. She'll compile all of her data into a picture-perfect portrait of the girl with the enviable body, who's already disappeared into a life far more dangerous than Jordi's.

Data is connection. Connection is power. Power is sexy. Feeling about as sexy as she ever does, Jordi whips open her computer and waits for its melodic mating call to tell her that it's time to merge with an unlimited supply of information. Taking a sip of her cappuccino, she leans back and waits for the rush.

Silence. The oval silver eye remains blank. Jordi taps the tiny ON button with the fingernail of her pinkie, making sure the machine knows who's boss. The laptop does nothing.

Jordi pushes her glasses up on the bridge of her nose. The plastic squeaks against her damp skin. She rubs the back of her hand across her lips; her hand comes away streaked with cinnamon foam. Her heart's hammering, but Jordi's not worried about a little tachycardia. She has already predicted the trajectory of her life, using statistics from an insurance database metacrawler. She won't die of cardiac arrest at the age of 25; with her family history, she's far more likely to die of breast cancer at the age of 84.

Right now she's only worried about her laptop's lifespan. Laptops don't live forever, and the computer is several years old. She fidgets with the keyboard, checks the power card. Her machine remains serenely unresponsive. A whimper wells up in the back of her throat. She looks around at the other patrons of Café Wifi, half of whom are happily bonding with their notebooks. *Help me!* she wants to cry, shattering their peaceful absorption. *Can't you see I'm not connected?*

'LIRA, lovely LIRA, please let me in,' Jordi chants under her breath.

Life sparkles on all around her. Schools of specimens swim around Jordi's table, girls she could be, women she would love to be, boys she wants, boys she will never have. Jordi clasps her hands over her keyboard and prays for reconnection.

'Mind if I sit here? There are no more empty tables.'

The chair next to Jordi has been occupied by a male entity holding a plate of almond biscotti and a cup of espresso. She drops back into meat-mind, examines him through the leftover haze of her anxiety. His head is cloaked in a gray hoodie. His eyes are olive green behind glasses with square black frames. He scowls like a monk with a grudge.

'My connection's dead,' Jordi's voice is a thread tied to a rising balloon of panic. 'I'm brainburger.'

'Brainburger?'

'Yeah. You know.' Jordi waves her hand impatiently. 'It's what happens when you get unexpectedly disconnected; your mind turns to meat.'

'Wow. That's intense. Doesn't sound healthy, somehow.'

She doesn't know how to explain to him that a disconnected brain is just a mass of unilluminated cells, energised by nothing but glucose.

'Here, let me take a look,' he says. 'I'm pretty good with computers.'

The monk cracks his knuckles. Jordi circles her machine with a protective forearm.

'This one's special,' she says.

'I can see that. And I'd really like to take a look. Trust me?'

'OK. But only because I'm desperate. She's never died on me before.'

Jordi turns the computer so that its impassive eye is facing the stranger. Jamming one of the biscotti into his mouth like a cigar, he shoves his sleeves above his elbows. A wrinkle forms between his eyes when he sees LIRA's screen. He squints at the pearly casing over the oval monitor, runs his fingers across the barely raised array of symbols on the flat keyboard.

'Never seen a laptop like this before. What is it? Some new release?'

'LIRA's mine. I built her. She's the only one of her kind.'

'LIRA. That's what you call her, huh?'

'Yeah. It's an acronym. L-I-R-A. She's the machine, the application, all of it. She's my baby.'

'What does LIRA stand for?'

Jordi gives the stranger a sideways glance. He doesn't look like the type of guy who would steal other people's brainchildren. When was the last time a guy, much less a cute one, looked at Jordi so intently? That look is bringing her dangerously to melting point; she could break down and give up all her secrets. She'd made a pact with her co-developers that they wouldn't give away the meaning of LIRA until the program was ready for its official release.

'Um, LIRA means Life in Real Application,' Jordi improvises.

'Wow. She's freaking wild.'

Panic and pride flutter in Jordi's chest as she watches his hands caress the computer.

'Sorry,' he shrugs. 'You're not only offline, you're stone-cold dead.' He pushes the plate of biscotti towards her. 'Have one of these. You look like you need some sustenance.'

Jordi shakes her head. Her hands are tingling. She presses them to her face. Her cheeks feel like ice. Dead. Yes, that's how it feels to lose that electronic artery to the universe of data that joins one person to another. Without LIRA, Jordi is not a secret agent, a spy, a visitor from another dimension, or even a run-of-the-mill infogeek. She's just a human girl with a piece of machinery that's become about as useful as the broken toaster on her kitchen counter.

'I don't know what I'm going to do,' she says.

'Do you use that thing for work?'

Jodi's hackles rise. She snaps LIRA shut, as if to hide the computer's nudity. 'This thing,' she says, '*is* my work. I am an interpersonal network architect. I'm designing a program that will allow people to connect in ways they've never imagined, to touch each other more intimately than they've ever thought possible.'

'Really? Like how?' He leans forward, forearms propped on the table. 'You make it sound hot.'

If he only knew. Now that LIRA is stubbornly refusing to Throb, or even to Thread, Jordi wishes more than anything that she could demonstrate her to this biscotti-eating, hoodie-wearing interloper. Besides Jordi, no one's ever experienced what it's like to fall into LIRA's iridescent world, to meet up with some other soul, to suddenly, unexpectedly, find yourself Throbbing, and to wonder how you ever settled for anything less than that kind of connection.

'She is,' Jordi agrees. 'She's extremely hot.'

For the first time Jordi notices a birthmark, the color of semi-sweet chocolate, above the right-hand corner of the interloper's upper lip. When he smiles, the mole rises like a punctuation mark, riding his mouth upward. Why can't she stop staring at it? And why is an evil little voice in the back of her brain daring her to touch it?

Jordi presses her lips shut and reaches for her notebook, placing a hand protectively on her smooth surface. LIRA is her top-secret project, the application she's been sweating over since college. While her dormmates were burning brain cells at keg parties and hooking up with frat boys like carefree rabbits, Jordi was drinking liter after liter of Mountain Dew and hammering out code, struggling to create the kind of connection that she really longed for. She's so close now, right on the edge of creating the perfect way to touch others without actually having to touch them. Four years of working in secrecy, and here she is about to hand over her baby to the first attractive male who's spoken more than five words to her since she can remember.

'Hey, we're in the same business, then. Only I deconstruct information systems, whenever I get a chance.'

'Who do you work for?'

He points to a large, multilevel building down the street. The building is a surreal structure, dreamed up by some architect whose imagination surpassed the city's budget. Streams of specimens, holding heavy bags and stacks of books, flow in and out of ogival doors embedded between blue pillars. A golden tower rises skyward over the whole structure.

'The library?'

'I'm on my break right now. I usually read, unless I see something more interesting.'

Jordi glances at the other tables, then back at the guy in

the hoodie. It takes her a few moments to realise that the 'something interesting' is her. She hides her pink face behind her wide white cup – it's empty, so she's stuck sucking out the last of the foam. Sexy move. So very sophisticated.

'So you're a librarian,' she says, coming up for air once her cup has been drained to the dregs.

'Nah. I dropped out of library school when I realised that the degree was going to interfere with my mission. I work as a shelver now. That gives me the opportunity to implement my own cataloging system. I'm sort of an anarchist.'

'Huh.'

Jordi squints at him. She can't tell if his grin is a form of flirting, or if he's just making fun of her. Jordi isn't what 99.9 percent of the male population would consider coffee shop pick-up material. She doesn't wear the right jeans; her round freckled cheeks make her look perpetually prepubescent; and her springy red hair always seems to be on the verge of flying off to a more elegant life on another woman's head.

'Come check it out sometime. I'll show you my secret system. This is going to blow Dewey and the Library of Congress out of the water. When I'm done here, I'm going to move on to some other town, some other library. All across the country.'

The scowling monk, when he's not scowling, has a smile that sets off a small cyclone in Jordi's heart. Lust? Maybe. Unless it's just too much cappuccino on an empty stomach.

If we kissed, our glasses would knock together, Jordi thinks, feeling herself flush from neck to forehead.

'My name's Nolan, by the way. Here, have the rest of these cookie things. I have to get back to work.'

Jordi stares down at the pale cylinders of baked Italian dough. Then she looks up at Nolan, who's standing over her. He's tall, he's angular, and his hip bones have all but poked holes through his faded jeans. In other words, he's way too cute to have dropped out of reality into Jordi's world.

'This is where you tell me *your* name,' he prompts.

'Uh . . . it's Jordi. That's short for something else.'

'Really? What?'

'I don't like to tell people my full name. I'm just Jordi.'

'Jordi. Nice. Different. Hey, why don't you stop by the library this afternoon? Free public internet access. The computers are dinosaurs, but at least you could check your email.'

He's right. Jordi's pulse thrums out a promising little drumbeat. She hasn't been inside a library since she graduated from college, but, all of a sudden, that building holds the promise of the fix she can't live without. She can already feel the juices coursing through her brain cells, her neural networks expanding like freshly watered flowers.

LIRA, the silent titanium traitor, is as functionless as a piece of modern art lying on the table. Jordi slips the notebook into her canvas bag and slings the bag over her shoulder.

'I'll follow you,' she says, trotting after Nolan. He's already weaving through the tables with his long legs, and Jordi has to rush to keep up. 'What does an information anarchist do, anyway?'

'I like to withhold the details until I've taken full advantage of the suspense,' he says. He tosses her another grin over his shoulder. 'I'm Machiavellian that way.'

In college Jordi would spend days at a time in the university library, but that was mostly because it offered her asylum from her roommates and the endless soap opera of their lives. At the university library she could hide with her laptop at one of the battered desks deep in the stacks, tapping out her code in blissful silence among the books that no one ever opened. In all her years at the university, no one ever bothered Jordi in her secret nook.

Except once. That one incident changed the course of Jordi's senior project, then it changed the course of her life.

Jordi was sitting at her favorite desk that night, the old-fashioned desk-chair combo with the sculpture of dried chewing gum under the right-hand corner and the plea 'Eat me . . . PLEASE!!' gouged in the surface by a clearly desperate hand. It was about nine p.m. on a Friday, three hours before closing time. Even though she couldn't imagine anything worse than going home to her apartment on a Friday night, Jordi was about to call it quits. She'd been banging her head over her senior project for weeks, but no amount of self-inflicted injury would knock her out of her uninspired lethargy. Four months before graduation, Jordi was suddenly convinced that she'd chosen the wrong major. She didn't want to be a computer programmer. She didn't want to specialise in information systems. She damn sure didn't want to design yet another metasearch engine to clutter up the cybersphere with one more way to organise data.

Jordi sighed and shoved the laptop away. Cheap piece of crap – it wasn't the machine she'd wanted, just the best she could afford. Her whole life seemed to be like that, Jordi thought, easing into self-pity like a warm bubble bath. Always settling for the next best thing, she never seemed to be able to get her hands on what she truly wanted.

'I don't even know what I really want,' Jordi grumbled to herself. 'Oh, shit!'

Brooding, she'd been resting her elbow on the space bar of her laptop. The last lines of code she'd written had been erased by a stream of blank spaces. Jordi made a strangled sound, something between a scream and a sob. She tore open her backpack and fumbled around inside until her fingers made contact with a bumpy oblong shape. One more Snickers bar – the last thing her rapidly expanding hips needed. But, with every line of code, every new idea, costing her a bucket of brain cells, Jordi had to have some way to replenish her energy.

Jordi munched away with angry gusto. She was chewing so loudly that she almost didn't hear the murmured voices on the other side of the bookshelf.

'It's OK. No one's here. Tell me everything.' It was a masculine voice, mellow and deep and somehow vaguely familiar.

'I can't believe it. I was such an *idiot*!' A female voice, higher pitched, with an edge of distress; it made Jordi think of a high-strung blonde (Katie? Carrie? No, *Kelly*) who sat beside Jordi in her Statistics class. The blonde was always twirling her hair around her pencil and staring at her split ends when she wasn't trying to copy Jordi's notes. 'I just feel so . . . stupid. I can't believe I let a jerk like Geoff ruin my life. He stole my bike, my grades are in the toilet and, to make things even more hellish, he's fucking my room-mate.'

'It's OK. Everything's going to be fine. We'll file a report with the campus police about the bike. As far as your grades go, don't worry about Stats. I've got you covered.'

'What about my roommate?' Sniffle. 'Every time I see that bitch, I don't know whether to kill her or have a nervous breakdown. I know Geoff is a creep, but I can't stand the thought of him screwing that skank-ho.'

'Listen, Kelly. After what I'm going to do to you tonight, you'll never think about Geoff again.'

Jordi's jaw froze, a wad of chocolate and peanuts stuck between her teeth. She half-rose in her chair, peeking through the space above a row of books. Sitting in this same spot, Jordi had often stared at those cracked spines and wondered idly why so many books had been written about the geographical history of Scandinavia. Tonight, the scene on the other side of the shelf knocked all thoughts of Scandinavia from her mind.

Kelly, the blonde from her Statistics class, was perched on the desk between the adjacent bookshelves. That desk was an identical twin to Jordi's, but Jordi never sat there because the right leg wobbled. The desk was teetering dangerously right now as Jake, the teaching assistant who led the tutorial for Jordi's Statistics section, rocked Kelly back and forth in his arms, petting her hair. He kissed the shiny golden crown of her head, murmuring to her soothingly, while Kelly whined as if she'd dropped her Popsicle in the dirt.

Was that all it took? Jordi seethed. You just had to act pathetic and helpless, and guys like Jake would go down on you in the library?

Because that's exactly what was happening. Jake sank to his knees, pushed Kelly's green suede skirt above her thighs with the reverence of a pilgrim approaching Lourdes, and parted her pointed knees. Kelly's pinched teary face turned soft and dreamy as Jake's hands went to work under her rucked-up skirt. His fingers were hidden by Kelly's skinny legs, but judging by the way her eyelids fluttered, and her thigh muscles began to quiver, the Stats instructor was doing something that had nothing to do with standard deviations.

Jordi took off her glasses and wiped the lenses on her blouse, then jammed the glasses back onto the bridge of her nose. Nope – book dust wasn't responsible for the scene unfolding before Jordi's eyes. She glanced at her backpack, wondering whether she should take out her cellphone and grab a few pictures. Visual evidence of a sex-for-grades scam would inject some juice into the listless university newspaper. Unethical behaviour was unfolding before Jordi's eyes, and justice demanded that she record it.

Voyeuristic lust, on the other hand, demanded that she shut up and watch. Kelly was getting to her feet now, wobbling as she leaned on Jake's square shoulders for balance. Of all the women who had enrolled in Stats this semester, maybe a third of them were taking the class to fulfill an academic requirement. The rest of the girls, and a few of the guys, too, had signed up just to have an excuse to drool over Jake Bennigan, a grad student in Finance. With his angular jaw, blue bedroom eyes under shaggy dark-blond hair, and sheepishly sensual smile, he could pass for a lost junior cousin of the Baldwin clan.

So why was he eating out Kelly, Jordi thought, when he could have his pick of any of the women in his section? Kelly had an endless supply of skirts and dresses, from pricey boutiques that you couldn't enter without looking like a famine victim, but, as far as Jordi could tell, her wardrobe and her blonde hair were her strongest points. Her face reminded Jordi of an anxious rabbit – her eyes were always pinkish around the edges, and her mouth twitched constantly – and her chest and ass were flapjack flat. What on earth did Jake see in her?

The mysteries of sexual chemistry fascinated Jordi.

Sometimes the connections between lovers seemed so obvious; other times, it would take a crystal ball to decipher those secret connections. Statistically, what were the chances of a hot smart guy like Jake choosing a dim-witted chick who looked like a blonde Olive Oyl? Probably slim to none, yet Jake couldn't keep his hands or mouth off her body.

Still on his knees, he unzipped Kelly's skirt and let the lined garment whisk down her thighs. With excruciating delicacy, he pulled down her lace panties (Hurry up! Jordi wanted to shout, let's see if Kelly shaves!) then lifted his face to kiss the light, furry space between her thighs. Kelly didn't even seem to mind that the green suede was lying on the tile with all the dust bunnies and dead bugs. Why should she care, when she was riding Jake Bennigan's mouth?

Her fingers clutching Jake's hair, Kelly rolled her hips, grinding her mound against her instructor's mouth. Kelly had rhythm – Jordi had to give her that. Jordi could practically hear the cheesy disco beat of a porno soundtrack as Kelly rocked away, Jake eagerly keeping time with his lips. The sound of Jake's tongue lapping Kelly's juices, and the moans that his tongue was inspiring, were making Jordi more than a little wet herself. She realised that she'd been wiggling in her chair, in time to Kelly's movements, and that the friction of the inseam of her jeans was doing a passable imitation of Jake's tongue.

With her foot tucked under her bottom, the heel of Jordi's sneaker had been nudging into the cleft of her crotch. Now that she was aware of it, Jordi worked that stimulation for all it was worth. Jordi couldn't remember the last time she'd had an orgasm. She had a vibrator, buried somewhere in her sock drawer, but she was too embarrassed to use it in front of her roommates and, anyway, she always seemed to be too stressed out or depressed these days to masturbate. But Jordi's flesh hadn't forgotten how much fun it was to rub and knead and grind those moist parts. Warmth spread, honey smooth, through Jordi's pussy as she watched Kelly throw her head back and buck against Jake's chin.

Before she knew what hit her, Jordi felt an orgasm rippling through her lower body, spreading upward to flood her chest, throat and face with heat. Clamping her hand over her mouth, Jordi barely managed to swallow the yowl of surprise that rose in her throat. Not that it would have mattered, with the animal cries that Kelly was making as she reached her own climax. When the last wave had shuddered through her body, Kelly collapsed slowly to the floor. Jake followed her, and the two of them disappeared from Jordi's sight. Still panting, Jordi heard the muffled sounds of more clothing being peeled off, followed by masculine groans, and the bump-and-grind of classic male-superior fucking.

Jordi sat back in her desk, catching her breath. She closed her eyes and listened to the growling sounds Jake made as he came; he was more subtle than Kelly, either out of decorum or just out of practice. Maybe he brought all his worried, distraught, failing female students here, for tutoring and counseling in the stacks.

Jordi stifled an evil snicker, thinking about how Jake had been using the dustiest, grimiest part of the library as his secret love nest. But she stopped laughing when she heard what he said after all the moaning and gasping, bumping and groaning, had died away.

'The first time you cried over standard deviations, I fell in love with you,' Jake said. 'I've been crazy about you ever since. God, I can't believe how lucky I am.'

Jordi froze. Love? When had love sneaked into this sordid little scene? She could tell that Jake was sincere. Men didn't speak in that hoarse thick voice, as if they were swallowing a mouthful of half-chewed Tootsie Rolls, if their confessions weren't genuine. His dorky reverence in front of Kelly's pussy, the glow of adoration in his eyes, his hungry devouring of her flesh, weren't part of his regular shtick, apparently.

He loved her, wanted her, and in the heat of those two states of being, an alchemy of desire had created something amazing.

How did two people connect that way? Jordi wondered. Was it just chance that brought them together, with a few shared hobbies and attractive body parts thrown in to seal the deal? Or could that sweet merging, that closeness she coveted more than anything in the world, be engineered somehow, so that everyone could experience it, even geeky introverts who couldn't separate themselves from their computers long enough to tolerate a date with another human being, much less bond for life?

That's how LIRA was born. To this day Jordi still doesn't understand exactly how LIRA came into being, but she has a vague comprehension of the recipe. Take one tediously boring senior project, one frustrated and lonely computer science major, two obliviously hungry lovers, and an emotional equation so complex and vast that all the information in the world couldn't solve it, and you got LIRA.

Sort of.

Mostly, LIRA is a mystery: part labor, part dumb luck, part divine inspiration. She's too incredible to share with the world, yet too incredible *not* to share. Once her senior project, The Most Tediously Predictable Search Engine Ever, turned into LIRA, Jordi took her underground, with only a few select computer scientists to help her develop her brainbaby. Nolan is the first person besides Jordi and her co-developers who's ever laid eyes on LIRA – and, at her debut performance, LIRA happened to be playing dead.

Walking into the library with her defunct laptop, Jordi feels like an alien stepping off a spaceship into the holding area of a new planet. She expected a silent sanctum, but the building is hopping, and it's about as quiet as an aviary at a zoo. A large central room opens upward to a series of balconies, where stacks of books are arranged in seemingly endless rows. Men and women in business suits, teenagers armed with backpacks, moms with flocks of tiny kids – apparently everyone in the city needs a book or a magazine, except Jordi, who doesn't do print on paper anymore. Nolan bobs and weaves through the lunchtime crowd. Jordi trots along after him and tries not to look up. Gazing into that vertical corridor of books makes her stomach drop, as if she were staring up into an elevator shaft.

'Where are we going?' she asks the back of Nolan's head, as he steps onto an escalator.

'Upstairs. That's where the public access computers are. That's what you're looking for, right?'

'Right. That's what I need,' Jordi nods.

Nolan leans back against the rail of the escalator, which seems to be taking forever to ascend, and looks down at Jordi. 'Need. That's a scary choice of words.'

'Why?' Jordi's mouth feels dry. Her pulse points are tiny hammers, trying to pound their way out of her skin. 'Doesn't everybody need to be connected these days?'

'Sure. But not everybody sweats when they haven't had access to a computer in thirty minutes.'

Nolan's grin seems diabolical. As the escalator continues

its crawl upward, past the array of books and desks manned by readers with laptops (does everyone on earth have access at this moment but Jordi, she wonders?), the information anarchist is starting to look more and more like Satan, himself. Jordi scratches at the collar of her shirt. Her skin itches all over. Maybe this is all part of a plot to destroy LIRA, or at least to undermine Jordi's sanity. Nolan could be the minion of a software giant, out to steal Jordi's creation. When Jordi doesn't have LIRA at her fingertips, she always tries to keep her password-protected, locked, and hidden from her roommate. Was she careless this morning when she went into the shower? Did she leave her baby exposed to the machinations of an evil genius?

Jordi should have known, back at Café Wifi, that Nolan had a secret agenda. Hot guys like Nolan didn't randomly approach Jordi at coffee houses. His show of technological incompetence was a clever charade; he's probably got advanced degrees in Math and Computer Science, and an extensive record for criminal hacking. In all his precocious travels through the labyrinths of computer code, Nolan's never seen anything like LIRA. Who *wouldn't* want a program that allowed instant connection, at the level of body and soul?

Now he's leading Jordi to some hidden inner chamber deep in the library, where she'll be stripped naked and forced to give up all her secrets . . .

'Are you OK?'

'Huh?' Jordi blinks. Images of forced nude confessions swirl in her mind, making colorful streaks in the stew of her paranoia.

'You look like you're going to pass out.'

'I'm fine.'

'You sure?'

'Totally.'

Nolan peers down into her face. As they reach the top of the escalator (finally!), he takes hold of her arm and guides her onto solid ground. Only a few yards away lies a bank of public access terminals. In front of each computer, perched on a high stool, is a happily connected human being.

'How do I get online?' Jordi asks.

Nolan points to a line of people, standing at a desk with a banner over it that blares, CHECK IN HERE. 'Check in there,' he says, with a hint of pride, as if he were handing Jordi the keys to a kingdom instead of herding her toward another bureaucratic obstacle.

'Doesn't anyone in the city have their *own* computer?' Jordi asks. 'I'm going to be here forever!'

A couple of patrons turn in response to her shrill question. Nolan rubs the small of her back, in a gesture so sudden and blissfully delicious that her skin tingles.

'It's OK, Jordi. Really. You're going to be fine. Everyone only gets forty-five minutes. You'll be here ten or fifteen, at most, before you get on. Go get in the line. I have to get back to work. Chaos waits for no one.'

He gives Jordi a slight push, and she stumbles forward. She gives him one last alarmed glance. 'Where can I find you, if I need you?'

Nolan gives her that grin again, melting any remnants of paranoid hostility in Jordi's heart. He spreads his arms wide. 'I'm always here. Just look around.'

'What if I can't get to the library?'

He reaches into the kangaroo pouch of his gray hoodie and fishes out a few cards. One is an ace of hearts, from a playing deck. Another has a silhouette of a naked woman and bears the jagged logo of a club called Misteek. The third he hands to Jordi. The cardstock is flimsy, and the text looks like it was printed from a home computer. There's a phone number, an email address, and the words:

Nolan Nelson
Information Anarchist
Dedicated to Correcting the Mis-Organization
of the World

'If you ever feel like you need to be reorganized, and you can't find me here, feel free to call,' Nolan says, with a bow that's only partly ironic. 'By the way, I also play in a band. You should come out and hear us; we're at Misteek tonight, if you want to stop by.'

'What's the band called? Just so I don't, um, show up for the wrong one.'

Nolan grins. 'Don't worry, you couldn't miss us. We're called Wreckage.' He stresses the last syllable of 'wreckage,' pronouncing it 'ahhge', as if it were French.

Baffled, Jordi stares down at the card. A cute guy's business card. An invitation to hear a band. The unexpected death of her precious LIRA. It's too much for an antisocial girl-geek to handle in one day.

Nolan lopes off to report for duty, to whatever unwitting supervisor oversees his secret mission. Jordi, feeling abandoned to a world of public bureaucracy, straggles toward the check-in desk, where she takes her place behind a man with stooped shoulders and a brave comb-over. Another line, another long wait to have some ephemeral desire fulfilled. And the end result will be nothing like she waited for, nothing close to what she wanted.

Across the room, at the corner of the bank of public terminals – 'terminal', what a dismally appropriate term for a machine linked to a chain gang on a network devoid of inspiration – a woman about Jordi's age is rising from her stool. Even with her glasses, Jordi can't see well at a distance. All she sees of the girl is an alluring blur of curves and shiny hair, a pretty smear that represents a face, but, in that moment of visual contact, Jordi feels a throb of connection, a buzz of conspiracy.

The woman has no idea who Jordi is, but she's smiling. Beckoning.

Why wait? I know what you need.

I know what you need. I know what you need. Sweeter words have never been broadcast to Jordi's brain. Somehow that stranger must have recognised the hunger in Jordi's face, noted the tremor in her hands. It's just so hard to be a singular, solitary entity, waiting around in a line of other isolates, when every cell in your being longs to be linked, connected, networked, *joined*.

Jordi looks around. The man in front of her is still shuffling obediently toward his online fix, while the two teens who've taken their place behind her are absorbed in a giggly inspection of a text message on one of the girl's Blackberries. No one seems to notice, or care, when Jordi darts out of line, following the hallucinatory summons of a woman who so clearly sensed Jordi's desire, and steals a seat in front of the only open computer in the room.

Chapter Three

Dana: Princess of Smorgasmia

Dearest Deviant,

Since when do they have beefy bald security guards
stationed at the doors of the public library? When did the
city decided that it needed to staff a desk with a brute who
would check you out with elevator eyes as you enter the
hallowed halls of public information? The bald Wrestle-
mania wannabe wearing the steel-blue uniform looked
like he wanted to strip-search me as I walked through the
door of my temporary home – not because of the bounce
in my hips, or the swing of my hair, but because I was
loaded down like a cat burglar heading out of town on a
camping trip.

Over my right shoulder hung the duffel bag that carried
every possession I'd been able to take, borrow or steal from
the penthouse, including an old sleeping bag from my
slumber party days. Over my left hung a garment bag filled
with three evening gowns that I couldn't bear to part with,
and a leather tote holding the matching shoes. The gowns
rustled nervously under the plastic, the silk and tulle
peeking from under the hem of the bag as if they were
trying to crawl out and flee to their cozy walk-in closet
back home.

'Where you headed, Cinderella? This is a library, not a

ANNE TOURNEY

ballroom,' the Wrestlemaniac said. His lip curled in a half-smile, half-sneer that said, damn, I'm clever. An allusion like 'Cinderella' must have been a real stretch for him.

I gave him a look that could have frozen the warts off his chunky fingers. 'I am komming from zee hohstel,' I announced, in my best Smorgasmian accent. I didn't really need to lie to the brute; I just preferred the fantasy of being a footloose exchange student to the reality of being a disowned nymphomaniac.

Things certainly had changed since I was a little girl. That's the last time I visited a public institution of any kind, other than the Department of Motor Vehicles. One of my au pairs, a dreamy bohemian refugee from Eastern Europe, used to take me to the public library every day, where she would pass several sweet hours holding hands under the table with a male grad student who pretended to be tutoring her in English, while I spied on them from behind a copy of *The Lonely Doll*.

Years later, I realised that my au pair must have been doing something a lot more interesting than holding hands under the table with her sexy tutor (even then, I could identify sexiness in a man, even when it took the more subtle forms of a wicked smile, or a pair of perfectly sculpted hands). I remember the way her waxy face would flush with pink, the way her tight mouth would blossom into a rose, the way her eyes would take on the sheen of glazed blue china as he manipulated her body under the table in the study room. They always planted me just outside the closed study cubicle, where my au pair could keep an eye on me. All the lewd things he did to her unfolded in silence before my eyes, like a pantomime behind the glass window of that closed door.

At the age of seven, I couldn't have told you what a

'voyeur' was, but I knew I didn't want to be one. I still don't like to watch. I like to get naked, jump right in and *wallow* in pleasure. Lips, hands, thighs, ass, pussy, hair, feet – I want to use them all. I want to feel a thousand textures against my skin while I'm making love; I want to taste, smell, see, hear, and touch the other body (bodies, if I'm lucky enough to have a plural) that I'm with. If I can't make a connection with my flesh, I'd rather just grab a smutty novel, a bag of candy bars, and my vibrator and take to my bed.

Damn. I knew I'd forgotten something. Though I'd packed a reliable vibrator, my very favorite sex toy, the vibrator with the whirring head that twirls in four directions at six exquisite speeds lay in my dresser drawer back home.

Not home. Not anymore. I felt a catch in my throat as I corrected myself on this point. There was no shelter for me, no security, no reliable source of income, in my father's penthouse. Everything I carried was my home now. I stood in the middle of the library's vast anteroom, suddenly feeling infinitesimally small, and welcomed myself to my new temporary residence.

It didn't take me long to note that I wasn't the only human snail hauling a portable world on its back. Call me self-absorbed, but as soon as I stepped into the library as a homeless woman, I began to see transients everywhere. There was the lady with the funny silver hat (was that a construction worker's helmet, or a colander on top of her head?) carrying three loaded shopping bags in each hand, and the furry guy with the Army coat and a duffel bag that rivaled the size of mine. In an isolated corner behind the Large Print books in the fiction section, I came across a man dozing on a sofa, and when I went to Ladies' Room to freshen up, I met a sister vagrant blow-drying her hair under the hand drier.

Reassuring? Not quite.

Standing in front of the sink, I studied my puffy unpainted face. The traces of last night's sex-and-gin binge still showed in the bags under my eyes, the droop of my mouth. I wondered if I looked pathetic enough to win back my father's heart, then remembered that he was in the mountains with Chastity, nursing his wounded paternal pride with warm brandy. By now, the locksmith would have come to change the locks on the apartment. I'd never get back in, not unless I was willing to slaughter my pride and crawl back to him, defeated.

Darling Deviant, your heroine doesn't crawl. Except during especially twisted role-playing scenarios, involving rhinestone collars and chocolate-chip cookies shaped like dog biscuits.

'Hey. Got a hairbrush I could borrow?' asked the woman with her head under the hand drier. 'Even one of those little plastic combs would do.'

'Sorry. I left my purse on the plane,' I lied. 'I just flew in from Paris, stopping in on my way to Milan. I'm a fashion editor. Always on the go.'

'Yeah.' The woman eyed the load of stuff that I'd dropped on the floor. 'And you had to drop in to take a pee at the library.'

'Overdue books,' I said with a sniff.

'Whatever.'

She combed her hair, which actually looked better than my own snarled mop, with her fingers, and left me alone in the bathroom. It was the first time since I'd left the penthouse that I'd had a moment to myself. Privacy, I was quickly learning, was a luxury when you were living on the streets. That epiphany made me feel hardened, gritty. I didn't want to feel that way. I wanted to feel pretty and silky, pampered and soft.

In the bowels of my duffel bag, I somehow found my cosmetic kit. Holding that bulky red satin bag, with its freight of expensive creams and lotions, sticks and paints and powders, grounded me in my personal reality again. I wasn't a disowned denizen of the public library; I was a beautiful young girl with a brilliant future ahead of her.

Or at least a brilliant face. Applying the familiar foundation, powder, eye shadow, mascara, and blush – and of course, my favorite PussyPink lipstick – I became a privileged beauty again, a girl with the world at her fingertips. I ran a brush through my hair, spent a few extra minutes primping, then marched out of the restroom to survey my new home.

Reality hit me, in the form of a stampede of squealing schoolgirls, as soon as I stepped out of the door. I had to flatten myself against the wall to keep from being trampled, as a frazzled woman cried imploringly for them to enter three at a time. Apparently the girls didn't speak English, and they didn't respond to cutting glares like the one I gave them.

'I'm so sorry,' said their chaperone. 'They're out of control. Field trip, you know.'

Her face was a husk, topped by a ring of yellow frizz. I felt that usual pang of pity that I usually get for women who have to work full-time to support themselves, before I remembered that not only was I one of those women now, but I didn't even have a job to speak of. I gave her a shaky smile, then edged my way out of the corridor and back into the lobby.

Feeling like every orphan, scullery maid and disinherited princess who's ever starred in a fairy tale or Disney movie,

I stood in the middle of the stream of library patrons, all of whom looked happily housed and employed, and tried not to cry. What the hell was I thinking when I decided this would be a good place to shack up for a few days? I surveyed all the display shelves of newly released books, their covers as shiny and colorful as fresh candy, and realized that I couldn't remember the last time I'd read anything that wasn't printed on the back of a box, bag, or bottle.

It wasn't always that way. When I was a little girl, overweight and sulky and non-verbal, I used to hole up in my room and lose myself in novels for hours. Nancy Drew, Laura Ingalls Wilder, and Katie John were my best friends. Later, as I sprouted new breasts and pimples, I enhanced my reading list with Jackie Collins and Judith Krantz, masturbating behind a locked door to sex scenes that were achingly hot. Once I slimmed down and learned how to talk to people without staring at my shoes, I discovered a much more exciting form of escapism; I began to pursue anything with two legs and a penis, and the legs were optional. Suddenly it was looking like I'd made the wrong choice. I should have stuck with Nancy, Laura, and Katie.

'Can I help you find something?'

I perked up at the sound of a mature male voice, deep and self-assured. When I saw who the voice belonged to, I was glad I'd put on make-up. He was tall, lean but not skinny, with fox-colored hair shot with gray and keen slate blue eyes. Those eyes didn't jibe with his hard narrow nose, or his economical lips. He looked like the type of guy who would block out an entire day for laundry so that he could sort, count, and match his clothes, before hanging them in his closet in a color-coordinated spectrum. Definitely too OCD for my usual tastes – I'm kind of a slob myself, and I find that most anal retentives have too many hang-ups about cunnilingus – but at the moment, any male presence was welcome.

I wanted to shout, 'Help me! I'm a highly sensual tactile female stranded in a world of print on paper!', and throw myself against his broad chest. Two things stopped me: one, I remembered that if I was going to shack up at the library, I'd have to stay undercover; and two, I was afraid that if I creased his blue Oxford shirt, he'd spank me.

'Um, I'm looking for a book,' I mumbled.

He smiled. The smile softened those thin efficient lips into something much more promising. I could swear I caught a flash of tongue crossing his even white teeth, and I wondered if those cunnilingual hang-ups really applied here.

'You've come to the right place. Anything in particular?'

I waved my hand in what I hoped was a regal gesture. 'No. Just browsing.'

'Browse away, then. The library is all yours,' he said, so gallantly that I almost went ahead and creased his Oxford shirt, anyway. 'Let me know if you need any help refining your search. You can find me at the reference desk up on the second floor. My name's Steffen.'

I watched him stroll away, his hands stuffed in his pockets. He walked like someone with a purpose, an inner compass. I could imagine him sitting behind a reference desk, holding court over a flock of people with questions on every imaginable topic. I could see him answering their queries with a calm, and very sexy, confidence.

I love a confident man. My radar honed in on Steffen's lean disappearing form. I tried to think of a fantasy about us, but my imagination wouldn't pump any juice. Juiceless – what a queasy, strange state! Feeling so dry made me want to break down and weep.

Then, in the middle of that crowd of strangers with real lives and real jobs, your homeless love junkie had an epiphany. The reason I felt so ungrounded wasn't just because I was carrying all my belongings on my back, but because I wasn't in love. And I couldn't even imagine myself being in love, or being loved, in the state I was in: my money gone, the penthouse gone. Knocked out of my orbit, I floated in dark cold space, a rogue planet with a duffel bag and bad hair.

I hiked my bag onto one shoulder, the garment bag on the other. Together, the bags were as heavy as fallen bodies. Stooping like a defeated soldier carrying his dead comrades, I marched toward the escalator. I had no idea where I was going, or what I was looking for: a vending machine; a novel to read; a dream to glue back together. I only knew that I needed to move, crawl, stagger, whatever, in some direction.

On the second floor, before the rows of books, sat a bank of computers. People sat on high stools in front of the monitors, their faces colored by a rainbow of expressions. Some looked curious. Others were clearly bored. A few were so enthralled by whatever they were staring at on the flickering screen that their faces sat slack in their hands. A couple of them looked like they were in danger of drooling on their keyboards. I'd never seen a group of human beings so deeply involved in worlds that were private, but not. They were making connections, capturing currents. Whatever they were finding – knowledge or titillation or love – I wanted a few handfuls of it for myself.

Buoyed on a little wave of hope, I hurried over to a vacant station. I was just about to hoist my bottom onto the stool, when I was shoved away by a six-foot Amazon wearing black leather wrist gauntlets, multiple nose rings, and a T-shirt that said *Eat the Rich – But Screw Them First*.

'I'm not rich anymore,' I babbled, withering in her flame-thrower glare.

'No. But you're butting in line. Go stand over there.'

She lifted a burly arm, one black-taloned finger pointing to a line that seemed eternal, under a banner that read CHECK IN HERE.

'OK,' I said, in a voice so tiny that I could barely hear myself.

I followed the trajectory that the Amazon's finger had set for me. The old Dana, who existed as recently as yesterday, never tolerated lines. Lines were for the under-privileged and the tired. Lines were created for people like me, so that everyone else would have to wait for the goodies that I would choose from first.

Today I took my place behind the others, and I waited. I tried to make eye contact with the serene silver-haired lady perched behind the desk – she could be my fairy godmother, poised to rescue the princess in disguise – but she didn't seem to see me. Neither did the heavyset man standing in front of me, or the bored blonde standing behind. I was one of them. I *was* them. Why should they look at me?

'Excuse me. How long have you been waiting?'

I tapped the heavyset man's back. He was so big, it felt like knocking on a wall. I love a big man. I love a man whose mass makes me feel small and dainty by compari-son, so that when he peels off my clothes with his enormous hands, I feel like a doll being undressed.

He turned to look at me. His eyes were the color of raw oysters, and just about as expressive; they didn't even register a flicker of desire when he saw my heart-shaped peach of a face.

'Forever,' he said, in a dirgelike tone. 'Once you get assigned to a computer, you could wait up to an hour for the other person to get off.'

'Waiting for other people to get off has never been my strong suit,' I quipped. 'I pride myself on timely satisfaction.'

To my horror, I found myself batting my eyes, shifting into fourth-gear Flirt Mode before I was even aware of it. I didn't even want anything from the guy, except maybe his place in line. Or a candy bar. My stomach was starting to rumble, and my head, already foggy from last night's overindulgence, felt like it could easily float away from my body.

What was I waiting for, anyway? I didn't even know. Whatever those other computer users had – ethereal, intangible – I wanted it too. Something to feed me. Something to distract me. Something to get those damn juices flowing, because I hadn't felt so parched in as long as I could remember.

My hungover belly was ordering me to ditch the line and head off on a quest for refined carbs, but I was too stubborn to give up my place in the wait for Purgatory. I felt my eyes glaze over, my shoulders slump, as I searched my memory for things besides food, sex, and love that had comforted me in the past. An image of myself, so old that I had to mentally blow the dust off it, rose to my consciousness. When I was thirteen years old, at the height of my lonely homeliness, absolutely certain that I'd die a virgin, I used to keep a journal. It was a little hardbound book, bound in pink satin and filled with wide-ruled paper, that my aunt had given me for my birthday.

My Aunt Cynthia undoubtedly thought I'd fill it with winsome poems about fairy-tale princes and purple unicorns. I scalded those pristine pages with sex fantasies that would have blistered her poor eyeballs. I scribbled out all my desires, and then some – I wrote like the possessed, horny, teenage fiend that I was. I wrote till my fingers cramped, and I still kept writing. Those fantasies, mine and yet so *not* mine, kept me sane in a whirlwind of adolescent chaos.

Miraculously, as if that memory had cracked open the gates of time, I found myself standing in front of the silver-haired librarian. My fairy godmother watched me expectantly.

'Go ahead, dear,' she urged. 'Sign your name and the time you're checking in.'

She tapped a golden fountain pen on the last blank line of a long form. I didn't know how long I'd been standing there, but she must have thought I looked like a zombie. Not a princess, just another spaced-out digit in the human equation, dazed by waiting for the object of her desire.

'I'm going to start a journal, to record my downfall,' I announced.

As if she were blessing my enterprise, my fairy godmother beamed.

'That's wonderful, dear. Now would you go and wait over there? You're holding up the line.'

She pointed to a row of chairs, then handed me a slip of paper with the number of a computer station on it. For the second time that day, I was being told to wait, but this time it didn't send me into a pit of despair. Clutching that scrap of paper, I floated over to a row of chairs to wait with the other hungry lonely people.

I felt ten times better after I'd written down my story of misery and injustice. My bags even felt lighter when I got up from the computer, my time having expired. Feeling strong enough to explore my new territory, I took up my duffel and dresses and set off in search of food and a place to sleep. *I could do this.* I wasn't just the pampered daughter of a Fortune 500 daddy; I was a survivor. After all, I'd made it through eight years of private schools with the most vicious evil girls produced by humanity. I'd survived two stepmothers with ridiculous names and a whole bevy of perky 'fiancées' sharing the penthouse with me. I'd had nannies and babysitters who tried to squash my spirits, and lovers who attempted to crush my ego after I broke up with them, and therapists who'd tried to cure me of my cravings, but I was still the same seductive sex fiend that I'd always been.

Which reminded me that I hadn't had an orgasm yet today. I added 'masturbation' to my mental to-do list, right after eating and finding a safe place to stash my stuff.

Passing the reference desk, I looked across the room and saw Steffen. Just as I'd imagined, he was surrounded by a small crowd of people waiting for him to answer their questions. Another librarian sat beside him. She scowled at a computer monitor, fingers flying over the keyboard, barely glancing at the girl standing in front of her. Steffen, on the other hand, sat with his hands folded on the desk. He watched the patrons with full attention, his mouth set in a smile that promised patience, that promised answers.

I love a patient man. I love a patient mature man, who takes his time learning the landscape of my desires before he shoves a wriggly tongue in my mouth, or tries to paw my breasts. I've had enough of those to know that slow passion burns a lot brighter in the end, than spontaneous combustion. I imagined that Steffen would be the slow-burn kind of lover. He'd cook me fine but simple meals; he'd feed me by hand at his table. He'd play Bach and Haydn for me, or Nina Simone, maybe Al Green. He'd hand me a glass of port to sip while I relaxed on the battered leather couch in a room lined with books. He'd bring me one of those books to leaf through, something profound and mystical but sensually suggestive, like Rumi. He'd watch me while I read.

Then, when I was loosened by poetry and wine, my mind and belly comfortably filled, he'd discover me. He'd pet my hair with those long hands before he'd even come close to my mouth. He'd nuzzle my neck, brush his nose against my cheeks, let me feel the slightly coarse texture of his fox-colored hair against my skin . . . all this before we even kissed.

Damn. Now I really needed to have an orgasm.

But first I needed to find a place where I could dump my portable world for a while. The duffel's strap was carving a ditch in my shoulder, and the bag of rustling gowns was starting to seem like sheer nonsense. The second floor of the library was a bustling human hive; it wouldn't take long for some snoop to find and plunder my stuff. I took the escalator upstairs to check out the third floor.

Literature, religion, philosophy. History, social studies, health sciences. Level Three was much quieter than Two. People sat reading silently, suspended in the classic hush that I remembered from childhood. I couldn't recall the last time I'd read a book with any meat, or contemplated anything more metaphysical than the precise color of a lover's eyes.

I ducked into the philosophy aisle, my bags still in tow. After I'd satisfied my hungry humming flesh, maybe I'd spend some time trying to beef up my mind. I'd start with the Greeks, read Socrates and Plato, then work my way through the history of human thought. I'd become so wise and learned that I'd attract a whole new class of men – quietly handsome philosophers, who would marvel at the scope of my intellect as they tasted the richness of my flesh.

I pulled a book off the shelf at random and glanced down at the cover.

Princess Daisy by Judith Krantz lay sizzling in my hands. The well-worn paperback burned my palms, like shrapnel from my adolescence. I'd read that novel, and masturbated to its sex scenes, more times than I could count in those lonely early teenage years, before Real Boys would have anything to do with me.

I glanced up and down the aisle. I saw no one, only the back of a book shelver wearing a gray hoodie. The thought of asking him if he'd like to take a break and watch me pleasure myself flitted across my mind, but before I could get his attention, he pushed his cart of books around the corner and disappeared. I hadn't even considered what he'd think, being propositioned by a girl who looked like a style-conscious hobo.

Less than 24 hours ago, I was urban royalty. I looked the part, like Disney's version of a princess, the kind you see simpering on little girls' birthday cards. I never had a problem making men fall in love with me; what hetero-sexual male doesn't want his own princess?

Fuck that, I thought. All birthday card princesses were identically perfect, identically insipid. I was creating a new princess, one with ragged fingernails and messy hair, one who washes in public restrooms and lusts after librarians. I was the princess, and the library was my castle. I wasn't condemned to live out my father's curse of poverty and bad hair; I could write my own fairy tale! I'd be the disinherited Princess of Smorgasmia, the mythical country I'd invented as a little girl. A chubby kid with a perpetual sweet tooth, I'd fantasised about a land of spectacular gluttony, where landscapes and interiors were crafted from delicious food, and everything the hands or lips touched was made of glistening candy. When my first addiction, to food, was later replaced by other appetites, the word 'Smorgasmia' took on a whole different meaning (nudge, nudge, wink, wink). But, for today, that vision of fictional joy glittered with its original innocence.

Armed with my paperback, a pocketful of candy bars, and my vibrator, I set off in search of a secluded nook where I could lose myself for half an hour or so in a smorgasbord of solitary delights.

I've always had a soft (and wet) spot for the girl/girl seductions in *Princess Daisy*. I found a comfy purple chair in an out-of-the-way corner on the third floor, curled up and turned straight to the passages I'd read a thousand times. *Princess Daisy* had been my intro to lesbian erotica. After reading it for the first time, I'd loaned the book to a girlfriend, and she'd been equally inspired. We muddled our way through some mutual fondling, nipple-biting, and licking, but the divine spark was never there for either of us. Still, when it came to masturbation, *Princess Daisy* and my vibrator were a foolproof pair.

So I whiled away the time in a contented haze of soft porn and chocolate, until I got so turned on by the moans and steamy clinches of Krantz's characters that I couldn't turn one more page. I pulled my trusty battery-operated boyfriend out of the pocket of my sweatshirt, flicked the switch, and let the device buzz its way down the waistband of my jeans. I loosened my fly just enough to let my little friend do his work. So trustworthy, so loyal, the vibrator never let me down. It didn't ask me to earn my orgasms by crawling on all fours and barking like a dog, or by kissing any hairy sweating places. It didn't beg me to have three-somes with the sleazy bottle-blonde waitress who served up its pancakes at the local greasy spoon.

My vibrator simply made me come.

And come, and come. I'd learned long ago how to give myself multiple orgasms with the wand, by teasing my outer lips, then the inner ones, then gradually working my way to my pussy's sweet gooey center before finally rewarding my clit with a climax all its own. I'd watched the whole delicious process take place, holding a mirror between my spread thighs. Nuzzled by the vibrator's nose, my labia majora would turn plump and pouty, darkening under the fine layer of copper fur.

I'd have my first orgasm before I'd even parted those petals, then I'd have a second one as soon as I'd pried open the wet mouth underneath. I'd penetrate myself with the buzzing tip, just a little at first, then with long lavish strokes. Orgasms three, four, and sometimes five, would follow, harder and more wrenching than the first two. As a grand finale, I'd draw the wand up the length of my vulva while I was still shuddering from Number five, then tease a shattering shower of pleasure from my clitoris before collapsing into a drenched, gasping heap as Number seven followed hard on Number six's heels.

Of course, those were my penthouse days, when all my problems could be defined as 'luxury lifestyle challenges'. Here at the public library, I couldn't even count on a few minutes of privacy for my much-needed masturbation session. Sure, it was a city building, but how could they deprive me of my favorite anxiety reliever? Homelessness was stressful. No one could argue with that.

Besides, it's not officially public masturbation if you have all your clothes on, right?

I snuggled back in the chair, threw one leg over the other and tilted my bottom so that I could insert the wand at a more pleasing angle. Though I hadn't touched my nipples, I could feel them getting painfully hard. I reached under my sweatshirt, glancing around first, and tweaked one of the buds through my bra. At the same time, my vibrator hit a nerve-rich spot just south of my clit and I moaned. I wasn't trying for sound effects; the sound just burst out of my mouth. It stopped me for a second. I flicked off the vibrator with my thumbnail and froze.

Someone was standing behind one of the bookshelves. I couldn't see him, but I could feel him. I knew without a doubt that my audience of one was a male. The sixth sense that alerts me whenever any man within a ten-foot radius has a hard-on was going off like a car alarm.

My body, always a traitor to my conscience, was responding. I knew I should have stopped. I knew I could be caught. But, as you've probably figured out by now, Dear Deviant, I love to put on a show. Instead of furtively pulling the vibrator out of my pants, I dug in deeper; instead of pretending that my moan had been a yawn, I upped the volume on the erotic sounds I was making.

Now I was sure that the watcher was male. It wasn't just the masculine energy radiating from behind the shelves; I could see his body now, as he leaned in for a clearer view. He hid his face cleverly between books, but I saw his broad shoulders, leading down to slender hips. I had no clue who he was. It could have been any guy off the streets, browsing for books, or one of the employees. It could be the reference librarian who'd caught my attention earlier. Whoever it was, I focused my attention on him and let myself go wild, letting the vibrator have its way with my lower lips as I pulled and pinched my nipples. I even lifted up my sweat-shirt so he could see the dusky rose points protruding from the lace of my bra. I wriggled and moaned; I mewled like a porn star.

When the tingly prelude to orgasm came over me, I stared straight at the point where his eyes were. If there was any doubt in the perv's mind that I didn't know he was watching, I wiped it out just before I came.

'Come get me,' I beckoned. 'You know you want to.'

When I came, the pleasure was for me, but the perform-ance was all for him. I turned my desire inside out and let it shine straight at a stranger. Shame couldn't touch us; public sex was an act of outrageous beauty. In the end, I was just a naughty little girl who craved attention, and we both knew it.

With all the noise I made, all the squirming and sighing, it's a miracle I wasn't caught by anyone else. Afterward, I curled up in my chair and closed my eyes for a little post-orgasmic nap. When I opened them, the Watchful Stranger was gone.

Later that afternoon, when the lights dimmed in the library and a solemn voice announced that the building was closing, I sat alone in that same purple chair and wished there were someone else to watch over me. Anyone would do. The Princess of Smorgasmia was never very good at being alone.

Chapter Four

Jordi: How 'Deep' Deep Is

The world looks different through the hungry, hyperfocused gaze of a voyeur. Riding home on the bus, holding LIRA against her chest like a sick infant, Jordi steals glances at the other passengers and wonders if they've ever committed a crime like hers.

It wasn't a crime, Jordi argues with herself. The girl left her blog open on the computer. She's obviously an exhibitionist; she was *inviting* someone to plunder her secrets.

Fair enough, Jordi's angelic side counters, but did she 'invite' you to hack into the account and steal her password, so you could log in again and read the rest of her deviant misadventures?

None of the other passengers appears to be chewing over the same ethical conflicts as Jordi. A man in a rumpled business suit sighs as he circles ads in a folded newspaper with a ballpoint pen. A girl with complicated Medusa braids idly narrates a boyfriend drama over her cellphone. Two elderly women wearing matching polyester pantsuits murmur to each other in a foreign language, and Jordi, watching the movements of their faces, realises that they are identical twins.

Growing up, Jordi had an ongoing fantasy about having a twin sister. As an only child, she never had to do battle with siblings over her possessions, or claw her way to the forefront of her parents' attention. She never felt like she missed out on the ordinary sister stuff; what she craved was a girl who looked exactly like herself, a double, someone so similar at cell level that she'd have to reflect Jordi at soul level, too.

Except the twin, as Jordi imagined her, would be more exciting. She'd be a figure of mystery and glamor, sexy and popular. Everyone at school would worship this fascinating girl and Jordi, by default, would bask in her light. After transferring from Westside to Eastside High School at the age of 15, Jordi even lied to her class that she *did* have a twin sister named Gillian, who had enrolled at the rival school across town. Gillian was a troublemaker, always getting detention for making snarky jokes in class, or for getting caught smoking behind the gym or for making out with boys in the boiler room. She looked exactly like Jordi, only she was charmingly trashy, alarmingly cute. She had a huge hoard of make-up, shoplifted from the local drug store, that she tarted herself up with in the school bathroom. She owned a closetful of slutty clothes that made their mother weep with frustration and shame.

The other kids bought into the fantasy at first, until Jordi's stories got so wild that a suspicious classmate decided to conduct a little research and discovered that there wasn't any 'Gillian' at that rival school. Never had been and most likely never would be – at least not a Gillian who lived up to the fantasy.

After the rock was lifted on her nest of lies, Jordi found herself eating her lunches and walking home from school alone. Girls didn't flock around her in the shower room after gym class to hear her give secondhand advice from her twin sister on bra-stuffing or blow job techniques.

Boys didn't sidle up to her at her locker to find out if her sister ever dated Eastside guys. Jordi without a twin was worse than Jordi alone; subtract Gillian from the equation, and you had a bookish chunky girl whose social appeal vanished along with her extravagant twin.

The girl who wrote the blog, Dana – how Jordi envies the sexy streamlined elegance of that name – wouldn't need to invent an alternate life. She had intrigue, romance, love in spades; even the story of her downfall and dis-inheritance was passionately dramatic. Disinherited because of her addiction to love and sex: what could be more romantic? Like a fairy-tale princess, reduced to rags and health-food bars, Dana had been cast out into the cruel landscape of reality. How would she get by, with her evening gowns and her duffel bag and her vibrator? Would she find her true self, somewhere in the stacks of books?

Would she find love?

Jordi glances at her watch. Six o'clock. She'd stayed until the library closed, reading and re-reading Dana's blog, then she'd printed out the pages so she could take them home and pore over Dana's words, sipping every drop of vicarious juice. Her new craving is almost – *almost* – enough to make her forget about LIRA, until the bus pulls up at Jordi's stop. As Jordi stands, LIRA's sleek casing slides down her knees, and the laptop almost falls. The shock of almost dropping her precious device brings her loss back to life and, with a thud, Jordi remembers what she is without LIRA.

Disconnected meat.

She hurries off the bus. Her feet quickly cover the half-block to the apartment she shares with an old college roommate, Samantha. Clutching LIRA to her chest, hoping her accelerating heartbeat could knock some life back into the machine, Jordi pounds up the stairs. Up until today,

LIRA had been so reliable that Jordi had never considered the obvious. Maybe the problem wasn't with LIRA, but with the signal at Café Wifi, that pretentious little fly-by-night coffee joint. As soon as LIRA was safely back in the embrace of a reliable wireless network, she'd work again, and Jordi would be Threading, Throbbing, and humming again.

Out of breath, Jordi bursts through the unlocked door of her apartment. She doesn't even notice the male body sprawling across the couch, until she trips on a pair of long, idly crossed, legs.

'Whoa, there.' A large hand, steady and warm, catches Jordi's arm in mid-flight. The hand keeps LIRA from flying out of Jordi's arms and Jordi herself from sprawling on the floor, but it can't stop her from tumbling face down into his lap. A weird noise, something between a squeal and a grunt, comes from her mouth. For a second or two, she can't breathe, and it's not just because she's had the wind knocked out of her. The lap feels good. *Very* good. Two thighs, like twin wooden columns covered with denim, lead up to a warm bulky hollow that Jordi recognises, with some shock, as a male crotch.

I am lying on a man's penis, Jordi announces to herself. Maybe it's not exactly where it's supposed to be, and maybe there are too many layers of cloth involved for it to count, but I am on top of a male sex organ.

'You know, if I were a spanking kind of guy,' muses a male voice, 'I'd be looking at paradise right now. Would you think I was crazy if I told you that you have a sexy bum?'

'No, but I'd think you were horribly rude,' Jordi snaps. Shielding herself with her computer, she pushes herself off the stranger's lap before he can explore 'paradise' any further. 'What are you doing on my couch?'

Jordi glares. The stranger looks wildly amused. Her face

is hot enough to fry an egg on; no wonder he's grinning like a Cheshire cat on crack. Reddish-brown hair flops over hooded hazel eyes and a nose as straight as a Grecian statue's. His lips, when he finally stops grinning, are so fleshy and sensual that they're almost obscene.

'I'm waiting for Samantha,' he says. He stretches his arm along the couch, his fingertips alighting close to Jordi's shoulder. His eyelids droop lazily over his green-brown eyes as he takes in Jordi's curvy figure. 'But now I wonder why.'

And her family wonders why Jordi gave up on the dating scene at such a tender age. She rolls her eyes, then narrows them.

'Samantha didn't give you a key, did she?'

'Well, as a matter of fact . . .'

With a certain lazy satisfaction, as if he'd been collecting women's keys for years, the intruder pulls a key identical to Jordi's own out of the front pocket of his jeans. Jordi sighs.

If she hadn't had such a weird crappy day, she might yank the key out of the guy's hand and send him back out into the night. But, really, she's too much of a mouse to be pushing men out of her apartment. Especially when they look – and, from what Jordi remembers, feel – so good.

What would Dana do, if she were sitting here beside a man who looks like an extra from a Gerard Butler epic? Not cringe against a sofa cushion, clinging to a laptop computer with white-knuckled ferocity. Dana would already have her hungry fingers all over that button-down fly, her lips parting as she sank down, a greedy swan, to taste the fruit she found there.

'How long have you two been sleeping together? A week? A couple of days?'

The words don't come out in the sultry siren's voice that spoke to Jordi from the computer monitor that afternoon; they come out in a crabby skeptical whine that she associates with someone much older and more jaded.

'A few weeks,' Samantha's lover says.

'Where did you meet her?'

'What are you, her parole officer?' he chuckles.

'Hardly. I just like to know who has keys to my apartment.'

'Fair enough. We met at the Smoothie Spot, where Sam works. I asked for a wheatgrass protein shake. She made my order. We looked into each other's eyes, and we fell for each other.'

Jordi can't hold back a skeptical snort. 'Just like that, huh? She gazed at you across a field of wheatgrass, and you both went *boom*.'

'You don't believe in love at first sight?' he asks, holding his palm to his chest as if her cynicism were an arrow to his heart.

I'd be a lot more likely to believe in love if you weren't panting down the neckline of my shirt right now, Jordi thinks. Somehow he's managed to inch his body so close to her that she can smell the detergent he used on his clothes. Covering that amount of distance without being perceived is an amazing feat, considering the length and size of his frame. His broad chest rises and falls, a bit faster now. Jordi's nostrils twitch. She's never been aware of how much she loves the scent of clean clothing on a man; the guy smells like he just stepped out of a Laundromat.

'I don't even know what your name is!' Jordi blurts, backing deeper into her corner of the sofa. 'It's Dave, isn't it? All of Samantha's boyfriends are named Dave. Or Steve. Or Jack.'

He smiles, tilting his head in a way that Jordi, in spite of herself, finds charming. 'No, I'm not a Dave, a Steve or a Jack. I'm a Kurt.' He squints at her. 'And you're Jordi. You don't remember me, do you?'

Jordi shakes her head. Kurt lifts one of the red curls that lies along her shoulder and toys with it, winding the ringlet around his index finger, then letting it spring back into place. She can't stop staring at his mouth – those juicy, almost petulant lips. Meat, for all its limitations, can be so delicious.

'Junior year of college. Advanced Calculus. You were the star of the class. I was barely passing.'

'I still don't remember,' Jordi says, almost in a whisper. All she remembers from Advanced Calculus is a vast green chalkboard, and a brilliant Pakistani professor scrawling equations across it with fanatic speed.

'I sat behind you on the right for the first three weeks. Then I dropped out,' Kurt prompts. 'I can't believe you never felt me breathing down your neck; I hung over your shoulder during every quiz.'

'Always sit behind the smart girl. If you can't figure out which one is the smart girl, find the chunky girl with glasses,' Jordi says, quoting every hairy-assed, beer-guzzling oaf she'd collided with during her college Math and Computer Science courses.

'Well, yeah. I knew you were the brainiest chick in the room. But I also just wanted to sit behind you.'

Jordi shakes her head. 'Why?'

'Because your hair smelled like fresh bananas, when they're just turning yellow all over. And you had these little birthmarks running down your right arm that looked like the Big Dipper.'

'The Big Dipper?' Jordi echoes dumbly. She doesn't

remember Kurt at all. Suddenly she wishes that she did. Memory . . . you could paint with it, tempt with it, seduce with it, the way Kurt is doing now. It was part of the way people connected and, more importantly, part of the way they fell in love. She had forgotten to write any capacity for remembered experience into LIRA. As soon as the machine is working again, she'll have sensual memory in her code.

'I might have been an idiot at Calculus, but I knew a few things about astronomy. I used to think about taking my pen and connecting the freckles, then seeing where else they'd go. You might say I was stargazing. See? There they are.'

Kurt's fingertip grazes Jordi's Big Dipper as he describes it. Her skin prickles in the wake of his touch. His eyes are bolder than his hand, following the soft inner curve of her upper arm up to her collar bone, across the clavicle, then sliding down the valley between her breasts.

Stargazing. Yeah, right.

Jordi scrutinises Kurt's way-too-handsome face. Somewhere behind those angelic hazel eyes, those sweetly pouting lips, there must be a joke waiting to burst out. Even as he leans in to bring those lips unbearably close to hers, Jordi sees the flashing lights of a warning sign over Kurt's head. DANGER: TREACHEROUS FLESH AHEAD. The body has its own agenda, urgent and mysterious, which Jordi has never been able to figure out. Much easier to follow the illuminated trails of the brain's network as it seeks those Threads and Throbs where one being intertwines with another.

Kurt's body is so close to Jordi now that his weight is pressing her laptop into her breasts. His weight, his bone and muscle, the sheer material *stuff* of him makes Jordi dizzy. She takes deep breaths to fill her panicked lungs, squirms in the cushions to find space. Kurt takes her gasping and wriggling as signs of passion and looms in, lips first. As that overripe, faintly moist mouth comes closer, closer, Jordi's heart rate skyrockets. With her pinned arms, she makes one last attempt to lift LIRA in front of her face, but she's too slow.

He kisses her.

So this is a kiss. It's been so long since Jordi actually kissed anyone that she's all but forgotten this collision of bodies, an accident of mismatched matter, an exchange of cells and matter that somehow feels divinely *good*. It's not that Jordi's never been kissed before; she's just never been kissed with such artful hunger by lips that are full and soft and resilient, all at the same time. Most men, she realises through the pink haze that's overwhelming her, have no idea what to do with their own mouths, much less how to use them to turn a woman's entire body into an electromagnetic field.

'You have the softest skin,' Kurt says.

'It's just skin,' Jordi protests.

'No. Never just skin, velvet girl, silk girl,' Kurt whispers into Jordi's mouth, as if he were feeding her with words. He's eased her down the sofa cushions so that she's halfway on her back, his chest directly over hers, one long thigh draped across her plump hip. There's nothing between Jordi and this stranger now but a thin electronic device and some assorted clothing.

'Here, let's get rid of this,' Kurt murmurs. He tries to tug LIRA away from Jordi's chest, but her forearms are a fiercely clasped X over the machine's pearly-smooth casing.

'No! I can't let go of her.'

'Why? Is it some kind of medical device?'

Jordi shakes her head.

'Then what's the problem? I don't get you.'

Kurt's eyebrows knit over his eyes. The sexy lips droop into a sullen pouch of disgruntled flesh. *I don't 'get' you.* Of course he doesn't. If they were Threading right now, through LIRA's serene circuitry, they could be experiencing a union of thought and feeling, even of sensation, that they'll never touch together here, tonight, on this old sofa. Under her back, Jordi feels a broken spring in the sofa's depths poking her ribcage. Crumbs from the pillows stud her back, where her shirt has ridden up around her waist. These are the kinds of nasty dull details that you can escape forever with LIRA. You don't have to smell the sour tang of beer on your lover's breath as he kisses you, or accidentally brush against the ugly patch of bristly hair on the small of his back when you put your arms around him.

Experience, through LIRA, is flawless. Bumpless. Sweat-free and stainless.

'Just take my word for it,' Jordi sighs. 'Either I hang on to my computer, or this doesn't go any further.'

'Well, OK.' Kurt shrugs. 'But can I at least get a little closer to that gorgeous skin?'

'As long as I don't have to let go of my laptop,' Jordi says stubbornly.

Permission granted, Kurt makes quick work of Jordi's clothes. His hands slide under Jordi's T-shirt, reaching behind to work the clasp of her bra. Suddenly she's so acutely aware of the texture of his hands that she can feel every groove, every ridge and soft plane in his palms and finger pads.

The skin isn't just a coat of cellular material, she remembers from some old physiology class. It's an organ, the largest in the body, receiving and transmitting sensations, processing and excreting the substances that flow in and out of our bodies through a world that's not always gentle or kind. At the moment, Jordi's skin has forgotten its practical functions and has turned into a sensual minefield. As Kurt's fingers tease, test, probe, explore her material self, she feels a hundred new responses from places she never knew held so much promise.

'What if we push this down just a few inches?' Kurt suggests in a husky whisper, tugging at LIRA again, 'so I can see what you've got on under that shirt?'

Half dissolved now, Jordi makes a non-committal moan. She'd forgotten how everything solid turns liquid in a high state of arousal; none of her nerves seem to be functioning the way they usually do. The light slap of cool air against her skin tells her that Kurt has pulled away her shield and removed her bra; her exposed breasts tumble out, peaked with nipples that rise like pink antennae to meet his lips.

A light buzzing static fills Jordi's ears. She closes her eyes and tries to bring herself back to the lovely things Kurt's mouth is doing to her, but the noise won't go away. The back of her throat tickles and her head feels helium-light. She's gazing down at the curly crown of Kurt's head as if he were exploring the topography of an alien planet, not her own all-too-familiar curves and valleys and rolls. Her stomach takes a sharp plunge, all the way to her feet and, though she's lying down, with Kurt's beefcake bulk pinning her firmly to the sofa, Jordi's overwhelmed by the panicky certainty that she's going to fall. The beige carpet below her, with its panoramic array of crumbs and stains, seems a million miles away. Her stomach does a mighty flip-flop.

'Let me go!'

'What's wrong? Are you sick?' Kurt asks, his arms tightening around Jordi as the willing body underneath him suddenly turns into a bucking, wriggling wild thing.

'Not sick,' Jordi mumbles. She finally breaks free, and stumbles through the fog to the bathroom. 'Disconnected. We're disconnected.'

'Huh?'

Jordi closes the bathroom door on Kurt's bewildered face. Her shaky hands find the doorknob and press the lock. Whatever's going to happen in the next few minutes is going to demand privacy.

Kurt knocks on the door. 'Jordi? Is it something I did? My breath or something?'

'I don't know. I think it's an allergy.'

'Can I get you anything?'

'No,' Jordi replies weakly.

She sinks down onto the tiles, kneeling among the hairballs and cast-away underpants, then presses her head against the closed toilet lid and closes her eyes. For a second back there in the living room, she'd been sure she was going to throw up. As one breath follows the other, the roiling sensations in her belly settle to a mild burble. Her head sinks slowly back into place. Gravity resumes its role in keeping her pinned to the earth.

This isn't the first withdrawal episode that Jordi's ever experienced, but it's definitely the most dramatic. Then again, she's never gone for so many consecutive hours without being connected.

Faint voices fill the rooms outside. Jordi recognises Samantha's melodious chatter, Kurt's masculine purr as he greets the girl he came to see in the first place. When silence replaces the voices, Jordi doesn't have to leave her post beside the porcelain goddess to know that Kurt has scooped Samantha into his arms, and that his mouth is already occupied with her roommate's flesh. Jordi still tastes the ghost of Kurt's lips on her own; he tasted musky, tangy, slightly sour.

LIRA doesn't allow its supplicants to feel, or smell, or taste each other – not yet. Jordi's working on that part, but she hasn't figured out how to trip the senses through the code she's written. Sometimes she wonders if anyone would notice if she left out the messy issue of sexual chemistry altogether. Who needs smelling and tasting when you can Throb and Thread? The only reason people are still drawn to the kind of anonymous face mashing that she and Kurt were doing on the sofa is that they haven't experienced the luminous intersection of lightpoints that LIRA, before she crumped, could offer.

'It's worth it,' Jordi mutters to herself, as another wave of nausea hits her. 'I'll work out this withdrawal glitch.'

And maybe it's not even withdrawal that's left Jordi feeling like she's been hit with a mild case of salmonella. Maybe it's the sushi she had for lunch. Or Kurt's sour beer breath. One of LIRA's best features is that by avoiding the skin collisions of everyday interaction, she eliminates the hazards of body odor.

'Jordi? You OK in there?'

'Fine!' Jordi calls back.

'Could I come in for a second? Kurt's taking me out, but I need to check my hair first.'

Samantha taps on the bathroom door. Jordi sighs. She should have known that she couldn't keep this refuge for long; her roommate can't be separated from a mirror for more than 45 minutes at a time. We all have our addictions.

Jordi lifts herself to a standing position and opens the door. Samantha slips in, graceful as a blonde cat, and rushes to her reflection as if she hasn't seen herself in months. Jordi scowls at her own pale face as Samantha anxiously fluffs her cap of feathery hair.

'I'm not sure if I like this new haircut,' Samantha frets. 'It's so much shorter than before. Do you think it makes me look like one of those choirboys at church?'

'When's the last time *you* were at church?' Jordi asks.

Samantha's lips rise into a Mona Lisa smile. 'Good point. That reminds me, I think I'm out of condoms. You wouldn't happen to have an extra two or three, would you?'

Jordi shakes her head. 'I don't do meat sex. You know that.'

Samantha frowns. 'How do you have sex without meeting?'

'We've talked about this a hundred times, Sam,' Jordi says with a sigh. 'I connect with people through LIRA.'

'Oh, right. Your *computer*,' Samantha sniffs.

People like Samantha, obsessed with hair and teeth and skin and the shallow connections that those tissues allow, are always dismissing LIRA as a piece of equipment. That's only because they experience the world as an endless array of solid objects, things they can touch or see or consume. The idea of a soul-level networking system boggles their brains.

One of these days, when LIRA is finally complete, Jordi's genius will blow them all away.

'LIRA isn't just a computer,' Jordi says. 'She's anything but just a computer.'

'Well, apparently she can't keep you from being in a bitchy mood all the time. You're not getting any *real* action. Why don't you let me fix you up sometime? There's this guy at work who fixes the computers ... he asked me out, but he's not my type. I could see the two of you hanging out. You have tons in common.'

'Let me guess. He's an introverted geek whose idea of

working out is lifting Pop-Tarts out of the toaster,' Jordi suggests.

'How did you know?'

'Oh, forget it. The answer to your question is, no, I don't have any condoms. Maybe Kurt does. He seems like he's ready for anything.'

Anything with just about anyone, Jordi adds mentally. She estimates that the amount of time that passed between her nausea attack on the couch and Samantha's return to Kurt's loving arms was less than five minutes. Now he's out in the living room, waiting to sweep Samantha off to a club where they'll twist and gyrate and pant into each other's ears all night, before staggering back to the apartment and making 'love' in a semi-conscious stupor on the sofa.

'Isn't he hot? I can't believe how lucky I was to hook up with him. He's sexy, he's sweet, he's got a good job . . . and he wants to date me exclusively. This guy could be the one, Jordi. You could be looking at a rock on this hand in a few weeks.'

Samantha holds up her left hand, ringless at the moment, and beams into the mirror like a girl who's just won a spot on *American Idol*.

Jordi smiles wanly back. Any words she might speak would fall from her lips in venomous drops, splattering Samantha's joy like battery acid: your dreamboat is a hound dog. You don't know what you're doing. Romance is related to love only incidentally, the way fire trucks are related to candles. Face it, romantic love is a lie concocted by the companies who manufacture greeting cards, lipstick, and condoms.

'Well, I gotta book. Kurt's taking me out to the Bamba Room. He's gonna teach me to *salsa*.'

Samantha snaps her fingers over her head in a lame rendering of something that looks more like flamenco than salsa. Then she squirts her neck with something musky that makes Jordi want to sneeze, and sweeps past her roommate to rejoin her boyfriend in the living room. Kurt, slouching against the wall, has the balls to wink at Jordi as she follows Sam out of the bathroom.

'Be good,' he says to Jordi, in a smoky tone that makes Sam giggle.

'Jordi's always good,' she says, and gives her roomie an affectionate half-hug before making her exit with Kurt.

Jordi's always good.

Good old Jordi.

After they're gone, the place seems deathly quiet. Jordi wanders to the kitchen, opens the freezer door, finds a carton of Ben & Jerry's ice cream. Chocolate chip cookie dough: the foolproof antidote to LIRA withdrawal. She's digging into the frozen block when Sam's cellphone goes off in the living room. Sam will have a fit when she reaches for her phone and can't find it, or when she realises that she's gone for a full hour without hearing from one of her galaxy of friends.

Jordi sympathises. The ice cream is cold and heavy in her stomach. Not even cold chunks of cookie dough can quell her gnawing need for LIRA. Mouth full, she walks back into the living room. Her computer sleeps on a sofa cushion, in the hollow that Kurt's big body left. Samantha's cellphone sits on the coffee table, where Sam must have exuberantly dropped it before falling into Kurt's arms.

Two useless pieces of communication technology, idling in wait for the humans who need them so desperately.

Jordi picks up the cellphone. She can't do anything about LIRA right now, but there's still hope for Sam and her beloved cell. Showing up at the trendy Bamba Room in sneakers, jeans, and a ratty T-shirt will be penance for Jordi's cynical thoughts. It's not Sam's fault that her lover is a dog. Maybe another guy will attempt to call her tonight, someone loyal and true. Jordi will be the handmaiden of serendipity, bringing her roommate together with a man who's actually worthy of her, instead of the shifty slimy Adonises she usually dates.

Like this Kurt character. Who the heck *was* he? Jordi shakes her head in disbelief as she reviews the incidents of the evening: coming home to find Kurt lounging on her couch; sitting down beside him; finding him; suddenly draped across her; confessing to a college crush. Then tonguing and groping her body in an urgent hungry way that made Jordi feel more like food than flesh. And Jordi, knowing full well that he was dating her roommate, had melted so fast that she'd been ready to let him have his way with her, right there on the sofa. If she hadn't been hit by a wave of withdrawal, Kurt would have had her pants down and would have been deep inside her when Samantha stepped into the room . . .

Deep inside her. The phrase alone leaves Jordi reeling with something between nausea and desire. How deep was 'deep', really? As subtly suppressed as the memory of a girl you liked in college? As profound as the distance between the root of a cock and the core of a vagina? As powerful as the impact of two souls meeting over a few scoops of protein powder at a Smoothie Spot?

Jordi knows there's something deeper. The rest of the world just doesn't have a clue yet. She gives LIRA a last lingering caress. Her pearly case is cool to the touch, like something dead. This is how 'deep' deep is; it's the tremor of two minds touching, without the layers of lies or the worn-out shells of reality that turn desire into a perpetually unreachable dream.

Not dead – sleeping, Jordi reminds herself sternly. It's only a matter of time, or technology, or . . . something until LIRA wakes up again. The thought of remaining disconnected is simply not thinkable.

Jordi pockets Samantha's cellphone and heads out on her mission of mercy.

Chapter Five

Dana: Sex for Sanctuary

Dearest Deviant,

One thing I can tell you about the public library at night: it looks a hell of a lot cozier when you're on the outside looking in than when you're on the inside looking out.

Flash back to Christmas Eve, last year. I'd done a bit of last-minute shopping before heading up to the cabin in the mountains, where we always opened our presents before a roaring fire. Holiday traffic crept through downtown. I was sitting on Broadway, idling in my beloved Jeep, listening to a Frank Sinatra Christmas album on my ultra-loaded car stereo. The heater blew a pleasantly toasty draft up my skirt, a creamy woolen number from Ann Taylor, which I'd topped with a knee-length suede jacket lined in lambswool.

I wasn't wearing any panties, and the gridlock wasn't showing any signs of easing, so I was seriously considering giving myself an orgasm. Pleasuring myself in the car has always been a favorite pastime, especially when it's dark outside, and pedestrians passing by could catch glimpses of my hot pink cheeks as I fingered my pussy. I'd often wished I could afford to buy a custom-made Jeep with glass doors, so I could be sure of having an audience for my auto-erotic adventures.

Actually, my father *could* have afforded to buy his little girl a Jeep with glass doors. He just wouldn't have approved. I had enough traffic tickets on my record.

I reached under my pretty winter skirt and found that puff of flesh and fur between my thighs. The inner lips were already moist; I was wound up from a day of shopping, one of the biggest aphrodisiacs I know. I'd spent the day surging in and out of crowds, wrestling with perfumed women over last-minute holiday bargains, pulling out my charge card over and over again, watching their balances rise to dizzying heights. By the time I rushed into Saks Fifth Avenue for one final fix, I was ready to come.

As you can imagine, I'm a girl with a lot of toys. I own things that buzz and things that whir; vibes that throb like miniature jackhammers; dildos big enough to make a donkey cry; blown-glass phalluses exquisite enough to have graced a lady's nightstand in a Hapsburg castle. Still, my favorite plaything remains the one I was born with: my right index finger. When I'm diddling myself, my pleasure is double; I get to relish the fleshy, slick warmth of my pussy – like popping my digit into a ripe mango – as well as experience the joys delivered by one of the most artful fingertips this side of the Rockies.

How do I know I'm that good at masturbation, compared to the billions of other sentient beings on the planet who practice self-stimulation? Well, I don't, but if experience counts for anything, I've got to be up there in the top ten. I still remember my first, shattering, self-induced orgasm, delivered while I was still wearing pink flannel pajamas with white unicorns on them. Since then, I've probably had climaxes in the quadruple digits. I'm that kind of girl.

So there I sat, in my cozy Jeep, listening to Frank croon out the carols as I swirled my finger around my hardening clit.

The little bud was so sensitive – all that friction of walking around without panties all day! – that I could have come within a minute or two, if I'd allowed myself to be that greedy. But I wanted to draw this one out, make it as leisurely as sipping a cup of cocoa on a frosty winter evening. When I felt that unmistakable keen tingle, I'd back off a little, slow down the rhythm, and the wave would withdraw.

The traffic light ahead changed to green, but only two cars made it through the packed intersection before the light switched to red again. I could be sitting here masturbating till Christmas morning at this rate. I sighed, spread my thighs a notch wider and leaned back in my seat as Sinatra eased into 'White Christmas'.

Floating in that sensory cocoon of solitary delights, I happened to glance over and see the public library to my right. Closed, obviously, but its windows were warmly lit, and the shelves of books stretched out in invitation, as if they were waiting for the right person to step through the glass and tour their contents. Maybe I was that special person, I thought lazily. I could wander through the empty halls of the library like Clara in *The Nutcracker Suite*, discovering the hidden delights that reveal themselves after all the grown-ups have gone to bed. Seen from the outside, the library was a castle of magic and mystery, the kind of place I used to dream of occupying when I was a chubby little bookworm.

Now that I actually did occupy that library, through circumstances so sudden that I was still trying to muddle through them, I realised that peering out into the night felt very different to peering in.

I had found a cleaning closet to stash my things for the night. I knew that the closet wouldn't be safe on a permanent basis; I just wanted to give my back and brain a rest, so that I could wander freely through my new temporary home. I'd already eaten three of my Lunar bars, but my stomach was rumbling, and I craved the warmth of a hot cup of tea between my hands. I knew that the public library was always battling budget cuts, but I didn't see why they had to turn the thermostat down to 'bone chilling' after hours. Didn't they ever consider the possibility that pampered waifs might be spending the night in the stacks?

Aside from a couple of summers spent at an elite summer camp, where 'wilderness' was considered any grassy space that wasn't regularly mowed, I didn't have much experience at roughing it. Standing on the third floor, staring out into the night, I made up stories about the people who were tucked safely into cars. They would be going home to hot meals, TV, clean sheets. I would be going to bed with a belly half-filled with snack food, on a sleeping bag spread out between European Literature and Literary Criticism.

I wished I'd thought to bring my iPod with me, or at least a portable radio. No library had ever felt so quiet, so devoid of life; the silence that I usually associated with the stacks, I realised, was actually full of the whispers and rustles of human activity. If you listened hard enough, you could hear people breathing, chewing gum, reading, even thinking. All I could hear tonight was the drone of an overhead security lamp, the occasional honk or siren from the streets outside. What I wouldn't give right now for the snore of a transient sleeping in one of the comfy library chairs, or the second-hand buzz of rock from some kid's Walkman! I had my cellphone, of course, and a network of friends I could have called, but what would I say when they asked me that *de rigueur* question of all cellular communication: *so where are you right now*?

I could call Dad. He'd answer, I was sure of it. But some hard and stony obstacle rose up in my throat when I imagined the sound of his voice, remembered the 'Dear Dana' letter he'd left me. What kind of father disinherits his daughter with a freaking note?

Screw the penthouse. Screw Bambi or Bootsie or Snowflake or whatever the new wife's name was. I'd make it here. Surrounded by information, I'd find a way out of this mess. So what if I didn't have the slightest clue how to start a new life? I'd pick up a book and steal someone else's.

I'd already read all the juicy parts of *Princess Daisy* earlier that afternoon. I'd even reshelved the book in its proper place in contemporary paperback fiction. In fact, I was discovering a weird new OCD tendency as I drifted through the shelves. Everywhere I looked, I kept finding books in the wrong categories. I found a fascinating exploration of sadomasochism jammed into a section on yoga, and an introduction to astronomy shelved with Chinese cookbooks. An old tract on physiognomy was wedged in between works by two American poets.

Something must be wrong with the staff here. They were either slacking in their organizational skills, or off their meds. The disorder was so crazed, in some sections, that the books looked like some schizophrenic postmodern art installation. I found a nearly empty book cart sitting in one of the aisles and began to fill it with the renegade volumes. With the help of a foggy memory of my research days in college, and a vague understanding of the Library of Congress cataloging system, I made my way through the library's semi-illuminated corridors putting books back in their proper places.

The work was pleasantly tedious, and surprisingly

satisfying. I'd never thought of myself as the AR type. Anal, yes – I loved having objects of various types inserted in my bottom, especially in tandem with a light tickling of my clit – but not anal-retentive. In the midst of my falling-apart world, I liked the idea of restoring order, in some small way. By the time I'd finished replacing the contents of my cart, which involved multiple trips up and down the elevator, I'd gotten the equivalent of an hour of Jazzercise and felt like I'd made a small dent in the entropy of the universe.

Best of all, my work had taken a healthy chunk out of the night. It was almost midnight when I sat down, my muscles pleasantly humming, to take a break. I plopped onto one of the couches on the second floor, in an open reading area. I'd grabbed a book at random out of the European Literature section, something nice and fat and weighty. I'd learned at a very young age that fat novels always seemed to have the best sex scenes.

With a smug little yawn, I curled up in the corner of the sofa and opened the book. Couldn't have made a worse choice, I thought, as I saw that I'd picked Joyce's modern classic, *Ulysses*. I'd done my time with that book in my junior year of college, struggling to wade through its wilderness of brilliantly discordant chapters before giving up and buying the CliffsNotes. Hard to write a term paper on a book you've never read, but I managed to do it by reading a few select passages ... well, one passage, really – namely, Molly Bloom's famous soliloquy.

Molly Bloom. Now there was a fictional invention after my own heart, a hungry sensual animal of a girl, with appetites so big that they exploded in her lush and earthy words. Molly, Leopold Bloom's singing, straying wife, the woman of the perpetual Yes, was me. Molly understood

74

that life was all about having all your holes, physical and otherwise, filled to the brim, filled to overflowing if at all possible. I flipped to the last chapter, the only one worth reading as far as I could tell, and let myself drown in her river of prose, with no punctuation to save me from that sensual submersion.

Within a few minutes, I was so absorbed in Molly's voice that I'd forgotten I was supposed to be hiding out here, not lounging around sampling books in an open area like a mouse nibbling the hors d'oeuvres at a catered wedding. My eyelids began to droop. I must have dozed off. Curled up in the corner of the couch, I imagined that the weight of the cushion was Molly's body, deep and warm, cuddling me like a sister, or a best friend, and then I slipped into sleep.

Say yes, say yes, that's all you have to do, lovely, Molly seemed to be murmuring to me. Don't struggle against the world; fall into it. Let it fill you. If you can't have a cock in your bum, try a cucumber...

Huh?

I jerked awake, heart in my throat. My drooping eyelids were suddenly wide open, and I found myself staring into the chalk-white face of the Angel Gabriel.

OK, I was dead. I'd died of starvation, hypothermia and a lack of late-night television, and here I was in heaven, with some divinely handsome creature hovering over me. Molly Bloom had been replaced by my guardian angel, who was here to conduct me into the afterlife. I rubbed my sticky eyes. In my afterlife, apparently, angels wore uniforms that made them look like rejects from the Village People. This particular angel looked like he'd auditioned to perform as a stripping postal worker, or maybe a traffic cop, but he'd flunked the auditions for both roles.

'What are you doing?' the supernatural being asked, in a voice that cracked like a human teenager's. His hand trembled as he reached for the holster on his belt.

I sat up fast. 'What are *you* doing?' I shot back, clinging to the front of my sweatshirt as if it were a silk négligée covering my bare bosom. 'Who are you? Why are you in my bedroom?'

'This isn't your bedroom, lady. It's the public library! How did you get in here?'

I looked around. I patted the sofa cushions. He was right. This couldn't be my bedroom. I didn't own nearly this many books, and my bed didn't smell like it had been slept on by several hundred humans. I had fallen asleep in the library. Even worse, I had woken up in it, and had no other place to go. But this wasn't only the library, I reminded myself. It was my new kingdom, Smorgasmia, where fallen princesses were granted asylum from snotty boys who weren't even old enough to shave yet.

'You're not an angel,' I said accusingly. I gave his holster a contemptuous glare. 'You're a security guard.'

His Adam's apple plunged as he swallowed. His face turned red. His hand was still shaking.

'Have you ever actually fired that gun?' I asked, heaping on the scorn. 'Outside of security guard school, I mean.'

Now it was his mouth's turn to quiver. 'I was the best shot at the firing range. Hit the paper target right between the eyes.'

Fully awake, I could see that the kid really didn't look like anything Michelangelo would have wanted to sculpt. My hyperactive imagination had given him beauty he didn't possess, but it had also left out a few juicy details. Like the way his mouth softened and grew deliciously unstable, like a soufflé about to collapse, when he was being humiliated by an older woman. And the way his fine brown hair stood out in staticky cowlicks, begging to be smoothed down. Or the cocky droop of his belt around his waist, which was so lean its circumference probably equaled one of my chunky thighs.

'You're not the Angel Gabriel,' I mused out loud. 'More like the Angel James Dean.'

He smiled. His smile grew into a shaky grin with a twist of something wicked, something just being born in his young libido.

My hungry heart, slumbering for the past 24 hours, was awake again. I stretched my arms overhead, elongating my body like a cat.

'What's your name?' I asked. 'No, don't tell me. Let me give you one. You're James. Jimmy. How's that?'

He shrugged his slender shoulders. Light was dawning in his blue eyes. 'Sounds good to me.'

I love a young, young man. I love an impressionable man, one who's soft and moist enough that I can leave my fingerprints all over him. And I especially love it when that young man is wearing a uniform, so I can strip him gently of his authority and turn him into my toy.

'How old are you, Jimmy?'

He cleared his throat. Blushed a few shades deeper. 'Twenty-five.'

'Tsk, tsk. I don't think so.' I looked him up and down. There was a promising swell in his creased khaki trousers. 'I'd say you're not a day over twenty-one.'

'Turned twenty-one last month,' he admitted.

'You shouldn't have lied,' I said sternly. 'Take off your pants.'

'Huh?'

'Your pants. Take them off. I'd start with that silly belt,

if I were you. Why they have you kids rigged out with guns, I have no idea.'

'It's not really a gun. It's a Taser.' His fingers floated help-lessly around his belt buckle as he looked around the empty library.

'Even so. It's a weapon. I don't play with boys who wear weapons. Take the belt off, pull down your pants and come over here.'

'Really? Are you sure?'

I lowered my voice to a honeyed purr. 'Please. Come. Here.'

He unbuckled his belt and pulled it free from his trousers. Then he unzipped his pants and let them drop to his ankles. His erection nudged its way anxiously out of the waistband of his white Fruit of the Looms.

Dear Deviant, by now you're probably thinking that your heroine is an incorrigible slut. You could be right on that point, but please keep in mind that every erotic encounter, for me, even the fiery clinches that explode and fade into showers of useless sparks, is also an act of love. I lay every one of them at Aphrodite's slender feet, a gift not only from my flesh, but from my heart. No, I wasn't in love with James/Jimmy, or whatever his real name was, but when he shuffled over to me, ankles shackled by his pants, and offered me his quivering cock to kiss, I loved him. Sex may be the motor that drives me crazily through life, but love is its fuel.

I held his taut pink shaft, which listed slightly to the right, bursting from a scanty nest of golden brown pubic hair. I pressed my lips to the tip and tasted seawater. A bead of pearly liquid was already trickling down the cleft in the velvet crown. If it sounds like I'm laying on the metaphors a bit thick, Dear Deader, remember that your Dana is an oral girl.

Also a very hungry girl, as my belly was reminding me. I was about to eat Jimmy's cock for pleasure, but I also wanted to eat it for dinner.

'I can't believe this is happening,' he whispered. 'Are you real?'

'Maybe,' I teased. 'Or maybe I'm just a wet dream.'

'That's OK. Just as long as I don't wake up before I come.'

'Ah, no need to worry about that. You'll come tonight. At least once.'

I smiled like a she-wolf as I reached between his pale moist thighs to fondle his balls. Nice tight balls, firm as crab apples, they were warm and resilient in my palm. He gasped and tensed when I squeezed a little.

I looked up into his face. Though he wasn't all that much younger than me, I could tell by the dreamy yearning haze in his eyes that I'd surpassed him in experience long ago. A hint of sensitivity blurred the edges of his features, making me wonder for a second if I'd named him after James Dean, or James Joyce. I could be Nora right now, overpowering the young author with her lusty aggression, grabbing his cock and making him come in his pants. Except the cock in front of me was already bared for my mouth.

I shifted on the sofa, moving down onto my knees. As I lowered my body, my mouth slid down Jimmy's erection, so that by the time I was kneeling on the library's mustard-yellow carpet, the security guard's prick was lodged deep in my throat. He tasted heavenly: young and fresh, with a note of soap and a tang of sweat. None of that overripeness that older guys sometimes have when they've been around too many mouths (and other orifices) for their own good. This guy smelled and tasted brand new.

A scary thought flitted across my mind as I deep-throated Jimmy: was I already overripe, too? I hadn't even made it to the quarter-century mark, yet I knew more ways to make a man come than most women learn in a lifetime. I couldn't even remember a time when I'd been innocent enough to shrink back at the sight of an erect male organ jutting into my face. More likely, I'd *never* shrunk back; blow jobs were in my blood, and I'd loved them from Day One.

'You can't be real,' Jimmy repeated in an awestruck murmur. 'Things like this never happen to me. Girls like you don't exist in my world.'

I moaned a denial – I *was* real, I *did* exist – through a mouthful of his tasty flesh. He'd woven his fingers through my hair and was now wrapping it around his fists, tugging at the roots as he tried to keep from thrusting too hard into my mouth. Hair-pulling is a huge trigger for me; that firm pressure on my scalp sends a signal to my brain that it's OK to act like an animal. After all, I'm being treated like one, yanked around by my thick copper pelt. When my hair's being pulled, I howl, I growl, I bite, I buck my hips and lift my ass. For once, my outside matches my inside, and I'm the perfect image of the insatiable little beast who lives inside me.

When a man pulls my hair as I'm sucking him, and uses my tresses like reins to guide my head, I'm doubly in heaven. It wasn't long before I felt Jimmy's glutes tighten, his thighs stiffen. I pulled the length of him out of my mouth just a few seconds before he reached his peak. He let out a lion's growl, a surprise from such a skinny boy, and, as his hips rocked back and forth, I let him spill across my open lips.

'Yum,' I sighed, wiping my mouth. 'You're delicious.'

'You're *amazing*.'

Panting, he stared down at me. Cheeks flushed, exhilaration turning his baby-blue eyes electric; he looked like he'd won a marathon and a lottery at the same time.

'Oh, I'm just me.'

I glanced down modestly. My modesty was a façade. I knew I was the bomb when it came to fellatio. I got off my knees, fluffed my hair, and tried not to look too pleased with myself as I rearranged my voluptuous form on the sofa.

'Can I do something to you – um, I mean for you – now?' he asked.

My gut, and something softer and furrier than my gut, told me to say yes. Oh, yes, yes, please do something to me, anything to make me feel as good as you do right now. Then a new voice, one that was sharper and wilier than my gut, told me to think again. Maybe I could get something more out of this relationship than an orgasm.

I patted the sofa beside me. That sway-backed piece of public furniture was starting to feel like Cleopatra's barge. 'Sit down. Let's talk. Why don't you tell me your name?'

The guard sat gingerly beside me. His blue eyes widened. 'It's Jimmy.'

'No, darling. Your real name. Not the one I made up for fun and games.'

He pointed to the badge hanging inside the lapel of his jacket. Above a photo of our hero of the night, looking bleached-out but cocky in his new uniform, was the name JAMES MCNAMARA.

Coincidence? Probably. A common enough name, after all. Since I'd made the library my temporary address, I was getting used to coincidences, odd tricks and twists of serendipity. The magic of serendipity was what the library was all about, or so I'd been told by an Eastern Philosophy professor who was trying to encourage me to spend more time in the stacks while slipping into *my* stacks at the same time. As we leaned over my term paper, marked with a humiliating red D and the words, 'Superficial research. Go deeper', he had slipped his arm around my shoulders and grazed the outer curve of my breast through the cashmere sweater I was wearing.

I might have taken him up on his tacit offer, since I've always had a thing for overeducated older men. But the cigars that he smoked made his breath smell like an old tire, and his tweedy shoulders never lost their layer of dandruff. I just couldn't get past those little flaws, no matter how much I loved the way his lips pursed behind his beard when he pronounced Sanskrit.

'I'm trying to get people to call me Jim,' the guard was saying. 'But Jimmy just sticks, for some reason.'

'It suits you. Obviously.'

I smiled. He blushed. When his cheeks turned fuchsia, hidden freckles stood out in relief against the pink. I liked this boy – a lot. I reached for his hand and held it. His palm was moist and warm. His fingers trembled in mine. We sat there like sweethearts. I almost hated to ask him for what I needed, but my life wasn't what it used to be.

'Jimmy, I need to tell you something about myself.'

'Sure. Anything.'

'I live here.'

'I figured you did. I live here, too. Here is, like, wherever you are, right?'

'Exactly. That's exactly what I mean. I live here at the library.'

A cute wrinkle appeared between his eyebrows. 'You can't. It's not allowed.'

'I know that,' I said patiently, squeezing his hand tighter.

'But I'm doing it, anyway. I have to. I'm homeless. I don't have anywhere else to go.'

'You don't have any friends?'

'Well, I do. But they don't know I'm homeless. And I don't want them to find out. They wouldn't understand.'

'What about your family? Don't you have parents or brothers or sisters or anything?'

'My family,' I said darkly, 'is the reason I'm here. My father kicked me out of the house. I've been disowned. Disinherited. I don't have anything from him, not even a dust bunny from the penthouse where I grew up.'

'Wow.' Jimmy's shoulders sagged. 'That's rough. He didn't give you anything?'

'Nope. I left with a few clothes and some other stuff that I own, and that's it. Which brings me to a very important question. I need your help. Can you help me?'

He nodded solemnly and sat up straight, shoulders squaring as if to accept whatever burden I might hand him. His voice deepened by a couple of notches as he replied, 'Just tell me what you need.'

I scooted closer, until my thigh pressed against his. 'Help me find a safe place where I can keep my things.'

His face brightened. 'Hey, I can do that. No problem. I've got a locker downstairs; you can use that. All I ever keep there is my lunch, and my coat when it's cold, and sometimes a Thermos . . .'

'And, more importantly,' I interrupted, 'I need you to help keep me hidden here until I can find someplace else to go.'

So it was official. I had become a woman who would trade sex for sanctuary.

His hand went slack in mine. I could feel him backing away, his shoulders retracting under his jacket. 'I don't know how much I can do, without losing my job. I mean,

I can let you use my locker, but, other than that, I can't help you break the rules. I'm not going to cover up any security cameras or lie to my boss or anything.'

'Cameras? Where?' I looked up at the ceiling. 'You mean someone was watching us just now?'

Jimmy's head retreated, turtlelike, into his wide collar. 'Maybe. I dunno. I don't think this reading area's monitored.'

'You don't *think* it's monitored?' My voice rose to a squeal. 'You're security. You're supposed to know these things!'

'Hey, I'm new,' he said. 'Listen, if I really thought someone was watching, I'd never have dropped my pants. I don't want to lose this job anymore than you want to be found out. So let's work together, OK?'

In the aftermath of lust, it was dawning on Jimmy that his complicity in the Public Library Blow Job behooved him to help me. Whether he wanted me or not, I was his problem now. Jimmy was growing up fast.

'Come on.' He rose, still holding my hand, and half-dragged me to my feet. 'Show me where your stuff is. I'll take you to the locker room.'

As he hustled me out of the open reading area, I added in a small voice that I was kind of hungry.

'You can have half my dinner,' Jimmy said. 'It's a meatball sandwich. My mom makes the best meatball sandwiches in the world.'

'Do you live with her?'

'Yeah.' The syllable had a defensive thrust. 'Saves me money. Nothing wrong with living with your parents, is there?'

'No. Nothing at all. In fact, I think that's just how it should be. Parents should look out for their children, no matter how old they are.'

I thought of where my father would be right now. Lying in his four-poster bed in the cabin, the one with the ridiculous antlers on the headboard. He'd be sunk in a deep blue sleep, a feather comforter strewn across his body, Wife #3 snoring daintily beside him.

That wrinkle popped out between Jimmy's eyes again. 'Doesn't your family want to know where you are tonight? I mean, you don't seem like the kind of girl who just gets thrown away.'

'I'm not. I'm really not.'

A scary stinging in the corners of my eyes warned me that I was about to cry, in big embarrassing gusts. My father could have called my cellphone, just to find out how I was doing, where I'd landed. But, amazingly enough, I hadn't gotten a single call since I left home that morning. It was as if my identity, everything I came from, had been cancelled with that note I found in my bedroom. In a fit of paranoia, I imagined my stepmother calling all my friends, telling them I'd run away in a fit of anger, suggesting that they didn't try to find me.

But Chastity wouldn't have gone to all that trouble. She didn't have enough brainpower to come up with a scheme like that, or the motivation to ruin me. If anything, she'd been better off when I was living at home; I was the perfect negative example of appetites run riot in comparison to her dainty asceticism. Chastity neither ate nor drank nor fucked too much; she was my father's flawless snow bunny. Naked, I imagined, her body would be one seamless tan continuum. She'd be as smooth as a doll, with no vagina or anus to mar her exterior.

'I'll take care of you. You don't have to worry about anything. Nothing bad's gonna happen to you as long as I'm around.'

Jimmy took my hand again, not with romantic intent this time, but with a shaky self-assurance, the way Hansel must have taken Gretel's when they were lost in the forest. I wanted to fall against his narrow chest and beg for him to take me home. I could picture myself helping his mother in the kitchen, stirring a big pot of meatballs, or pressing the slacks of Jimmy's uniform. I'd be like one of the family. Hell, at this point, I'd even be their pet.

But he didn't take me home. Instead, he let me lead him to the cleaning closet where I'd temporarily hidden my things.

'What's all that?' Jimmy asked, eyeing my duffel bag, the heap of fluffy, frivolous evening gowns. 'No way is that all going to fit in my locker.'

I dropped the bag and clothes on the floor. We stared down at my stuff together, as if we were considering which of two hapless castaways to rescue from a desert island. No question, really, the gowns had to go. Where did I think I was going to wear them, anyway?

'I'll ditch the gowns,' I said. 'They're useless now.'

Jimmy knelt on the floor. In a gesture that I would never have expected from a male of his age or station in life, he fingered the lacy hem of one of my dresses. It was the dress I'd worn to an awards ceremony last year, where my father had been presented with a certificate of honour for public service to his community.

Service to the community – sure, he could handle that. Helping his wayward daughter was another question altogether.

'I bet you were a knockout in these,' he said. He grinned up at me, then leered at my figure in a way that was much more typical. 'But then, you're a knockout in jeans.'

'Thanks.' I ruffled his fine feathery brown hair. He stood

up, pulling the garment bag with him. I shouldered the duffel bag again.

'You could sell those dresses, you know,' he suggested. 'My mom runs a consignment shop. She'd get you a good deal.'

'Really?' My heart did a little skip at the thought of money. They were designer gowns. All together they'd be worth thousands, even on consignment. But something had shifted inside me, since the night began. I hadn't even been aware of the change, but subtly, everything was altered.

'Your mom can sell the gowns if she wants,' I said. 'But I don't want the money.'

'Are you serious?'

'Very. It would be bad juju. I desperately need to improve my juju right now.'

'Gotcha,' Jimmy said, with a grave nod. 'I can respect that.'

As it turned out, the duffel bag did fit in his skinny locker, but just barely. I had to cram it in, then give it a shove with my shoulder before the door would clear.

'I'll get rid of some more stuff tomorrow,' I promised. 'It's not fair for me to take up all your space.'

'You can have all the space you want,' he said. 'You need it more than I do.'

Jimmy brushed my cheek with the back of his hand, then he leaned in and planted the world's tiniest tenderest kiss on my lips. I wasn't surprised to see a glistening tear-trail on his knuckles when he took his hand away.

I wasn't feeling sorry for myself, Dear Deviant. Quite the contrary – I was suddenly almost giddy with my freedom. Freedom from what? I didn't exactly know, but something heavy and sodden had been lifted from me along with those silly evening gowns. I hadn't felt so light since the time I lost ten pounds on a diet of fresh pineapple, green tea, and daily coffee enemas at Spa Ba-Lo-Hai.

I threw my arms around Jimmy and squeezed, making the bag of dresses rustle with alarm.

'Thank you,' I said into his ear.

'For what?' he laughed. He hugged me back. Either he was hard again, or his Taser had taken on a mind of its own and wandered around to the front of his pants. 'You're the one who gave me the incredible blow – I mean, uh, good time. Wish you'd let me return the favor.'

'I'll take a rain check,' I said. 'Right now, I've got to roll out my sleeping bag and go to bed.'

'You won't have much time to sleep. The next guard comes on shift at six. It's four-thirty now.'

He pointed to the clock in the security locker room. He was right. I sighed. I'd accepted the fact that I'd be sleeping in a bag in a public building instead of on a mattress in a skyscraper, but I hadn't realised that dawn was coming to steal my small gift of rest. A new day was already breathing down my neck. I had no plans: no shopping, no gossip, no lunch dates, no appointments. My calendar was not only clear; my calendar didn't exist.

So why did I still feel so damn *happy* all of a sudden?

Chapter Six

Jordi: Learning to Tingle

The Bamba Room is in the heart of downtown, if Jordi remembers correctly, somewhere between 17th Avenue and the Clocktower. She peers out of the window of the bus as it creeps through the crowded streets. The city, on a Friday night, is a smear of red-and-gold light, laughing mouths and flashing bare legs. For most people, this would be a typical night of revelry at the end of another work week but, for Jordi, who never leaves her apartment after eight p.m., tonight is an anthropological tour of an alien urban subculture.

She's grateful for the distractions outside the window; they help her forget about that little wrestling match with Kurt. The flavour of his tongue, too close to liverwurst for comfort, lingers in her mouth. She thinks she can still feel the pressure of his fingertips on her breasts, where he kneaded them. Who did he think he was, handling Jordi's body as if her boobs were loaves of bread that he was testing for freshness? Some guys apparently thought the whole female gender was an endless buffet, laid out for their pleasure. If they saw something they liked, all they had to do was grab.

Still, there's a ghost of a tingle in the pit of her belly when she remembers how he kissed her. Tingle. Why shouldn't LIRA allow its users to 'tingle'? Jordi makes a mental note to investigate Tingling as a prelude to Throbbing. Another shade of experience would add subtlety to the application, make the connections more real.

But LIRA's connections *are* real. LIRA isn't just a way to find a relationship; LIRA is a relationship itself. LIRA will be the best thing that ever happened to love, Jordi reassures herself, the way she does whenever a tentacle of doubt about her project tickles the back of her mind. She hasn't given up her life (fill in the blank before 'life' with 'social', 'love', or 'sex') in vain.

It just feels like that sometimes. Especially when her computer is comatose.

Jordi pulls the bell to stop the bus. She's not sure if this is the right intersection, but thoughts of LIRA are giving her those withdrawal twinges again. She needs fresh air, motion. Somewhere in the Netherlands, in Japan, in San Francisco, and in a tiny town in Indiana, the people she's been Threading and Throbbing with must be wondering where she is. Or maybe they're not; maybe they're just connecting happily without her on their own laptops, experiencing those flashes and swells and surges of desire with no thought whatsoever of the girl who wrote the stupid code.

As if she'd sent a summons through the air, Jordi's phone goes off. She pulls it out of her mini-backpack. It's a text message from Tuan, in San Francisco: CANT THREAD U WASUP?

Jordi smiles. She imagines Tuan in his cramped basement studio apartment in the Haight. He's nervously raking his fingers through his crest of maroon-streaked hair, while munching Skittles between bong hits.

LIRA CRUMPD, she texts back.

A moment of nothing. Then, FUK. Spelling is not Tuan's forte.

YEAH. CANT FIX HER.

WANT ME THERE?

Jordi's skin tingles – that tingle, she's got to learn how to code a Tingle – as she texts, YES!!!!!! Tuan was the first of the guinea pigs who Threaded with her back in the beginning. Their connection is still the strongest; if she tries hard enough, Jordi and Tuan can create a Throb without any electronic intermediation at all. Every so often, after a night of steamy dreams of writhing in Tuan's wiry golden arms, Jordi wakes to a message from him on her pager: DID U THROB ME LAST NITE?

She's never actually touched Tuan. They spent three weeks together, when Jordi needed proximity with her Threaders to reassure herself that everyone was connecting happily, but during that whole time, skin never met skin. That was part of the unspoken contract – none of the developers could touch any of the others. Ever. Once LIRA was out on the market, its Threaders would be free to take their connections wherever they wanted, even as far as meat sex, if they were so inclined. But, in development, no meat could meet.

WHEN CAN U COME? Jordi texts. I NEED HELP.

She stands on the street corner, waiting, while a stream of half-drunk pedestrians jostles her like a floating leaf.

Help. The word drifts from her mind up to the sky, towards the Pacific Ocean and Tuan.

The electronic display goes blank. Jordi shakes the device, close to shrieking in frustration. Maybe she's developed some sort of magnetic force field that's causing every instrument around her to break down. More likely, in her distress over LIRA, she just forgot to recharge the damn thing.

'Get yourself together, Jordi,' she mutters to herself,

shoving the pager into the backpack. 'Paranoia is the last thing you need.'

She steps off the high cliff of her consciousness into the night's blur of noise and color. This definitely isn't the right corner, she realises. The Bamba Room is in an entirely different neighborhood, one of those gentrified face-lifted former ghettos. This neighborhood is still pretty much just a ghetto. The lights bleed from the barred windows of liquor stores and pawn shops. A street lined with warehouses stretches away into the arms of a freeway overpass. The thrust of the crowd's motion is aggressive, predatory. People are wearing strange headgear. A few of them shoot razor-sharp looks at Jordi. Most of them push past her as if she doesn't exist.

The next bus won't come by for another half hour. Jordi considers waiting, but some primordial instinct kicks in, telling her to square her shoulders and *move*. Though Jordi is not a merger by nature, she manages to squirm her way into the stream of pedestrians. She lets them carry her along on some mission that's not her own, past murky alleys and shadowed grocery shops whose shelves are stocked with fruit and vegetables in the phosphorescent shades of Mars and Neptune.

Why are all these people out at night? They all seem to be hunting, but for what? The kid in front of her walks with a feline sway, hips angling forwards with each stride. In his baggy jeans, muscle shirt and green bandana, he's on the prowl. His bare muscular shoulders have a caramel sheen that makes Jordi's belly growl, but she couldn't swear that she's hungry for food. She fixes her eyes on the green tail of Cat Boy's bandana. Experimentally, she flexes the part of her mind that Threads, reaching for the part of *his* mind that would Thread, if he knew what Threading was.

Jordi feels a flicker. Cat Boy glances to the left, a frown wrinkling his aquiline nose. He flinches and grunts, as if someone had shot him between the shoulder blades with a rubber band.

Jordi flexes harder. If Cat Boy turns to look at her, offering her something more than that tantalising flash of his profile, he won't look twice. But if she can weave herself through his mind's eye, she'll be in solid. And if she can Thread a total stranger without LIRA's mediation, who can tell what miracles she'd be capable of?

I know there's something in you that sees me.
Hello?
Do you feel me?
DO YOU HAVE A CLUE, MORON?

Cat Boy freezes in mid-stride, hips knocked out of synch. Jordi's heart goes into a brief arrhythmia, the way it always does when her mind has hooked another. That 'gotcha' moment of pure connection – she lives for it. Give her another millisecond, and she'll slip inside this sexy stranger's caramel-colored mind. She'll be the sudden star of his pornographic dreams, and he'll be the slut of her cerebral harem ...

Just before that millisecond clicks into being, Cat Boy breaks from the crowd, and away from the invisible finger that stretches yearningly from Jordi's curly red head. A girl, slim streak of astral blonde, glides out of the night and into his golden arms. Astral Girl and Cat Boy hold each other at arms' length for a long moment, beaming into each other's eyes, before coming together and devouring each other's mouths in a most tangible way.

Jordi sighs. Move along now, show's over. There'll be lots more to see, more kissing and gazing and mutual devouring. But Jordi's not enough of a voyeur tonight, or enough of a masochist, to lurk around and spy on the happy couple.

The stream of people seems to have hit a logjam. The crowd turns into a mass, which thins into a line, and suddenly its goal becomes clear to Jordi. She's standing at the end of a very long queue, in front of an anonymous block of a building. The sidewalk under her feet pulses. Jordi shudders. Techno – ugh. She's standing in a line of shifting, strutting, preening thugs and gangsta chicks waiting to get past some dweeb, dressed in head-to-toe black, who's guarding the entrance. The dweeb revels in his own power as he scans each would-be clubber, then pulls back the rope in front of the door or gives them the Hand of Disdain and sends them to the back of the line.

Jordi pushes her way out of the queue. Commercially sanctioned social rejection? No thanks. She scuttles down the street in what she thinks is the direction of the bus stop. Once again her inner compass proves to be broken; nothing looks familiar, and Jordi wishes she could plop down on the sidewalk and cry. No one would notice a chubby redhead sitting in the middle of the street crying. Except muggers and rapists, and maybe an undercover cop.

Don't cry. Keep moving.

There must be a bus stop around here somewhere. Following Cat Boy's sensual footsteps, Jordi must have been led off the main drag. She turns down a side street, hoping it will connect to something more familiar. The street is dark and goes nowhere. The lights, the catcalls, the thrust and grind of the crowd have disappeared. Though she's not exactly overflowing with urban wisdom, Jordi knows better than to assume that the absence of visible life forms means that the street is deserted.

Arms wrapped tight around her waist, she backtracks at a trot. A sudden eruption of trash, a scrabbling of claws in a dumpster, and Jordi breaks into a run, heart thundering. Panic whistling in her chest, she huffs and puffs around a corner.

I've got to get in shape somehow, she thinks wildly. And then, I hope that isn't my last conscious thought.

The blue letters on a sign over a shadowed door catch her eye. The word is familiar, but its meaning doesn't register until she's close enough to the building to feel like her life is no longer in danger.

MISTEEK.

Jordi blinks at the word, wondering where she's read it before. Unlike the club a few blocks away, this one looks like no one's cracked the door open for years. Instead of an effete doorman, the doorway is guarded only by a single empty malt-liquor bottle, turned over on its side. If not for the raucous medley of indistinguishable noises coming from inside – human roars, percussion, the random screech of amplifier feedback – Jordi would have assumed the place was deserted. It's not the kind of club she'd ever go to in a million years, but then neither is the Bamba Room. Jordi's ideal nightclub would exist in the interstices between brain cells.

But a raucous refuge is better than no refuge at all. Jordi opens the door and hurries inside, only to find herself bouncing against the wall of a very broad human chest. With a grunt of surprise, she peers up into a scowling slab of a face that resembles one of the stone heads of Easter Island.

'Hey! Five dollar cover!' Stone Head's voice rumbles through his chest, emerging as a growl that's loud enough to make itself heard through the cacophony inside the club. 'And I gotta see some ID.'

Though the bouncer's torso hides the rest of Misteek from view, Jordi is vaguely aware of a knot of arms and legs roiling against a stage where several musicians are chopping away at the set, at the crowd, and at each other, with electric guitars.

Jordi opens her backpack, praying she has some cash. It seems to take forever for her to fish out her wallet, while Stone Head glowers down at her.

'I've only got three bucks!' she screams up at him. 'Can I just stand here in the lobby and appreciate the music from a distance?'

She's not sure how to interpret the bouncer's responding stare: contempt, confusion, or both?

'Don't send me back outside. Please! It's scary out there. I don't know this neighborhood. I have no idea where I am. Please let me stay, please?'

It's hard to beg when you're screeching at the top of your lungs, but something in Jordi's plea seems to touch Stone Head's heart. He tugs the crumpled bills out of her hand.

'Good luck,' are his final, ominous words, before he steps back and lets Jordi enter the pit. She hangs back at the fringes of the crowd, flattening herself against a black wall to avoid being sucked into the bruising brouhaha of percussion-driven flesh. What's worse, she wonders, the hidden threats of the streets outside, or the more immediate dangers in here? The club reeks of spilled beer and body odor, a fragrance she hasn't smelled since college. Though she can't determine the gender of the bodies tangling ecstatically in front of the stage, Jordi's pretty sure that 99 percent of them are male.

In fact, she may well be the only patron of the club, at present, who boasts a pair of breasts. I ought to demand my cover charge back, she thinks.

Flesh. Bone. Muscles and tendons and sinewy things – all of it snarled in a tangle that heaves to the grating abrasion of hands on steel guitar strings. The noise is enough to strip away Jordi's skin. She begins to inch along the wall, pressing her face to the side to skirt another wave of smelly boys. If she can just get to the corridor to the left of the stage, where she knows there must be a restroom, she'll have enough of a break from the chaos to make a phone call. She'll call Samantha, call her mother in Michigan, call a crisis hotline. She'll call anyone sane and calm and quiet, who can talk her down from this peak of sensory overload.

As if on cue, a phone goes off. It's not Jordi's but Samantha's. With Jordi's nerves already on edge, the unexpected vibration feels like a rattlesnake in her pocket. She jumps, screams. Her scream is swallowed by the mosh in the pit. A scrawny boy, bandy arms covered with tattoos, takes Jordi's screech as a sign of jubilation and tries to drag her into the fray. She twists out of his clammy grasp and makes a break for the restrooms. By some miracle, Misteek actually has a ladies' lavatory. It's probably a legal requirement.

'Help me!' Jordi shouts into Samantha's phone, as she cowers in one of the stalls.

'Jordi? What's going on? Where are you? Where's my phone?'

Jordi's anxiety triggers Samantha, and the two roommates begin shrieking at each other: for help, for answers, for solutions to all the crises of their very different lives. After a few minutes, they simmer down.

'Sam, come get me,' Jordi pleads. 'I went out looking for you tonight, to give you your phone back. I ended up at some nightclub . . . with a mush pit.'

'You mean a mosh pit,' Samantha corrects her.

'Whatever. It's a big gang of guys that smells like a herd of cattle. The music here is a nightmare. It's all a nightmare.'

'What are you doing there? Why didn't you just call a taxi?'

'I only had three dollars on me. I spent it on the cover charge at this hellhole. Can't you and Kurt come get me?' she begs.

'Kurt's Jeep broke down on the way to the Bamba Room. That's why I was calling you. I went to look for my phone, and it was gone. I figured I'd left it at home, so I called it, thinking you'd pick up. I just thought you'd still be back at the apartment.'

'Why didn't you call me on *my* phone?'

'I forgot you had one.'

'Oh, Sam. Don't be an idiot. Of course I have a cell.'

'Seriously, I didn't think you ever called anybody, Jordi. You and your friends are all psychically connected through your computers.'

Jordi rolls her eyes. 'Listen, Samantha, I just need a way out of this neighborhood. If I stay in this club five minutes longer, I'm going to end up deaf. If I leave, I'm going to end up dead. Can't you and Kurt get a cab and come get me? Samantha?'

Silence is followed by a popping sound, a twitter that sounds like a distorted version of Samantha, then more silence. Sam's phone goes dead. If not for her inherent respect for electronic equipment, Jordi would be banging it against the toilet tank to the beat of the racket going on outside. There can't be any other explanation; she's mysteriously developed a syndrome that Tuan calls the Touch of Death. In his day job as a systems administrator, he sees the Touch of Death in certain co-workers who can't look cross-eyed at a computer terminal, a printer, or a server without bringing the machine to its knees.

Jordi stifles a sob. She's too big to cry, too frustrated not to. She gives in to a storm of weeping, the release delirious and fast, then blows her nose into a handful of tissue and opens the door of the stall. Her face, reflected in the bathroom's speckled, streaked mirror, looks like a stewed tomato. Not as if any of the club's patrons will notice that her face is streaked with tears.

'Hey. What's wrong?'

Miraculously, the place has gone quiet enough that she can hear another person speaking at normal volume when she steps back into the club. She looks up – a nanosecond before bumping into the speaker's chest – at a guy with shaggy dark hair and glasses.

Of course, with bad luck following Jordi like a scrap of toilet paper clinging to her shoe, who else would it be but the only cute non-obnoxious male who's spoken to her in recent memory? He's swapped the gray hoodie for a black Misfits T-shirt, but there's no mistaking the beaky nose, or the gently keen eyes of the Information Anarchist.

'I didn't know you'd really show up tonight,' Nolan says, bending down to peer at Jordi's puffy eyes. 'Did our set suck so bad it made you cry?'

'Well, sort of,' Jordi sniffles. 'Among other things.'

Misteek. Now she remembers where she saw that word: on the card that Nolan pulled from his wallet at the coffee shop. He'd said he was in a band ... Wreckage. She hadn't realised, at the time, how appropriate the name was.

'We weren't at our best,' Nolan admits. 'The lead guitarist was out of tune.'

'You mean you could tell?' she asks incredulously.

'Yeah. When he hit me over the head with his axe,' Nolan grins. 'We get pretty intense out there. It's chaos. I'm surprised you showed up. Most girls I know can't stand acoustic anarchy.'

'I didn't come out tonight expecting to hear acoustic anarchy. To tell you the truth, I didn't come out to see you at all. Not on purpose, anyway. I just ended up here when I got off at the wrong bus stop.'

'That's how most of our fans find us. Through misdirection,' Nolan says. His voice drops an octave, but she can still hear him. 'I'm glad you came.'

It occurs to Jordi that the sensual contact on her upper arm is Nolan's hand. He's touching her at the hem of her shirtsleeve, his fingertips stroking the underside of her arm, where she's always been ticklish. Whatever Nolan's doing to her right now, it definitely doesn't tickle.

'What instrument were you playing?' she asks. 'I never saw you.'

He points across the room, to a tiny square of glass embedded in the wall beneath the rafters. 'I was running the lights. I do lights, sound and sometimes I bang on the drums, when they let me. Tonight I was kinda in the mood to illuminate things. That's how I knew when you came in. You were the hottest girl in the room.'

'Yeah,' Jordi says. 'And the only girl in the room.'

'Nah. There were at least three other chicks out there in the pit. They just look like pro wrestlers. You, on the other hand ...'

Jordi is dying for him to go on, but Nolan simply looks at her. What could he possibly see, besides a girl who eats too many candy bars and spends too much time sitting in front of a computer? Yet he picked her out at Café Wifi that morning, among the thinner, hipper, sexier girls, the girls with tattoos and piercings and a colorful array of erotic fetishes. Now he's gazing at Jordi as if he couldn't have made a better choice.

A green-haired boy, spewing wrathful curses, shoves past Nolan, breaking off his sentence.

'We're blocking the way to the bathroom. We'd better get out of the...um...'

Jordi's words trail off at the end as Nolan peels a strand of hair off her cheek, brushing her lips as he lowers his hand. Jordi's face shimmers in response. His touch is so different from Kurt's that they might as well belong to two different species. Kurt's species would definitely be some-where lower down on the evolutionary ladder. How can one set of fingers, running along her face, make her feel like she's eaten a bad California roll, while another makes her faint with desire? Is it just a matter of technique? Is it a projection of her heart? Or is it a response from tender parts lying south of her heart?

'Blocking the bathroom isn't a safe thing to do, in a club full of angry punks sucking down beer,' Nolan agrees. 'I'm done here for the night. And I'm starving. Want to join me for dinner?'

'I'm kinda broke,' Jordi says. 'Wherever we go, it'll have to be cheap. Or free, really.'

'I was thinking of my place. I heat up a can of ravioli like no one else on earth.'

Nolan smiles. One side of his mouth rises higher than the other, bringing out a groove in his cheek that's too long to be a dimple, but too adorable to be called anything as practical as a 'groove'. He's holding both of her hands now, swinging them back and forth as he waits for her to respond. Jordi smiles back.

'So what do you think?' he asks.

'I think I like being misdirected,' Jordi says.

'When I first started disorganising the books,' Nolan says when they're standing by the stove in his postage-stamp sized kitchen, 'I didn't do it on purpose. It was an impulse. I was tired, I was bored, I was sick of reading the numbers on spines and having faith that the sequence meant something. I shoved a book onto a shelf at random. One book. Then another book. Then I just repeated it over and over. I was mad. I didn't care if the books went back on the shelves in the "correct" order; why should I?'

Nolan hovers over the stove, a spoon poised over a pot of canned ravioli as he delivers a lecture he calls Information Anarchy 101. Jordi leans against the counter. She's half listening, half concentrating on the way Nolan's biceps twitch when he gestures with the spoon. The tight black T-shirt and black jeans are a huge improvement over the baggie gray hoodie he wore earlier. Punk beats monk by a long shot.

'I mean, it's like the whole Library of Congress cataloging system is some sacred cow, and we're all supposed to bow down to it. Melvil Dewey is a *god* to some of these librarians. Why?'

Jordi stares. Eyes flashing, all intense and bothered, Nolan radiates more passion than Jordi's felt in months. It isn't just a romantic cliché that links passion with heat. The human heart is carbon, pure fuel, and when it's ignited by emotion, it *burns*. She waits for Nolan to go on, but he doesn't break their gaze, and she finally clues in that he actually expects her to answer. 'Why?' Nolan repeats, even more insistent than the first time, burning even brighter.

'Uh, what was the question?'

'What's so important about enforcing a cataloging system?'

Jordi's lips open, close, as if she were trying to talk underwater. Then: 'It helps you find stuff.'

'Well, what if you're not looking for books the same way everyone else does? What if that one book you waited for your whole life could be right within reach if it weren't shelved in some order that someone else invented, something that's as random as a car accident?'

'But what you're doing is random, too. It's random on purpose. When an accident happens on purpose, and it's done over and over again in a publicly funded building, isn't it an act of terrorism?'

Nolan's face lights up. He grabs Jordi's hands and squeezes them so tightly that if they'd been oranges, the juices would be flowing all over the countertop. Juices, in fact, are starting to flow at the moment, softening the crevice between Jordi's thighs.

'Exactly! That's what I do. I design public accidents. That's what information anarchy is all about.'

'But why? I still don't get it.'

Jordi's voice sounds muzzy to her own ears. The light on the other side of the window in Nolan's postage stamp of a kitchen is lifting from deep blue to green. Dawn's coming. An image takes shape in Jordi's mind, more delicious than the scent of tomato sauce to her empty stomach: it's a visual of herself lying naked in Nolan's arms, in his bed, which she pictures as a micro version of a library – a library where a bomb has exploded.

Nolan, still holding Jordi's hands, uses them to pull himself closer to her. He's leaning over the table as he replies softly.

'I have faith in disorder.'

'And misdirection?'

He smiles that smile again, the dimple emerging like a star. 'Right. And, even better, I have faith that misdirected things or people find a better place for themselves than if they'd gone the "right" way in the first place.'

'Tell me how that works,' Jordi says, though she's already thanking whatever serendipitous force in the universe dumped her off at the wrong bus stop tonight.

'Here. I'll show you, instead.'

Nolan reaches out with his left hand to turn off the burner under the ravioli, while with his right, he pulls Jordi closer and leans in to touch his lips to hers. It's just a slight kiss, a shadow kiss, no tongue. But that kiss makes the invisible hairs on Jordi's skin rise, then fall, then rise again down the length of her body, in a delicious wave. A purr forms in her mouth, and Nolan takes that as a cue to kiss her harder, deeper. This time she feels his tongue. Unlike Kurt's, it doesn't taste like liverwurst. And it doesn't insist on taking up more space in Jordi's mouth than she's willing to give.

Nolan's hands course quickly across her body, skimming the outer edges of Jordi's figure before coming to rest on her shoulders.

'Know why I like touching you so much?' he asks.

Jordi shakes her head. She waits for the usual compliments, the kind that women want to hear from their bosses but not from would-be boyfriends: smart, dependable, hard-working.

'You're curvy,' Nolan says, squeezing her hips. 'Now let's eat.'

He gives Jordi one more quick kiss on the cheek before turning to the sink to pull out a couple of spoons. He squints at the spoons, then hands one to his guest of honour.

KISS BETWEEN MY LINES

'Nothing's stuck to it,' he says. 'Nothing visible, anyway. Maybe a few microbes, but they're probably harmless. You hungry?'

Jordi's ravenous. Not even the absence of bowls – she doesn't bother to ask, just assumes that eating utensils are scarce around here – discourages her from diving into the ravioli along with Nolan, as they stand side by side in front of the stove. Every now and then her hand brushes his, or his elbow nudges hers, and she feels that tingle again. Apparently the Tingle is an experience that requires actual, spatial proximity, unlike Threading and Throbbing, which can happen through the ether.

'I've got to learn how to duplicate this,' she mumbles through a mouthful of pasta and tomato sauce.

'Duplicate what? My can-opening technique?' Nolan asks.

Jordi glances at him in surprise, unaware that she'd spoken out loud. 'No,' she says. 'I was thinking of something totally different.'

'Like what?'

'I'll tell you someday,' Jordi says mysteriously. 'It has to do with my project. Maybe I'll use you as a guinea pig.'

'Just say the word. I love being a guinea pig. I did a whole research study last summer on this experimental drug that was supposed to improve your focus and make you more organised. Sometimes I wonder if that's why I'm so obsessed with disorganisation now.'

'I think you were probably always like that,' Jordi says.

Nolan nods. 'You're right. I was. Come here.'

She lets her spoon clatter into the empty pot, and Nolan draws her close again. He wraps his arms around Jordi's waist, hands dangling below the small of her back, and rocks her back and forth, as if they were slow-dancing in place. His mouth is so close to hers that their lips could touch, but they don't, and the tiny chasm of space between them somehow excites Jordi more than a full-on French kiss. The tips of their noses whisk against each other each time Nolan subtly swings her. The frames of their glasses touch lightly too, just as she'd imagined they would, clicking like transparent castanets to the rhythm of their bodies.

At this distance, Jordi can see the gold freckles that circle the irises of Nolan's dark green eyes.

Dancing without music, they stand at the stove until their closeness takes a new turn. Jordi can't tell if the heart that's beating so fast is her own, or Nolan's. His breathing turns husky, and, as he leans in to speak into her ear, the skin under his stubbled cheek is warm to the touch. He's warm below the waist too as he turns Jordi against the countertop and nudges his hips against hers. Warm, urgent and hard, his pelvis presses her bottom against the Formica. Another kiss, this time a serious one, is unavoidable now. To hell with Threading and Throbbing; Jordi gives herself up to Tingling as her tongue dances with Nolan's, tips skirting each other's mouths, then plunging deep, only to retreat again.

'I want to take you to bed,' Nolan says, fondling the top button on Jordi's shirt, 'but I think it's too soon.'

Jordi had been thinking the same thing – the ridge underneath his fly had set off sparks of alarm – but she still feels a twinge of disappointment, along with the buzz on her lips where Nolan's mouth used to be.

'Definitely too soon,' she says. 'We need to know each other better.'

'Yeah,' Nolan sighs. He rests his head against her shoulder, nuzzling her in a way that makes her want to cling even tighter to his lean back. 'I tend to fall in love too fast. Then everything gets mixed up, and the whole relationship goes to hell before it even started.'

'I thought you liked things to be mixed up,' Jordi says.

He pulls back and looks into Jordi's eyes. His pupils move slightly back and forth as he searches her from inside.

'Not love and lust,' he says. 'I don't want this to fall apart, like my last crush did. I had a thing for this librarian for months and, when I finally got up the nerve to talk to her, the talking turned to naked confessions in the administrators' break room. We both almost got fired, and she hasn't spoken to me since.'

Crush? Did Nolan just use that word in connection with Jordi, outside of the context of orange soda or a literal flattening of matter? Jordi scans his face for signs of a hidden joke, or a big mistake on her part. She sees nothing but a furrow between his eyebrows that she hadn't noticed before.

'So, is it OK if we just get to know each other slowly before we rip off our clothes and fall into bed?' Nolan is saying.

It dawns on Jordi that she hasn't felt a single wave of nausea since she left her apartment that night. In fact, since she's been with Nolan, she hasn't felt anything but a strange glittering sense of weightlessness that fills her like helium.

She hasn't even been tempted to try Threading Nolan. Not one single time. Surprised to find herself Throbbing and Tingling without LIRA, Jordi wriggles inside her meat-self as if it were a sexy new dress.

'It's way better than OK,' Jordi smiles.

Then something else occurs to her. 'Listen, could you

meet me Monday at the library after you get off work? There's something I have to show you.'

'*After* work?' Nolan scoffs. 'Hey, drop by anytime.'

'Your manager doesn't care if you sneak away to look at something with me?'

'You can't sneak away from the cultivation of chaos,' Nolan says grandly. 'Just come find me. I'll drop everything for a bombshell redhead. Except sleep. That I gotta have. '

One more peck on the cheek, and Nolan walks Jordi downstairs and up to the nearest bus stop. And with the words 'bombshell redhead' bouncing through her brain cells, lighting up her neural networks like a pinball machine, Jordi finally finds her way home.

Bombshell, she thinks, her footsteps so springy that they almost lift her into the air. He called me a bombshell.

Chapter Seven

Dana: The Kindness of Librarians

Darling Deviant,

I don't know what you think of me after my sex-for-sanctuary escapade with Jimmy the security guard, and you know what? As much as I love you, I really don't care about your moral opinion. If you have one, fabulous; if you don't, that's even more fabulous. I'm just trying to survive in the dog-eat-dog world of the public library.

If you think I'm kidding about the dog-eat-dog stuff, you should hear some of the conversations I've picked up on in the ladies' room. The library, which I was starting to embrace as my fairy-tale castle, turns out to be a seething hotbed of envy, competition, and sexual intrigue. Yes, it's true, Darling Deviant, the meek, homely librarian is a myth. Hiding in a bathroom stall this morning, waiting for the library to officially open, I heard a tidbit of gossip that would have made my hair curl, if it weren't already curly.

One female employee, with a taste for restraint, met a reference librarian on the staff with complementary fantasies. This woman's fantasy, apparently, was to be tied up and left alone in the dark for hours by a mysterious, dark, and dominant stranger, who would come back for her at some undisclosed time and inflict all kinds of delicious torments on her flesh. Well, she didn't have hours to live out the fantasy, but she did have 30 minutes for lunch, and a co-worker who was willing to play the 'dark and dominant' stranger (although he himself was as pale and domineering as a mushroom).

So according to the anecdote I overheard in the ladies' room, Master Mushroom had Miss Bondage strip down to her bra and panties in one of the janitorial closets. He then bound her in soft nylon rope, blindfolded her, and ordered her to sit obediently on an overturned bucket while he went out to pick up a sandwich. Imagine the heroine of this bit of nasty gossip squirming as she waited for her captor to return! Across her bare skin she'd feel the dark coolness of the closet's interior, even as she inhaled the aromas of Pine-Sol and book dust. With each footfall in the hallway outside, her nipples would tighten and her skin break out in gooseflesh as she thought about what would happen when her Master returned.

Hours seemed to pass as she waited on the overturned bucket. By this time, her squirming had a large component of irritation. Where the hell was her not-so-dark, not-very-dominant stranger? Annoyance turned to panic as a bit of experimental wriggling proved that, although Master Mushroom had the personality and appearance of a turnip, he was damn good at tying rope.

He was also late – very late. By the time she finally heard his footsteps hurrying down the hallway, our lusty librarian wasn't very lusty anymore. In fact, she was ready to rip the head off her captor as soon as he threw open the door of the closet.

'How could you do this to me?' she shrieked, as the door flew open. 'I'm cold, I'm hungry, and I'm about to pee all over myself.'

Imagine our heroine's surprise when her blindfold was lifted away, and she found herself glaring into the face of a sweet local historian. The historian was visiting the library for a fundraising luncheon, where she'd knocked over an entire urn of coffee. In a fit of humiliation, she'd run to the janitor's closet for a mop, only to find a scene straight from *Private Detective* magazine.

Master Mushroom, as it turned out, had been delayed by a parking ticket.

I could have crouched in the bathroom listening to tales like this all day, but I had more pressing things to do. Like figuring out where to take a long hot bath laced with almond oil. Bathing in public sinks has never been my thing, but stripping down to my bra and scrubbing my armpits over the basin seemed to be my only resort. Fast and furtive, I washed my upper body, then pulled on a clean T-shirt and peeled off my jeans to wash the lower half. If I was going to be caught, I wanted to be caught only half naked. That way, I figured, my mortification would also be cut in half.

It wasn't so much my nudity that bothered me, though I've never liked that roll of pudge around my waist, or the fringe of extra flesh under my upper arms. It was that I couldn't bear the haste of that five-minute toilette, the total absence of pampering. Mine was a body that had been lovingly, lingeringly cleansed and lubricated and combed and brushed for 24 years. Now my flesh, which I was deeply attached to, was being daubed with handfuls of paper towels – the brown scratchy kind, no less – in the same sink where thousands of library patrons and employees washed their hands.

We haven't even talked about washing my hair yet. My hair isn't a flowing stream of silken tresses; it's more like an overgrown shrub. When it's properly conditioned, tamed and straightened, my hair settles into a semblance of civilised beauty. Otherwise, it springs out all over my head and down my back like the burning bush itself, only without any prophetic statements to make. For the moment, I decided to tie the mass of it back with a scrunchie and do my best to forget about it. Glamor was a luxury I hadn't figured out how to afford yet.

How do you start a day with no agenda? More importantly, how do you start a day with no coffee? My body, without its usual morning dose of fresh-ground black Sumatran, felt like a buzzing ball of irritation; each uncaffeinated cell cried out for something to zap it back to consciousness. The library wouldn't open to the public till ten, which was normally the time that your heroine would be stretching and yawning in her bed, lengthening her limbs like a plump Persian cat and thinking about getting up to pour a mug of java from the pot the maid had brewed, before checking her schedule for any pressing obligations. Nine times out of ten, there weren't any obligations, pressing or otherwise. The day would be devoted to a bit of freelance work in Daddy's home office followed by lunch with girlfriends, a round of light shopping, cocktails and, of course, a rendezvous with the lover *du jour* that would last until dawn drove me back to my beautiful bed in the sky.

Today I had nothing to do but wander the stacks, read, brood, blog and hide. Until the library officially opened, hiding, reading, and brooding were my only real options. Once the ladies' room was clear, and I'd taken my pitiful whore's bath with paper towels and hand detergent, I found a dusty corner in the last row of shelves on the third floor. Since there was no one to help me now beside myself, it seemed ironically appropriate that I'd ended up in the Self-Help section.

My father would have sobbed with joy to see me crouching on the floor of the public library, perusing books with titles like *Love: One Addict's Journey to Hell and Beyond* and *When the Fairy-tale's Over, Who Keeps the Castle?* At one time, he had tried to rehabilitate me discreetly by planting books like these, in their paperback version, on my dresser and in my Jeep. He'd even left a couple of them in the bar behind the gin. I read those books. I read about women who loved too much, too little, and not at all. I pored over the confessions of porn junkies and adulterous soccer moms. I beefed up my self-confidence; I opened my heart; I illuminated my spirit. I popped those self-help books like chocolates, then let their wisdom glide through my mind with laxative ease.

Now that I was trapped for the next 45 minutes, those books had become my fellow inmates. I picked up *When the Fairy-tale's Over* and tried to read. But it's tough to focus on the pitfalls of romantic love when you have to look up after every paragraph to scan the ceiling.

I'd been in the library less than 24 hours, and I was already starting to get paranoid. After what Jimmy told me about security cameras, I was starting to look for their blank beady eyes in every corner. I found myself clinging to walls, ducking into corners whenever the back of my neck started to prickle. It was only a matter of time before someone would spot my lurking form and say, 'Hasn't that woman been here four days in a row – wearing the same clothes? And look how flat and matted her hair looks; you can tell she hasn't used conditioner.'

On the other hand, the thought of being caught on tape having wild, reckless, semi-public sex in the library did set off a few sparks in my loins. I imagined a group of slack-jawed guards and library staff huddled around a monitor, watching a grainy black-and-white version of myself bucking and moaning in the throes of passion, and those sparks roared into a bonfire. Paranoia versus exhibitionism: which would win in the battle for my soul?

I didn't really have the attention span to sustain any specific paranoid fantasy. The flip side of self-consciousness is vanity, and I've always loved to be the center of attention. If possible, I'd rather have positive adoring attention, but I'll settle for the sleazy voyeuristic kind.

Meanwhile, I wasn't the focus of anything at all in my cramped self-help corner of the world. I decided to take my chances and get up to explore the building. Still skirting the open areas, I crept down three flights of stairs to the basement to check out Multimedia. This would be a good place to fritter away some time, I figured; with a pair of headphones stuck over my ears, I could get lost in music and forget my more practical woes.

The lights over the banks of CDs were still dimmed. The Multimedia room was empty. I drifted along the shelves, running my hand along the CD cases. So much at my fingertips, yet I couldn't actually touch any of it, or listen, not yet. Vivaldi, Enya, Nina Simone . . . so much pleasure for the ears, all of it hovering on the other side of a barrier of time. Delayed gratification was such a new experience that I almost didn't recognise the gnawing throb.

Want. That's what it was. Not the desire that already sees its object in reach, but the gut-deep absence of some-thing that I knew would fill me. It was hell for a hedonist, being tantalised like this; no wonder hermits had to go out into the bleak desolate wilderness when they wanted to meditate on God or the Great Pumpkin or on whomever it was they contemplated. Life in the thick of the world was just too packed with sensory treats.

'In the mood for anything in particular?'

I froze, my hand poised somewhere above the blues. Somewhere in my primordial brain, that voice registered as male, beautifully male. I love a man with a butterscotch voice, rich and mellow, not too deep, but deep enough to hit that sweet spot in my ears that somehow connects straight to my pussy.

I opened my mouth. A sound came out, but it didn't make much sense. All I could think of was that I'd been caught, maybe fatally caught this time. Then I saw the man who'd addressed me, and my mind veered off in a totally different direction. This was a man, yes, but a man from a different time. Tall and slender, dark and elegant, he wore a crisp white shirt that set off his sleek black hair and olive skin to perfection. A trimmed mustache punctuated a mouth that would have been too vulnerable on its own. Break my heart, Mr Multimedia Librarian, I thought. Let me drown in those almond-shaped brown eyes, and take my last breath through those divine lips.

'We're not actually open yet.' He cocked his head. 'How'd you get in here, anyway?'

'I ... uh ... walked through the door,' I stammered. 'One of them was open. Upstairs.'

When he smiled, his eyes crinkled at the corners, and I mentally clicked off the 'maturity' box on his list of assets.

'Really.' It was a statement, not a question.

'Yes, really. Somebody must have made a mistake. I just assumed the library was open already. I didn't know better. I swear.'

Not many men could make me babble anymore, but this one stripped my verbal faculties to the bone.

'Don't worry. I won't tell. You don't have anywhere else to go, do you?'

I shook my head.

'You know, I could recommend a good women's shelter here in the city. It's quiet, it's small and it's relatively safe. You haven't been on the streets for very long, I'm thinking.'

He eyed my clothes, my hair. I'm not sure how he'd reached the conclusion that I hadn't been 'on the streets' for very long; as far as I could tell, I looked and smelled like I'd been wandering the wide world forever.

'What's your name?' he asked. He smiled again, the eyes half-disappearing behind those sexy crinkles. 'Or should I call you Cinderella?'

'I'm Dana.' My lower lip felt dangerously wobbly.

'And I'm Christopher.' He held out his hand. I took it. He squeezed my palm and fingers as he studied my face with those liquid eyes. 'Let me take care of you. Just for a little while.'

If he kept going in that direction, I was going to break down and throw myself against his cotton-clad, washboard torso and beg him to take me home. What did I care? I'd left my pride back at home, with my hairdryer, my jet-stream Jacuzzi bathtub, and my collection of Clinique cosmetic products. I'd be Christopher's live-in maid. I'd be his pet. I'd sleep on a blanket on the floor at the foot of his bed; I'd wake at dawn to do his bidding.

Prince Christopher, may I have the honour of washing your feet this morning? I'd ask. And he would let me bathe his feet with warm water and essential oils, and dry them with my hair à la Mary Magdalene as I knelt before him. We'd share a kind of love I'd never experienced before: the kind where I wasn't the center of the guy's universe, but a satellite planet, rotating in his orbit.

Hey, I'd try anything for a warm bath and a hot toddy.

'Come back to my office. I'll put on a CD for you,' Prince Christopher was saying. 'What's your preference?'

I thought about it for a second, then I chose Nina Simone. Her wistful husky voice seemed like what I needed this morning, the smoky melancholy of another woman in pain.

'Good choice,' he said. I felt blessed.

Prince Christopher was still holding my hand, mostly because I was clinging to him like a life preserver. He didn't let go as he found a recording of Nina's greatest hits for me, then lead me to a cubicle behind the Multimedia Department's information desk. The walls of his immaculate cubby were lined with photos of musicians from a dizzying range of genres: Billie Holliday, Itzhak Perlman, Joni Mitchell, Sid Vicious. In one corner sat a small stereo, equipped with a pair of headphones (a real set, not the little bud kind that buzz in your ears like bugs). But what really caught my eye was a large paper cup topped with a cone-shaped white lid, sitting next to a croissant that looked as huge as one of Cézanne's haystacks, rising huge and golden on its napkin.

God, I hope this crazy chick doesn't drool on my breakfast, Prince Christopher must have been thinking, but he was too gallant to say such a thing. Still, I held back when he nudged me toward his chair. Maybe I did have a smidgen of pride left. After all, I hadn't jumped on his croissant and ripped it to flaky shreds.

'Have a seat, Dana. Go on. It's fine. I'm not going to give you away to the Library Police. '

Prince Christopher pulled out his ergonomic chair for me. I sat down. He brushed my hair away from my ears, and settled the headphones over my head. Then he opened the CD case, pressed a few buttons on the stereo, and Nina's voice filled my ears. Perfect. She sounded exactly like the inside of my head that morning. I closed my eyes and listened to 'Lilac Wine', and, for the first time since I found that awful letter yesterday in the room that used to be my bedroom, I felt OK.

'These are for you, by the way. You're not caffeine-free, are you?'

I opened my eyes. Christopher picked up the coffee and croissant and set them within my reach.

I stared up into his eyes, twin pools the color of root beer. His lips curved under the perfect mustache. Prince Christopher's beauty didn't originate with the flawless symmetry of his features, or the smoothness of his olive skin, or even those devastating eyes. On the other hand, all that stuff didn't hurt.

'I am so *not* caffeine-free,' I reassured him. 'But are you sure you want to sacrifice your breakfast? Don't you want all this?' I waved my hand at what suddenly looked like a banquet to me.

'It's not a matter of whether I want it. It's a matter of whether you need it. Enjoy.'

With that, my prince departed. I was worse than Blanche DuBois; I not only relied on the kindness of strangers, I was getting free caffeine fixes from them. My hand shook as I reached for the coffee; a true addict, I neglected the food and went straight for my drug of choice. One sip, and I was back in my skin again. Bless Prince Christopher, he'd bought himself an Americano that morning, my favorite. In between sips of that blissful near-bitterness, I took bites of the croissant, which turned out to be stuffed with warm ham and Swiss cheese, and I listened to Nina, and I was in heaven.

I couldn't even thank my benefactor, because he'd not only given me coffee, food, and music; he'd given me a safe place to be alone with my thoughts for a while. Safety, privacy, and solitude were luxuries too. I'd never appreciated them, of course. Between pleasure and appreciation stretched a black hole that I'd never attempted to cross. I did not savor fill-in-the-blank (food, coffee, sex, life); I gobbled and reached for more.

And I had to stop that train of thought before it lead to canonization. A little gratitude goes a long way. Too much is a dangerous thing.

I reached for the croissant.

In four flaky bites, Dear Reader, I gobbled someone else's breakfast.

I wouldn't have minded lolling around in Prince Christopher's cubicle all day, but I knew he'd be back eventually to reclaim his workspace. I didn't want to get caught in the crossfire of anything like 'work'. I threw away the empty coffee cup and brushed the croissant flakes off his desk, and figured that would be my hard labor for the day.

Trying to survive in the cold cruel world of public computer access was work enough for this displaced princess. Because the library's doors had literally just opened, I assumed I could go straight to one of the computers and continue hammering away at my misadventures in my blog. I was wrong. By the time I arrived at the check-in desk, there was already a small snake of people shuffling their feet and scratching themselves as they waited their turns. From the shifty unwashed looks of them, I assumed they all needed their daily free porn fix. Then I remembered that I was as shifty and unwashed as the rest of them, maybe more so.

(One more lesson in humility, Dear Deviant, and your heroine was going to give up her noble life of poverty and become a high-class hooker.)

Porn could be an interesting diversion, I mused as I waited for my turn on the computer. I could see myself getting lost in its lurid wet tentacles, drowning my sorrows in the pink-and-brown-and-purple world of internet flesh. Hell, I was so in awe of the library's anti-censorship stance that I almost felt morally obligated to become an online porn freak. But watching strangers wrapped in each others' sweaty limbs, tongues laving each others' moist pink orifices, wasn't what I wanted. I wanted those fleshy delights for myself. I craved skin. I trembled with the need for kisses.

I was an addict, after all, and each second away from my source took me deeper into withdrawal. Could it really be less than 48 hours since I'd been caught lying naked under Blake, his cock between my breasts as we bumped and banged joyfully against the headboard? It felt like forever. The episode with the security guard had been sweet and tender, like a dumpling appetiser at a Chinese wedding, but I wanted the orgiastic feast itself.

I sighed as I pulled myself up onto one of the high stools in front of a public computer and finally got back to my blog. I was determined to be one of those brutally honest journalers who rips their soul, and panties, open for the world. Hold nothing back – that would be my philosophy. Faithfully recording all my fantasies, my encounter with Jimmy, my near-romance with Prince Christopher, I felt like an adventuress in the wild alleys of the heart.

I only had 45 minutes on the public computer to spill my most recent confessions, so I made the most of the time, pounding madly at the keyboard till I'd emptied my soul.

A couple of other people glanced at me with bleary morning eyes, squinting in irritation at the racket I was making, but I didn't care. Having a psychological catharsis is like having an orgasm – when it's coming on, you have to let it flow. I wanted to grab the world, at least the small segment of it that might stumble onto my blog, by the balls and make it know who I was. Homeless love junkie, sex-starved sensualist, and who knew what else?

By the time the computer kicked me off my session, I felt drained. Light-headed and trembling, I gave up my seat to a bored kid with a Mohawk and walked away.

'Writing a love letter? Or your memoirs?'

The reference librarian I'd met yesterday stood in front of me, blocking my path. With his wire-rimmed glasses and fox-colored hair, he was as neatly groomed as ever. He was very tasty. I'd eat him, given half the chance. Today he wore a tweed jacket over another Oxford shirt and jeans. I liked that look, casual but academic, like one of those professors who might slip his hand under your skirt during a mid-semester conference, if the skirt was short enough, and you flirted intelligently enough, while lifting your thighs at the right angle.

'Both,' I said. I tilted my head and batted my eyelashes a couple of times. 'Why, are you interested?'

'I think I'd be interested in anything you had to say.'

'Even if it was racy?'

'Especially if it was racy. Who wouldn't want to read the erotic memoirs of a beautiful woman? I've got a small collection of them, in fact.'

Steffen. That was his name. I was starting to like him. I've always been a sucker for a man who calls me beautiful but, with my ego lying somewhere in a Dumpster along with the excess stuff Jimmy and I had thrown away last night, I blossomed under Steffen's admiring gray-blue gaze.

'Were those memoirs written by lovers of yours?' I asked.

'Some of them. Most are classics – Anaïs Nin, Fanny Hill –'

'Hey, Fanny doesn't count. That was a novel, and it was written by a guy. John Cleland.'

Steffen smiled. 'English lit major?'

I smiled back, punctuating the smile with a flutter of eyelashes. 'How did you guess?'

'I don't think anyone else would recognise Fanny, or know the author's name. When I read *Fanny Hill* for the first time at fifteen, she became a real woman for me. Very much like you, I suspect.'

Now this librarian was really getting interesting. 'How so?'

Steffen assessed my face, my hair, my figure, apparently without noticing the fact that 1) I had no make-up on, 2) my hair was a flattened rat's nest, and 3) I was wearing the same clothes he'd seen me in yesterday.

'You're voluptuous. Sensual. A woman of strong appetites, with an earthy sense of humor and an unapologetic hunger for life. If I were Cleland, I would have had someone very much like you in my mind when I created Fanny.'

I've been compared to lots of women – mostly ex-girlfriends, renowned high school sluts and the occasional overweight actress – but never to a classic erotic character. I didn't know how to take Steffen's compliment, with spice or salt or both?

'What are you thinking?'

Steffen lowered his voice to ask the question, and I suddenly imagined him saying that to me in bed, as we lay together in a post-coital fog. I love a man who cares about what I'm thinking. I love it even more when he takes the trouble to ask.

'I was just thinking how much ordinary people hide. I'd never have guessed that you have an erotica collection at home. Or that the women you work with like to be tied up naked in the janitor's closet.'

'Very few people are ordinary once you get to know them,' Steffen said. 'And which one of my colleagues likes to be tied up naked in the janitor's closet? That's a bit of gossip that hasn't gotten around to me yet.'

'You should hang out in the ladies' restroom once in a while.'

'I'm not quite that much of a pervert, I'm afraid.'

'Oh, I don't know. I'd imagine you lead a fairly twisted life, when you're not sitting behind the reference desk.'

'Ah, but the life of a reference librarian isn't half as tame as you'd think. Nor is the librarian himself.'

We were in full-blown flirt mode now, which is why it didn't seem strange at all when Steffen asked me to join him for dinner that evening – at his house, only a few blocks from the library.

'That way, you could check out my private collection,' he said. 'I think you'd enjoy it. Immensely.'

Darling Deviant, I know what must be going through your mind right now. If you grew up nourished on the brilliant repartee of Beavis and Butt-head, you're probably thinking something along these lines: 'He said "view my private collection", heh, heh, heh.'

To be perfectly honest, I was thinking the same thing. And when Steffen took my hand, and brought it to his lips to give it a wry, mock-gallant kiss, I thought I'd like to view anything he had to show me. He left a trace of sandalwood soap on my skin and, for an hour after we parted, with arrangements for me to meet him at his place at seven-thirty (he offered to pick me up at 'home', but I quickly dodged that one), I kept rubbing my nose with my fingers so that I could breathe in that spicy mysterious scent.

I love a spicy mysterious man with a houseful of books. Especially when his dirty secrets are neatly covered by a layer of tweed, and his house holds the potential for a long hot bath.

The day unfolded at a leisurely pace, too leisurely for an addict in need of a fix. I busied my hands for a couple of hours with more reshelving, but my mind roiled with lewd images. I couldn't stop thinking about the librarian who'd arranged to have her co-worker tie her up in the janitor's closet. I kept imagining her, naked and squirming. In double darkness – the dark of the closet, and the dark behind the blindfold – she would have been all alone with her dread and lust. Fear and desire: now *that* was a potent cocktail, strong enough to give me a second-hand buzz.

It's not as easy as you might think, Dear Deviant, for a woman like me to find a willing playmate, especially when my needs are a little more exotic than usual. As I peeked around the tops of the books and the corners of the book-shelves, hunting for a potential playmate, I realised that the type of men I usually go for don't hang out in the library during the day. Most of the men sitting at the tables or browsing the online catalogs looked like sporadically employed novelists or retired civil employees. Buried in books, their faces had the intent furrowed look of people with minor obsessions or major anxieties. They wore cardigans in earth tones and button-down shirts with missing buttons.

I felt like a lioness trying to hunt for game in a desert filled with prairie dogs. If any of these fellows were going to tie me up naked in a closet, I'd have to overcome their fixations on Norse mythology or the history of Watergate.

I soon gave up and drifted downstairs. I let my hand drag along the rail of the escalator like a disgruntled and horny Scarlett O'Hara. Here I was in this temple of information, source of answers to almost any conceivable question, and I couldn't figure out where to meet a guy who would tie me up naked in a closet. He didn't have to be Rhett Butler; he just had to be a kinky, reasonably attractive gentleman with a mildly sadistic streak.

Lo and behold, there he was, dark and mysterious, more perfect than I could have hoped. Christopher the multimedia librarian ambled across the foyer, his sleek black hair and mustache gleaming under the lights.

'Christopher? Christopher!' I waved frantically from my descending staircase.

He looked up. When he recognised me, his lips formed a promising smile. I'd wondered earlier that morning, when he fed me breakfast and left me alone with Nina Simone, if Christopher might prefer the company of his own sex. He still triggered my gaydar; there was something about a man who would give up his breakfast without even trying to grope me that somehow seemed odd. On the other hand, if he'd been willing to sacrifice an Americano for me, who knew what else he'd be capable of?

'I need to ask you a favor,' I panted, catching up to him in the lobby. 'And I have to warn you up front – it's kind of kinky.'

'Why doesn't that surprise me?' he asked. His eyelids crinkled around warmly smiling brown eyes. 'Somehow

I guessed that you'd be a woman with unusual tastes. What can I do for you?'

I wondered how he could have guessed that I had such diverse erotic appetites, when he'd only seen me in a state of utter destitution. I left that question up to the same mysterious forces that led me to the conclusion that Prince Christopher was gay. Maybe those forces were right; maybe they were wrong; most likely we all had far more erotic potential than we ever gave ourselves credit for.

I stood up on my tiptoes to whisper into Prince Christopher's perfectly shaped ear, stealing a whiff of his musky aftershave as I did so. First I spilled the gossip about the librarian who'd been tied up in the closet, then I asked him if he'd be willing to do the same thing to me. Describing my fantasy to a near stranger was like slipping a note into a wishing wall; I had no clue how he'd respond, or whether he'd respond at all. I was sending my desires out to the universe on a breeze of sheer faith.

When he'd heard my request, Christopher stepped back. He studied me curiously, one black eyebrow rising like a wing.

'I didn't think the favor would be *that* unusual,' he finally said.

My heart and my libido sank in unison. 'Too kinky for you, huh?'

'Not necessarily too kinky, but possibly too risky. I work here, after all. I can't go tying up women and leaving them in closets. Besides, I wouldn't know where or how to start tying. I don't bring blindfolds or long lengths of rope with me to work every day.'

I pondered his objections, gave them careful weight, then tried to wheedle him out of them.

'But you wouldn't have to leave me for very long,' I begged.

'Fifteen minutes, max. And I've got all kinds of ideas for things you could tie me with: socks, electrical wire, packing tape. I'm creative and resourceful. Please?'

I was also horny, lonely and desperate for a little edgy excitement to distract me from my problems, but I didn't tell Prince Christopher any of this. That would have been too much pressure. He must have seen the despair on my face, however, because the wariness in his eyes was turning into a gleam of interest.

'Fair enough,' he said, 'but, if we do this, we'll have to meet each other halfway. If I agree to help you fulfill your fantasy, you have to agree to fulfill mine.'

Dear Deviant, this scenario was getting so much better than I thought! I agreed to any variations on the fantasy that would please Prince Christopher, and we arranged to go downstairs to the multimedia room in the basement. His first condition was that we had to use a different closet, one on his turf. He knew the ideal place: a locked storage area where some of the older media were kept. His second condition . . . well, I would find out about that soon enough. Christopher smiled at me, and I felt that warm sunburst of joy behind my ribs that always hits me when I'm in the presence of an exceptionally beautiful man.

'Soon enough' was still way too long.

The interior of the multimedia storage room was cool and smelled of dust. Sitting on the ergonomic chair from Christopher's cubby, my hands tied behind me with packing tape, I felt more like an abandoned piece of office furniture than a sexy damsel in distress. My blindfold, the scarf that Christopher had worn to work that morning, was the only sensually appealing detail in the scenario so far. Feathery soft cashmere, faintly scented by cedar, it reminded me of the handsome librarian who'd left me captive here.

'I'll be back soon,' he had whispered to me, before leaving me and locking the door behind him. 'And then we'll play out *my* part of the fantasy.'

'How soon is soon?' I asked. I had decided long ago that 'soon', along with 'never' and 'no' and 'celibacy', was one of the most vile words in the English language.

'If I told you, that would spoil my fun. And yours,' Christopher said.

So I waited, shifting my bare bottom on the scratchy seat and trying to find a halfway comfortable position. Being naked alone in the dark wasn't nearly as exciting as I'd thought. I tried to relax and imagine what sorts of evil things Christopher was going to do to my body, but all I could think about was food. My stomach kept rumbling, asking for club sandwiches with potato chips, hot fudge sundaes topped with cherries, Porterhouse steaks heaped with sliced mushrooms. The croissant that Prince Christopher had given me that morning was a memory by now.

As if hunger weren't bad enough, I was getting cold. For some reason, I'd never taken room temperature into account when I played out this fantasy in my mind, but the multimedia storage room was starting to feel more like a meat locker, and my poor nipples were turning into ice cubes. I could feel a dust-induced allergic spasm building inside my nose, but the tickle wasn't strong enough to bring me any relief. Your poor little sex junkie was not only horny; she was hungry, cold and she had to sneeze. So much for anticipatory thrills.

A key turned in the lock, and the door opened. Light sieved through the blindfold, but I couldn't see who was standing there. What if it wasn't Christopher? What if it was some other librarian, or an administrator, or some other member of the staff? What if it was one of the security guards, not my lovely little Jimmy, but some brute with a taste for naked redheads wrapped in packing tape?

'Hello?' I said. 'Christopher? Is that you?'

'Shhhh.'

The door closed behind him. I heard footsteps, but I had no idea to whom they belonged. I lifted my nose, trying to catch some sort of clue from the person's scent, but all I could smell was dust, dust and more dust.

I sneezed.

The person in the room with me didn't say 'Bless you', or offer to wipe my nose. That was my first indication that this stranger might not be my generous, chivalrous Prince. The second clue was the way the stranger circled me, then gripped my hair in his hand and pulled my head back to kiss me at full throttle. Prince Christopher had a mustache; this guy, whoever he was, did not. Still, he was a hell of a kisser, a master of lip music and, most importantly, he knew how to handle a handful of springy red hair. That firm tug at my roots yanked me out of my daydreams and my discontent; as soon as his tongue penetrated my mouth, I was smack in the present again. A large hand fondled one of my breasts, squeezing the nipple. The hand was strong and assertive, but the skin was as smooth and cool as ice cream; clearly this guy didn't do hard labour for a living.

Christopher's fingers, I remembered, were slim and tapered. These fingers were blunt and broad.

'You're not Christopher, are you?' I whispered.

His only answer was to gently part my thighs with his knee and reach between my legs. Somehow, in spite of my angry belly and my icy skin, I'd managed to get wet while

I was waiting. His fingers, too blunt and demanding to belong to my courtly Prince, slipped easily between the folds and set to work pleasuring me. Now this was more like it. I had turned into one of those bound-and-blindfolded dames on the covers of old detective magazines from the 1950s, only I was that dame after the lights went out, when she and her captor were alone.

Those deft fingers brought a mewling sound from my lips, but it was mostly swallowed by the stranger's kiss. He hadn't stopped kissing me; by now I was beginning to feel like I was floating blissfully underwater. When he began to rub me lightly along the length of my pussy, from my bottom all the way to my mound, I began to drown. Ten minutes ago, when I was shivering alone in the chair, I never dreamed I'd be on the brink of an orgasm right now. But here I was, so excited that I could hardly breathe. I could moan, though, and mewl and whimper, and beg him not to stop, and I did all of those things through the stranger's lips as he kissed me all the way to a climax. I bucked in the chair until the delectable tremors subsided, then I went limp.

I almost didn't hear the shuffling sound to my right. My loosened muscles suddenly went stiff.

'Someone else is here,' I gasped, when he broke our kiss to let me come up for air. 'This was supposed to be a private fantasy, not performance art.'

'Hush, Dana. It's OK.'

It wasn't the man kissing me who spoke. It was Stranger #2, standing in the corner. Stranger #2 sounded suspiciously like Prince Christopher, only he couldn't be *my* prince, because Christopher wasn't kinky enough to bring someone else into the room to pleasure me while he watched.

Or was he?

'Why are you both here?' I asked. The more I thought about this twist on my fantasy, the more intrigued I was.

'Because we both think you're absolutely beautiful.'

Someone lifted the cashmere scarf off my head. I looked up to see two male faces gazing down at me. There wasn't much light in the storage closet, except for the thin fluorescent strip that outlined the door, but there was enough illumination for me to recognise Christopher. Standing next to him was another man, tall and blond. Stranger #1 was built like a Viking and dressed like a male model from an L.L. Bean catalog. The man who'd just made a blindfolded naked woman come looked more like he was ready for a jaunt in the woods with his Labrador Retriever.

'I'm Jeff. I do systems administration here,' said the preppy Viking. 'Chris and I are roommates.'

'Jeff and I have a few fantasies in common,' Christopher said. 'One of them happened to be this one. I couldn't resist bringing him in. I apologise if this isn't what you wanted.'

'Not what I wanted?' I repeated faintly. 'It's so much more.'

Christopher stroked my shoulder. 'I'm so glad. We wanted to do something special for you.'

'For me?' I echoed.

'And for ourselves, too. We're not saints.'

Something salty and lumpy seemed to be stuck in my throat. It felt suspiciously like a ball of tears, and I didn't want to break out sobbing in front of these two gorgeous males.

'I'd better get dressed,' I said. 'And you guys had better get back to work, before you get caught and spanked.'

Christopher and Jeff exchanged a smile that told me they were considerably more than roommates. Whatever they were to each other, wherever they lived, I wanted to move in with them. We could play games like this every night. I'd cook and clean for them, and iron their khaki trousers and button-down shirts, and we'd be a happy kinky family.

But I knew that would never work. Chris and Jeff had their own lives together, just like my father and Chastity. Everyone had someone; lids were settled snugly on pots; partnerships were comfortably established.

I, on the other hand, was taped to a chair, alone.

Chapter Eight

Jordi: Love Is Rarely Attainable

Jordi dreams that she's Throbbing. There's no one in the dream but herself and some nameless, faceless Threader on the other side of a sea of ether, but the attraction radiating between them drenches her brain cells in light. Each pulsation heightens her sensual pleasure, drawing her nerves together like the delicate strings of a cat's cradle. Though she's never clearly aware of the fact that another flesh-and-blood human is orchestrating her Throb, she never loses consciousness of her partner either. Her lover could be male or female, animal or mineral; it really doesn't matter when she's climbing to the heights of nirvana.

Before she can reach that peak, Jordi's dream takes a detour into reality, and she's suddenly sitting up in bed, surrounded by her co-developers. One of the drawbacks of having such intensive neural connections with Tuan, Caryn, Fleek, and Bob is that they tend to pop up in her mind at any waking (or non-waking, as the case may be) moment, armed with opinions or objections.

'You're not really "coming" if the genitals aren't involved, Jordi,' complains the dream version of Caryn. A triathlete with a degree in neurobiology who works as an auto mechanic in her spare time, Caryn is the most pragmatic of the bunch, and the most deeply engaged in meat-life.

'If there's really any kind of orgasm taking place, we haven't been able to establish a direct link to Throbbing.'

Bob, horny net geek extraordinaire, rolls his eyes. 'Come on, Caryn. I had my first cyberorgasm in 1989, and it was from a scorching hot email that turned out to have been written by some geek. No, I couldn't establish a direct link between my orgasm and the text on the screen, but if you're such a hardcore materialist, you should stick to running marathons and fixing radiators.'

'They're both smoking crack, Jordi,' Fleek interjects. 'What we're trying to achieve here is neither material nor immaterial. It's a mystical union of minds with resonance in the flesh. Caryn wants LIRA to be another dating site. Cumshot Bob wants to infect it with the immanence of porn. This is sooo far from the vision we had in the beginning, Jordi.'

'OK, guys, time out.' Tuan pats the air with his hands in a simmer-down gesture. 'This is Jordi's experience. If she says she's having an orgasm, who are we to say she's not? Our goal is to create the experience. How the Threader defines that experience is up to her. Or him. Or it, or them, or whatever.'

Jordi sits up, clutching her pillow. 'Would you all just stop it? I'm not having an orgasm. I'm not even Throbbing anymore, thanks to you guys.'

'I thought you wanted us here. You called us,' Fleek points out. His sensitive philosopher's eyes are reproachful.

'Did I?' Jordi sighs. 'I guess I did.'

'We just wanted to help,' says Caryn. 'I've been feeling weird since yesterday.'

'Me too. Withdrawals, big time,' says Tuan. 'I can't hold down food, and I have a headache as big as the Ritz.'

'I thought it was food poisoning,' adds Bob. 'I didn't know

we were in for this kind of thing if the system crashed. I guess that blows your approach out of the water, Caryn. If we can have physical withdrawals from LIRA, we can have authentic orgasms.'

'Why are you all so fixated on genitalia?' Fleek complains. 'We try to take human relationships to a higher level, and we end up right back in the Freudian muck.'

'Let's just get LIRA up and running again. We can finish this discussion later. Jordi? You're going to have to wake up and work with us, girlfriend. This withdrawal thing is starting to suck.'

Someone is shaking Jordi's shoulder. She groans, rolls over, tries to mummify herself in her blankets, but the shaking only intensifies.

'Jordi? Hey, it's me. I just got off the red-eye from San Fran; the least you could do is get up and make me some pancakes.'

Jordi opens her eyes to find herself staring into a fiery nest of hair. Confusion is elbowed out of the way by joy as she recognises Tuan's oval face.

'Tuan? Are you really here?'

'How else would we be having this conversation? We can't Thread anymore, and I don't see a phone next to your ear.'

'Can I . . . I mean, should I . . . could I hug you?' Jordi asks.

'Hell, yes. You'd better. I need some meat contact right now.'

Tuan reaches for her, and Jordi rises out of the warm tangle of blankets to take his slender body into her arms. Through the leather of his jacket, through the layers of skin and muscle and bone, she feels the eager percussion of his heart. His cheek is cool and smooth against hers; his breath is warm and dry and smells of fake tropical fruit.

'Have you been eating Skittles already?' Jordi asks. 'The

way you pound sugar, I'm amazed that you have any teeth left.'

'Couldn't help it. My material being was crashing. Candy was the only thing that could save me. How are *you* holding up?'

Tuan breaks away from her and sits down on the bed, bouncing a little. A perpetual motion machine, he's always bouncing, jittering, jiving. His brain is just as active; Throbbing with Tuan is an ecstatic electron dance.

Which leads Jordi to wonder ... what would meat sex with him be like?

'You know, I'm not doing too bad,' Jordi says. 'Kind of odd, isn't it? I designed LIRA; you'd think I'd feel it the worst. Last night I felt horrible for a while, but this morning I'm OK. Better than OK, actually.'

Tuan narrows his eyes at her. 'You didn't go out and get laid, did you? I mean, literally laid?'

Jordi feels her cheeks getting hot. 'No.'

'But you did something, right? You had flesh-on-flesh contact. I can tell.'

'How? How could you possibly know that?'

'Because you're not sick, like me and the others. We've all been puking and rolling around with headaches since yesterday morning. You, on the other hand, are glowing, girlfriend. Who's the ignoramus who thinks you like meatboys?'

'Maybe I do like meat-boys,' Jordi says defensively.

'One in particular. Am I right?'

'Yes, you're right. I like a meat-boy. I like him a lot. I went to his apartment last night, and we ate ravioli in his kitchen, and I let him kiss me. So you know my dirty secret. Are you happy now?'

Tuan's sallow frowning face looks anything but happy.

'Yeah. I'm happy for you, if you're happy. But you're breaking our agreement. We all said we wouldn't have a "real" relationship until LIRA was out of beta. We didn't want to dilute the connections, or break any of the Threads with physical contact.'

Jordi hangs her head. 'I know, Tuan. But this sort of just happened.'

Tuan throws up his hands. 'That's always how it is. Sex "just happens". Love "just happens". It's all random and messy and accidental. Exactly what we were trying to avoid! Love, as humanity knows it, is a disaster. We go out searching for the fairy-tale fantasy; we end up with a bad sitcom. That's why we started this project in the first place. Remember what LIRA stands for?'

'"Love Is Rarely Attainable",' Jordi drones in a sing-song. 'But I'm thinking of changing that to "Life Is Really Annoying". I didn't ask for any of this to happen, Tuan. Do you think I'd want my life's work to crash on me? Or that I wanted to let you guys down? Nolan doesn't want to fall in love with me. He just wants to help me.'

'So that's his name. Nolan? I'm getting an image of a renegade nerd.'

'He *is* sort of a renegade nerd,' Jordi admits. 'How did you know?'

Tuan taps his temple with his index finger. Then he does the same thing to Jordi's forehead. 'You forget, we're permanently Threaded. I know you, Jordi. I know all your secrets, all your fantasies, all your dirty thoughts.'

'You do not!'

'Well, OK. Maybe I don't. But you're a geek, so it only makes sense you'd fall in love with a nerd. And that he'd be a rebel, because in your sweet little good-girl heart, you want a bad boy.'

'In my heart, I don't want any boy.' Jordi throws her blankets aside and swings her legs over the bed, almost accidentally kicking Tuan. 'I just want my computer to work again so my life can get back to normal and you'll all stop bugging me in my dreams.'

But her definition of 'normal', Jordi realises as she stomps off to the bathroom to wash the sleep out of her eyes, has changed overnight. 'Normal' looks and feels and smells different to how it did 48 hours ago, when her daily routine consisted of hours spent in the ether, sending out tendrils of desire to people she couldn't see or hear or touch.

'So when are you and Nolan going to do the nasty?' Tuan asks from behind the closed bathroom door.

'We're not!'

'Oh, come on. It'll be delicious. You can't wait to get your hands all over this guy's meat, and you know it. You'll not only have the base thrill of boinking someone, you'll have the sweet taste of treachery.'

Jordi opens the door and looks her friend in the face. 'I'm not betraying any of you. I'm trying to have a life,' she snaps.

Tuan shrinks back as if she'd slapped him. 'LIRA *is* your life, Jordi. Mine, too. How can you say that?'

Tuan's dark eyes are glinting with ... tears? Jordi wants to hug him again, like she did before, but touching him still feels strange. Spontaneity, with LIRA, has no fleshly component. Any deviation in the dance is strictly neural.

'She's still my life,' Jordi says. 'But she's not my whole life. Not anymore.'

'Your life couldn't have changed that much in less than two days,' Tuan says, shaking his head. 'You fell into a meat crush, Jordi. Enjoy it, if you have to, but don't take it too seriously. You could screw up everything we've worked for, and for what? Tell me.'

All Jordi can think of, in response to Tuan's question, is Nolan's eyes, with their freshwater currents of moss green and root-beer brown. She feels his mouth, when he kissed her gently, his tongue probing without attacking. She remembers him telling her that she was the most beautiful girl at the club and, though the compliment meant nothing in a roomful of sweaty ugly guys, Jordi never doubted that Nolan meant what he said.

'I'm not going to screw up LIRA,' Jordi says softly. 'I promise.'

Without thinking this time, or asking permission, she steps through the bathroom door and kisses her friend on the cheek.

'I don't think it's a microchip problem,' Tuan mutters to himself. 'But, hell, if I can figure out what's wrong with her.'

LIRA is lying in pieces on Jordi's kitchen table. She can't avert her eyes, but she can't bear to keep looking at her beloved dissected computer, either. Tuan glances at her over his shoulder.

'What's wrong, Jordi? You're green.'

'It's like watching your kid have open-heart surgery,' Jordi says. 'I can't stand to watch, but I can't leave.'

'Why don't you go out for a walk? Get some fresh air. You need more fresh air now that you're *in luuhhhv*. Gotta keep those lungs healthy for all that snorkeling – I mean, kissing.'

Jordi cuffs Tuan on the shoulder. Touching him is getting much easier, especially when he's being irritating.

'I'm not in love. We're just friends.'

'Friends who snorkel.'

'We kissed once! And there was no tongue involved. I breathed normally through the whole thing.'

'Then you're missing out. French kissing is fun,' Tuan sighs. 'I remember it well. But I've been willing to sacrifice all pleasures of the flesh for our project.'

'Stop trying to make me feel guilty,' Jordi says. 'It's not going to work. Besides, I didn't meet Nolan until LIRA broke down. If I'd been connected, I wouldn't even have noticed him in the first place.'

Surprisingly, that thought makes her shudder. The vision of a Nolan-less world seems somehow bleak and flat. Was my whole life bleak and flat before yesterday? Jordi wonders, as she leaves Tuan with the mess of computer parts that used to be the ultimate alternative to meat love. She hadn't planned to walk to the library, only to stroll down to the corner to buy vanilla lattés for herself and Tuan but, before she knows it, Jordi is boarding the bus and heading downtown.

All five of Jordi's senses seem to be clamoring for her attention as she takes in her surroundings. The garish upholstery of the seats assaults her eyes; the smell from someone's hotdog wafts through her nostrils and hits her belly like a cannonball. People are chattering into cellular headsets, singing along with their iPods. One guy, wearing what appears to be a pile of rags, preaches some unknown gospel to himself. Her nerves are so brightly awake that she tastes her own tongue; it tastes like an apple. If mass transit is such a sensual orgy all of a sudden, what would sex be like?

The thought gives Jordi chills, deliciously icy rivulets that course up and down the length of her body. By the time she walks through the library's double doors, she's trembling inside and out. She takes the elevator upstairs and wanders through the stacks in search of a serious-looking, intense, dark-haired guy in a gray hoodie. The only evidence of Nolan is a copy of *Being and Nothingness*, shelved among books on weight loss.

Passing the reference desk on the second floor, she decides to take a chance. The man in with the wire-rimmed glasses and tweed coat looks promising. He strikes Jordi as the type of man who would know everything, somehow, but never divulge his sources. She stops in front of him and waits for him to turn the page of a book he's reading. *Fanny Hill*. Jordi's never heard of it.

'Excuse me, have you seen Nolan?' she asks. 'He works here.'

The librarian looks up at her and smiles. His smile sets off a flutter under Jordi's ribs. He reminds her of the kind of man she tended to have a crush on in high school, someone safely mature and unattainable, like her best friend's father, or the history teacher who headed her chess club. He takes off his glasses, folds them, and sets them on the desk. Without his glasses he looks ten years younger, young enough that Jordi realises that he's not really all that safe.

'Nolan works?' he asks. The question has a wry twist. 'Funny, I've never thought to call it that.'

The librarian's steady gray-blue gaze makes Jordi want to wriggle, but she settles for shifting her weight. He really is attractive. Would Jordi have noticed that one day ago?

'Anyway, I'm looking for him,' she says, feeling as awkward as a teenager. 'Is he around?'

'No, but I am. Can I help you find something?'

A life, Jordi thinks. A social personality. A way to talk to appealing males without feeling like a paralysed chunk of flesh. Like that sex goddess who wrote the blog – Dana. Dana would know how to handle this man and any other male who might come her way.

'Um, maybe,' she says.

He motions to an empty chair in front of the desk. 'Have a seat. Tell me what you need.'

'I don't want to bother you ...'

'Bother me? By asking me to do my job? Nonsense. Sit down. Tell me why you're here, besides looking for that miscreant Nolan.'

'How do you know I'm looking for anything else?' Jordi asks, sliding into the chair.

'You have a hungry look on your face. By the way, your face is very pretty. You should pull your hair back. It's distracting.'

Jordi finds herself pulling her hair away from her face. She winds her curls into a loose clump at the back of her neck and sits there awkwardly while the librarian watches her.

'How's that?' she asks.

'Much better. Now there's nothing in the way of your lovely mouth. Talk to me.'

Jordi's not sure if she should want to talk to an older man who's just complimented her mouth, but she does want to. Very much. She's never looked at her mouth, or even thought much about it. Two lips surrounding a cavity where she inserts food and liquids so she can hammer out code or play in the ether for hours on end – that's what Jordi's mouth means to her.

Apparently it means something very different to this gentleman.

'I'm Steffen, by the way, if that makes you more comfortable. And you are?'

'Jordi.'

'Is that short for something else?'

She clears her throat. 'Yeah. But I don't tell anyone.'

'Why not?'

'I don't like the sound of my full name. I never have. So I shortened it.'

'Well, the short version suits you. I won't press for anything more than that. You can't always have everything you ask for. Or wish for.'

Jordi stares down at her hands, which she's twisting in her lap. Her palms feel sweaty. If this scene were playing out in reality the way it's unfolding in her imagination, she'd be wearing a short plaid skirt and chunk shoes, a white blouse and a little black tie. Under her skirt, she'd be wearing white cotton panties. Her hair would be tied up in pigtails, so that the disobedient red curls wouldn't distract attention from her mouth. Where did *that* fantasy come from? She must have picked it up in the ether. That was one of the hazards of playing around in sensual head-space: sometimes another person's fantasies clung to your own brain and hung there like the fuzz from a pink cashmere sweater.

'When you walked up to the desk, you looked like you had an urgent question in mind,' Steffen says. 'What was it?'

'Hey, you were reading when I came up to the desk!' Jordi protests. 'You had your nose stuck in a book. You didn't even see me till I asked about Nolan.'

'You'd be surprised at how many things a person can do with their nose stuck in a book. Over the years, I've learned how to do everything while reading. Well, almost everything. There are a few things that are too pleasurable to be shared with an absent author.'

This is the weirdest conversation Jordi has ever had. How

did she end up in this maze of sexual innuendos? Men never flatter her, flirt with her, or ask her questions that make her sticky.

'What if you do want to share those pleasurable things with an author?' Jordi asks. 'Like someone with a steamy sex blog?'

'Ah, a steamy sex blog. I can see the allure of those online confessions, but your participation, as a reader, is strictly second-hand. You aren't really sharing anything with the author at all. He doesn't even know you. He probably gets very aroused by the idea of being read, but your identity doesn't mean much to him.'

'She,' Jordi corrects him. 'The author of this blog is a woman. A very sexy slutty woman. And she lives here, at the library.'

Steffen's eyebrows rise. 'A sexy slutty writer living at the library? I can't say I've met her.'

'Neither have I,' Jordi sighs, twisting her hands in her lap. 'But I'd like to. You wouldn't believe the way she writes about sex. She's addicted to men, sex, love; she goes for anyone she wants, and she always gets the guy. I want to know everything about her: who she is, where she came from, how she got so brave.'

'What makes you think she's brave? Maybe she's more scared than you are. She'd have to be. Think about it. If she's living here at the library, she must have nowhere else to go. I'd be terrified if I were an attractive young woman, alone in the world, stranded in the library. Her high libido probably only adds to her stress.'

An odd idea is creeping through the back door of Jordi's mind, so sly and strange that at first she can't even admit to it. What if Dana's blog weren't written by a 'Dana' at all, but by someone else altogether? Like, say, a bored, mildly perverted, male reference librarian? Jordi studies Steffen more closely, searching his clothes, hands, face for signs that he could be harbouring an alternate feminine identity. All she sees is neatly dressed, soft-spoken, middle-aged male with sexy blue eyes.

We all want to be someone else, at least some of the time. Jordi knows this better than anyone. Maybe Steffen is a lonely bachelor who decided to craft the woman of his dreams out of text and bandwidth. With every RSS feed, his desire would spool out into the world of shy and slack-jawed readers like Jordi who longed for Dana's daily update on her lustlife. Meanwhile, Steffen (or whoever was writing the blog) would get his vicarious thrills with every caress, kiss and climax that filled Dana's confessions.

'You haven't seen anyone like Dana around here, have you?' Jordi asks, setting a trap for him.

'I don't know. I have no idea what your Dana looks like. But I do know most of our homeless patrons, at least by sight. I haven't seen anyone who looks like a brave, sexy, lusty writer named Dana. But if I do see Dana, or Nolan, I'll send them your way. Care to leave your phone number?'

Jordi can't read Steffen's smile. It is a small smirk of triumph at side-stepping Jordi's little maneuver? Or is it a subtly patronising grin, the kind that suggests that he doesn't mind indulging a crazy girl's delusions, as long as they're sexy? Jordi stands up and shakes her hair out, so that it falls over her face again. Conversations with librarians are supposed to leave you feeling comfortably informed, set on the right path. They're not supposed to make you feel like your familiar world has been knocked out of orbit.

'Nolan has my number,' Jordi says coolly. 'And Dana

doesn't need it. I'll find her, eventually. She's not just some-one's fictional creation; she's exists.'

'If you believe this Dana is real, then for all intents and purposes, she is,' Steffen says. He smiles, then returns to his book, all detached professionalism again.

Jordi's not 100 percent certain, but she thinks she's just experienced what her roommate Samantha would call a mind-fuck. And in an odd squishy way, mind-fucking feels more exciting than what Jordi usually thinks of as 'the real thing'.

Leaving the reference desk, Jordi goes back down to the second floor. No sign of a gray-clad information anarchist in any of the aisles, so she heads for the public computers and checks in. Once she's online, Jordi types in the blog's URL, username and password. It had been surprisingly easy for Jordi to hack into Dana's site; only a few keystrokes, and she'd been in, almost as if she were meant to be there from the beginning. Holding back a smirk of satisfaction is impos-sible as she watches Dana's blog unfold itself on the monitor, its fresh content as moist and juicy as a mouth opening.

Darling Deviant, I don't know what you'll think of me after my sex-for-sanctuary escapade . . .

Jordi props her chin on her hand and falls into Dana's life. If only she were allowed to eat candy at the public computers, she'd be chewing a Snickers bar right now, and life would be perfect. Becoming someone sexier, more desir-able, more beautiful, if only for the time allotted on a public computer, is such a sweet escape that Jordi doesn't hear her cellphone buzzing in her backpack, over and over again, frantic as a pissed-off bumblebee.

Guilt drives Jordi home as soon as she's logged out of her session with Dana. Tuan's probably tearing his hair out, going through caffeine withdrawals and cursing his missing friend. *You were supposed to run out for fresh air and lattés!* he would cry, all storm and drama. *What happened to you?*

Jordi wouldn't mind knowing the answer to that question, herself. What *has* happened to her, since LIRA crashed? Everything reliable, predictable and 'normal' in her life is being stirred by some force in the universe that she doesn't understand. She doesn't believe in fate, or destiny, or any of those other romance-novel delusions, but she doesn't believe that life is a totally random neutron dance. Something inside her is unfolding. Something is swelling into wild wet life, and whatever it is, it's making her do things she never thought she was capable of. Making out with her roommate's date. Walking into a mosh pit. Kissing some obsessive nerd from the library over a pot of ravioli . . .

Her cellphone's going crazy in her backpack. Jordi fumbles in the cluttered pack till she finds it. The number on the display looks vaguely familiar. The voice that answers when she says hello is definitely familiar; it makes Jordi break out in a riot of sparkling goosebumps.

'Jordi? Hey, it's me. I gotta talk to you.'

Hey, it's me. Nolan doesn't bother to identify himself; does that translate into 'I feel intimate enough with you that I trust you'll know my voice', or 'We're just buddies and I wouldn't bother to tell you who I am anymore than I'd declare myself to my favorite pair of socks'?

'Where are you?' Jordi asks. 'I was just at the library, but I couldn't find you anywhere. Now I have to get home.'

'Oh, I was there. Here. Wherever. I'm at the library right now trying to figure out what the hell is going on.'

'You don't sound like your usual cool anarchist self,' Jordi remarks. 'What's up?'

Nolan barks something into the phone. The connection goes punk, and his words shiver out through a field of static. The bus is packed with passengers, half of them standing in the aisle. Jordi tries to push her way through the crush of shoulders, bellies, and armpits, but she can't forge a path through the wall of flesh. Fear tickles the back of her throat; it's been ages since Jordi had one of her panic attacks in public, but a smelly crowd can still set one off. At the next stop, she dives off the bus as if she were plunging from a burning building. She sits down on a bench, takes deep breaths, wonders if she still has a Xanax left from the bottle that her therapist prescribed for moments like this.

'Jordi. Jordi, are you still there?' Nolan's back, deep and clear this time. Her phone is slippery from the sweat on her palm.

'Yeah,' she pants.

'You OK?'

'No. I just...I had...I got stuck in a flesh-field,' she says.

'A flesh-field,' he repeats. 'What does that mean?'

'It's when I get stuck in a whole bunch of bodies and can't get out. When people get to be too much for me, I can't breathe.'

'Sounds like we're both in bad shape,' he sighs. 'Look, I'm about to head home right now. I took the rest of the day off; I'm too much of a wreck to work. Something's happened. I need to tell you what's going on – you're the only one who might possibly understand. Can you get to my place from wherever you are? No, forget that. I'll come find you. Where are you right now?'

Jordi looks around. She's sitting on a street corner next to a hot-dog stand on wheels.

'I'm sitting on a bench next to the Rolling Weenie, on the corner of 18th and Massachusetts Avenue,' she says.

'Cool. You're only a few blocks from the library. I'll be by in a few minutes – just sit tight. Don't go anywhere.'

As if Jordi would go anywhere, with Nolan's voice in her ear, and the memory of kissing him last night still swimming through her consciousness. On those rare occasions when she knew she might kiss a guy – at a friend's wedding, for example, or on a blind date – Jordi always steels herself for the kiss. Kissing = disappointment, in Jordi's limited experience. Kisses that taste of liverwurst, kisses that feel like having her lips pried apart by a can-opener, kisses that leave her feeling like she's just ripped a gas mask off her face: every kiss seems to hold its own special horror.

Kissing Nolan had been sweet. And unexpected. That gentle contact with his lips had made her toes curl. So is it OK if we just get to know each other slowly before we rip off our clothes and fall into bed? he had asked. No guy has ever asked Jordi that question before, or bothered to ask her anything, really, before groping a handful of her plentiful flesh. The memory of Nolan's soft query ignites a shower of sparks in the pit of her belly. The sparks radiate to her inner thighs and spread along the soft crease between them.

The vendor at the Rolling Weenie, a heavyset man wearing a red beanie with a propeller on it, is squirting violently yellow mustard onto a bun, while a teenage boy looks on. How often do we get what we really want from the world of the senses? she wonders, watching the boy chew his lip in anticipation. That hot dog won't taste as good as the kid thinks it will. He'll take one bite, and his taste buds will shrivel up in disappointment, and he'll wonder what happened to The Ultimate Hot Dog that filled his fantasies as he strolled down the street to the Rolling Weenie.

Sex, for Jordi, is very much like that hot dog. No matter what she slathers it with, or how she decks it out, she's always disappointed with the reality of lying naked with another person. When a lover finally touches her, her body never responds the way she hoped. She always ends up shrinking back, confusing the poor boy with her uncertainty, her shyness. Will Nolan be any different, if they ever get beyond the point of squirting mustard on each other's libidos?

The kid walks over to the bus stop, chewing in time to his footsteps. He sits down on the bench next to Jordi. His cheeks bulge with each bite, and there's a streak of yellow mustard across his nose. He catches Jordi staring at him, and grins.

'Best hot dog ever,' he says, beaming through a mouthful of meat and bread. 'You oughta try one.'

Disappointed? Not even remotely. If there's hope for meat on a bun, maybe there's hope for love in a body.

'Jordi! Geez, I couldn't wait to see you.'

Nolan lands on the bench beside her, backpack landing with a thud on the sidewalk. Without warning, he wraps her in a tight hug and nuzzles her neck. Then he's kissing her cheek, her ear, the tip of her nose, planting butterfly kisses all over her face. Stunned, Jordi stares into space. With no time to process the ten thousand feelings that Nolan's hands and mouth are creating, she sits stiff as a board and watches the Rolling Weenie vendor slather mustard and relish on another hot dog.

'I haven't stopped thinking about you since last night,' Nolan says.

By the time he finally pulls back, holding her at arm's

length, and stares intently into her face, Jordi can hardly breathe. With the warmth of his lips still radiating across her face and throat, she feels like she's going to dissolve into a puddle of longing. She'll be nothing but a pool of lust on the sidewalk, topped by a pair of glasses and a pile of red hair.

'Your face is all pink,' he remarks. And then, unbelievably, 'You look gorgeous like that. I'm starting to rethink my idea about getting to know each other before we fall into bed. What do you think?'

Jordi's face turns even redder – there's a four-alarm fire in her cheeks at this point. She stammers something that doesn't resemble any human language she's ever heard.

'Yeah, I agree,' Nolan sighs. 'We should wait at least a few more hours. I need to talk to you, anyway. There's something seriously amiss at the library.'

Mind reeling, Jordi clutches her head. 'Wait a second, Nolan. Give me a chance to catch up.'

'What's to catch up with?' he asks, puzzled.

'Sex. Your job. Let's talk about one thing at a time.'

Nolan takes a deep breath. 'Someone's *organizing* me. I just found out this morning.'

'What do you mean, organizing?'

'I'm talking about my life's work. Someone's putting all the books back in that old, suffocating order. Someone's trying to wipe out serendipity.'

'Huh.' Jordi ponders this for a second. 'But that's got to be an occupational hazard, hasn't it? There are other shelvers in the library, not to mention the librarians, the public, et cetera. Don't they ever notice that you've put things in the wrong place?'

Nolan gives her a pained look. 'Jordi, I'm trying to put things in the *right* place. There's nothing "wrong" about misdirection; don't let the negative prefix fool you. Sure, a lot of people don't agree with what I'm doing. Most people are addicted to the organizational systems that they're born into. They can't imagine any other alternatives. Naturally they're going to try to re-establish those systems wherever they go. And, yeah, the other shelvers put my books back in LOC order all the time. But not at this speed. Within the past twenty-four hours, someone deliberately and willfully made a concentrated effort to redirect my books.'

He finishes with a chopping gesture, a flattened hand emphasising each syllable in the phrase, *redirect my books.*

'Who do you think it could be?'

'Someone with motivation. None of the guys I work with has enough of that to wreak this kind of devastation. It's got to be someone with time on their hands. Someone who's figured out that my anti-system is actually a system; it's not just the end result of a bunch of slobs randomly putting stuff back on the wrong shelves.'

'Well, the first thing I'd do, if someone were messing with my life's work, would be to figure out who's doing it. Maybe we need to spy on your co-workers.'

'But it could be anyone,' Nolan objects. 'More likely, it's someone who's unemployed and has obsessive-compulsive tendencies.'

'Wait a second.' A memory is rising to the surface of Jordi's consciousness, a scrap of text. 'I think I know who it is.'

'Who?'

'The girl who lives in the library. The one who writes the blog that I found on the public access computer. It's her! It has to be. And you know what?' Now Jordi is the one squeezing Nolan's hands. Her heart beats fast. 'This proves that she's real. Dana really exists. She's altering the material world.'

'I don't know who you're talking about.'

'Dana's a girl who lives at the library. She's addicted to sex and love. She used to be rich, but her dad kicked her out because she wouldn't get over her addiction, and she just moved into the library a couple of days ago. At night, she puts the books back in the places where they're supposed to be. I mean, where she thinks they're supposed to be.'

Nolan scratches his head, making his dark hair look even more mussed than it already does, and fixes Jordi with a look of profound confusion.

'No one sleeps in the library,' he says. 'It's not possible, much less desirable.'

'I didn't say she was sleeping, did I? She was up till after midnight last night rearranging books. That's what she does, when she's not having sex with security guards.'

'I gotta meet this chick,' Nolan says, shaking his head slowly. 'That blows my mind.'

'Mine too,' says Jordi. 'But listen. I know what we have to do.'

'What?'

'Tonight, we'll spend the night at the library. If she's a flesh-and-blood woman, and she's the one who's replacing all the books, we'll find her. But first, I have to show you her blog.'

They'll find her. Grab her. Pinch and squeeze and bite her – anything to prove that Dana exists. If you believe this Dana is real then, for all intents and purposes, she is, Steffen the reference librarian had said. But Jordi doesn't simply believe – she knows. Somewhere in the library is a juicy beautiful meat-girl who packs a vibrator, gives blow jobs to security guards, and gets tied up naked by beautiful male librarians. She couldn't be a construct of Jordi's imagination; in her wildest fantasies, Jordi could never conjure up a creature like Dana.

In her own sex-crazed, overblown way, Dana is as real as Jordi.

Maybe even more so.

Chapter Nine

Dana: Delayed Gratification

Darling Deviant,

By the time the library closed for the evening, your heroine needed food, a decent bed, and a scalding hot shower. I also craved the sound of a baritone reading me Shakespeare's sonnets, a warm brandy, and the feeling of a tongue coaxing open the folds of my pussy, but those pleasures were lower on my list of priorities, for once. For the first time in my misspent life, I was on the right place in Maslow's pyramid; I could honestly say that I needed nourishment and shelter more than poetry and cunnilingus.

My hopes for getting laid – and fed, and pampered, and praised for my beauty – were still high as I got ready to go over to Steffen's house. If nothing else, I'm an optimist. A girl with a can-do attitude. A fucking Pollyanna, if need be; survival has been the name of my game these days.

As the library closed, I walked through the lobby with the rest of the crowd, as if I were just another book lover on my way back to a warm meal, a clean bed. It didn't occur to me, until the doors closed behind me and I found myself out in the nippy night, that I'd just severely restricted my options. Either I could spend the night at Steffen's house, or sleep somewhere on the streets, or I'd need to find a homeless shelter that catered to disinherited rich girls.

If I got desperate enough, I could always go back home and beg my father and Chastity to take me in, but they were most likely planning to hide out at the cabin in Aspen until I died of exposure and deprivation. Besides, I wasn't ready to grovel . . . not outside a bedroom.

'Dana? Where are you going?'

I turned to find Prince Christopher, bondage hero of my fantasies, falling in step with me. He wore a burgundy cashmere scarf (the same one that had covered my eyes only a few hours earlier) over a black trench coat, and he looked like he'd stepped off the pages of *Anna Karenina*.

'Uh, I'm just heading out for the night,' I said, with a vague wave of my hand. 'Where's Jeff?'

'Working late. He got a little distracted by an incident in the Multimedia Department,' Christ said with a wink.

His lush brown eyes, twinkling down at mine, were as soft as an animal's, and when he smiled, those fine wrinkles radiated from their corners. He was really too beautiful to be a public servant; Prince Christopher and Prince Jeff deserved nothing less than to be the masters of a harem of worshipful girls and boys.

In fact, I was seriously thinking about offering to be part of that harem. I could start things off by giving my two princes a night of exotic pleasure, every moment so erotic-ally charged that for the rest of their days my name would never be far from their lips. He would forever remember me as Dana, harem slave extraordinaire, the girl with hair like fire and a pussy like molten lava . . .

'So where are you camping out, Dana? Or are you staying at one of the shelters around here?'

Christopher's question, asked with such kindness, blew my harem fantasy out of the water. I imagined what he must see when he looked down at me with those limpid brown eyes: a straggly haired girl with no make-up, trying to hide from the world under a bulky ski jacket. I didn't even ski anymore in my new life.

'No,' I replied, lifting my chin. 'As a matter of fact, I'm going to have dinner with a friend. A *gentleman* friend.'

I'd hoped to see a flicker of jealousy cross Prince Christopher's face. I saw surprise, instead, and something that looked suspiciously like pity. Pity is the one of the last emotions I'd want to inspire in a man – somewhere down there with 'disgust' and 'amusement'.

'Dana, you don't have to go to that extreme,' Christopher said.

'What extreme? I don't think he'll be cooking anything all that daring. He looks like the soup and salad type.'

He lowered his voice. 'There are all kinds of places to get a free meal in the city. It's not worth taking a risk.'

'What? You mean, you think I . . . I'd trade sex for dinner?'

'I didn't say that,' he said delicately, placing a protective hand on my arm. 'I just want you to be safe. You're a lovely girl. Life on the streets is rough.'

Safe. Now, there was an interesting term. Safety was something I considered when having sex with new partners, or when making a left turn against traffic, but I'd never associated safety with my life itself. I'd always been so secure, so utterly cherished and protected.

For the umpteenth time in the past two days, I wanted to throw myself into a man's muscular arms and wail. I didn't. I stopped in my tracks, held my ground, and looked Christopher straight in the eye.

'Don't ever feel sorry for me,' I said. '*Libraries* are to be patronised, not women. Especially not women like me.'

Just before I stalked away, I caught an infuriating twinkle

in his eye. I held my spine and head erect, as if I were striding off in a pair of Louis Vuitton calf leather pumps and a Chanel suit instead of a ski coat and hiking boots. In my mental movie, Prince Christopher watched me depart, his lean silhouette dark against the falling snow, his eyes moist with remorse. In reality I'm sure he shrugged his shoulders, chuckled to himself, and headed home to open up a bottle of cabernet and listen to Thelonious Monk with his golden-boy roommate, Jeff.

Steffen and I had arranged to meet at 7.30, which gave me over an hour to kill. That gap of time seemed to stretch on and on, chasmlike; with no money in my wallet, what was I supposed to do? I wandered over to the outdoor mall, glancing into shop windows and wishing I'd at least thought to steal a couple of Chastity's credit cards before I left home. The scents of lilac and jasmine wafting from Bellissima drew me inside. Bellissima had always been my favorite store for bath-time indulgences. Lotions and soaps, bath beads and powders, oils and exotic soaks were weaknesses of mine, and all of the salesgirls knew me by name. I'd dropped so much money there over the years that they should have had a plaque over the door with my name on it.

'Can I help you?' asked a petite young woman named Helen. Helen was the shop manager, one of those doll-like country club blondes who doesn't really need to work, but takes a job for purely social reasons. She was eyeballing my coat pockets as if she thought they might be stuffed with depilatory cream and rose-water hand soap. I couldn't really blame her for her suspicion; the bulges did look odd.

'Helen, it's me. I just stopped by to, um, browse.'

Her Wedgwood-blue eyes turned to slits. 'Do I know you?'

I planted my hands on my hips. 'Of course you do. It's Dana. Don't you remember my weekly routine? Two bottles of almond-honey massage oil, four packets of hibiscus crystals, and a jar of that pineapple wax that strips off the most stubborn pubic hair. *Dana.*'

Helen shook her head, mystified. Clearly the brain under the flaxen hair couldn't form a connection between those pricey products and the female yeti towering over her.

'Dana.'

The weak delayed echo was not encouraging. Helen's eyes darted to the wall phone behind the cash register. It was almost closing time, so she'd be the only employee in the shop; she was undoubtedly assessing her backup right now. Bellissima wasn't exactly the kind of place where they'd keep a sawed-off shotgun under the counter.

'Don't worry, Helen,' I reassured her. 'I'm leaving.'

Taking slow steps backward, I moved toward the door. As soon as Helen turned to go back to the register, I shot out my hand and snatched a bar of Luscious Lavender soap from a display beside the door. Necessity had driven me to theft; the candy pink detergent in the library's soap dispensers was turning the skin on my hands to Velcro.

Fortunately, Steffen didn't live far from the mall; I was too weak with hunger to take a long hike. I gave in to a few tears of self-pity along the way, but only enough to make my eyes sparkle fetchingly when I climbed the steps to the librarian's door.

Steffen lived in one of those old brick row houses downtown, the kind that used to house factory workers and now sell for obscenely high amounts to young professionals with a yen for architectural history. An old-fashioned brass knocker with a lion's snarling head graced the narrow wooden door. I lifted the knocker and let it fall a few times in ladylike percussion. I then stepped back and primped, to the best of my ability, while I waited for Steffen to open up.

When no one answered after a few minutes, I rapped with my knuckles. Then pounded with a closed fist.

The old door was impassive. The brass lion sneered at me. My empty stomach, primed for its first real meal in three days, complained loudly. My feminine ego, which hadn't been stroked by any prolonged male attention since that ill-fated encounter with Blake, deflated like a leaking balloon. Steffen had forgotten our date. He was probably out at a dimly lit bar, wherever librarians congregated after work to get plastered, drinking blended scotch and reading Lady Murasaki.

'Overly literate fucker,' I muttered, and kicked the base of his door.

I'm usually a lot more gracious and forgiving, Dear Deviant, but I was hungry. And lonely. And cold.

'Well, hello there. I didn't realise I was late.'

'I didn't realise I was early,' I shot back.

Steffen was walking up the steps. He held a paper sack of groceries in one arm and a bouquet of white roses in the other. I checked out the food and flowers with a wary eye. My heart wanted to fall apart and forgive him, but in my short time on the streets I had already developed a skeptical edge. The flowers could be for some other woman, the one he'd accidentally penciled into the same slot as me. She'd be the type of woman who could stroll into Bellissima and buy their whole stock of pineapple pubic wax without arousing any suspicion at all.

'Hello, lovely,' he said softly.

Steffen bent down and kissed my cheek. The wintry air had chilled his lips. A fine layer of snow had sifted through his hair, mingling with the foxlike shades of red and gray. He smelled of wool and woodsmoke.

'Would you do something for me?' he asked.

'Sure,' I said, already weakening.

'Reach in my coat pocket and grab my keys. My arms are full. The roses *are* for you, by the way, in case there was any doubt.'

How did he know I'd doubted him? In his gray-blue eyes, I thought I'd seen something sly and knowing. I see through walls, those eyes seemed to say, behind the scholarly glasses, including yours. I wasn't sure I wanted Steffen walking around inside my head.

'I don't do naked mind games,' I said. 'Not on the first date, anyway.'

His eyebrows rose a fraction of a centimeter. 'Thanks for the warning. I generally don't do them either, not without a cerebral condom. The long key opens the door; why don't you let us in?'

I found the key he was referring to and unlocked the heavy door. The foyer was small, too tight for two people, but we stood there anyway for a moment, just looking at each other in the manner of two people who know they're going to end up screwing like rabbits, but don't want to rush the process.

'Let me take your coat,' he said.

'Let me take a bath,' I countered.

'That's an interesting request. The bath usually comes after the food, the wine, the reading and the love making. It often happens between the afterglow and Round Two, I believe.'

'I haven't bathed in almost seventy-two hours,' I said. 'Please don't ask any questions yet. I'll tell you the whole story, but right now I need soap and water – desperately.'

'All right. Let me get you some clean towels. I'm afraid my bathtub isn't exactly Roman, but you're welcome to use it.'

Steffen set down the groceries and flowers on a table beside his front door and led me down a short hallway to the bathroom. He hadn't lied about the tub; it wasn't anything to write home about. Back at the penthouse, I had a bath fit for Cleopatra, complete with a marble head-rest, whirlpool jets and a set of artfully terraced shelves to hold my lotions, trashy novel, and champagne glass. Steffen's bathroom was the typical utilitarian bachelor setup, with a shower/tub combination wedged into a corner between the sink and toilet. On the positive side, the bathroom was immaculate and smelled of musk candles. Any man who has the aesthetic sensibility to equip his bathroom with candles can be forgiven for many short-comings.

'Would you like a fresh bar of soap?' he asked.

'That's OK. I brought my own.' I held up the stolen bar of Luscious Lavender.

'Perfect. I'm sure that suits you better than mine.'

'I think I'm all set now,' I said, putting my hand meaning-fully on the doorknob. In other words: no, you don't get a free nudie show from the chick you picked up at the library; you'll have to wait and want me for a while.

Steffen lingered in the doorway, his face a bit wistful, but only for a moment or two before leaving me to the fresh towels, the clean tub and a brand new bar of soap. The water pouring out of the faucet was clear and hot. The soap was smooth and fragrant in my grubby hand. The towels were fragrant with the detergent Steffen had washed them with. I'd never been so grateful for the basics of a bath, but there was something more: inside the stack of neatly folded towels, he'd tucked a volume of Kahlil Gibran.

This time, my heart really did fall apart. I couldn't help it; I'm a sucker for *The Prophet*. What sex junkie weaned on romance novels and sweaty back-seat groping doesn't secretly yearn for a love that's mystical, deep and pure?

I filled the tub with hot water, just enough to displace enough volume to let my zaftig mass sink in. When I peeled off my clothes, my skin cried out in voluptuous relief. I'd always been a compulsive clothing-changer, wearing several outfits per day in childlike faith that someone else was laundering them. I'd never, ever worn the same clothing for 24 hours in a row, much less 72.

As I was slipping into the water, Steffen knocked on the door.

'Dana?'

I yanked the tartan shower curtain across the bathtub. 'Not now! I'm naked!' I hollered.

'I thought you might need to wash your clothes,' he said through the door. 'I'd be happy to throw them in the laundry for you.'

His voice was muffled, but I could hear its gently gloating tone. I know what you need, he seemed to be saying, before you need it. I know everything about you; I've touched the recesses of your psyche. I am already acquainted with the hungers of your skin, your lips, your pussy. I am always a step ahead of you. There's no way for you to escape me, even if you wanted to.

The thing is, Darling Deviant, I didn't want to escape Steffen. Snug and safe in my primal pool of warm water, I was at peace. I could feel my body opening up again, a soft sensual creature eager to be fed in a dozen different ways.

'Come on in,' I called. 'My clothes are on the floor.'

Steffen opened the door. I lazily half-opened the shower curtain to smile at him. Well aware of the erotic impact of a fresh dewy-faced nude soaking in a steamy bath, I lifted my chest so that my firm nipples peeked above the surface of the water. Steffen cleared his throat. The steam had fogged his glasses so I couldn't see his eyes, but I could feel the energy coursing between us, sweetly tensile, and I knew that stolen glimpse of pink and white had gotten to him.

Chalk up a point for Dana, Dear Reader; I wasn't the only one who was going to be knocked off guard tonight.

I took my time in the bath, scrubbing and lathering myself over and over until the water went cool and the Luscious Lavender soap was worn down to a thin slice. When I finally stepped out of the tub, I saw that Steffen had left a fluffy terry-cloth robe draped across the sink. I patted myself dry, then stepped into it, nude, and wrapped the sash around my waist. A man's garment, it engulfed me with a generous warmth. Wearing a man's shirt or dressing gown is always a huge turn-on for me. Even when it's been washed, I can always catch a trace of his scent, a ghost of his person, on the fabric. The size makes me feel smaller than usual, safe and protected; at the same time, there's something deliciously transgressive about being cloaked in something he wears right next to his skin.

Stolen pleasures are always the sweetest, especially when you know you're going to get caught.

I toweled off my thick hair and let it hang in damp curls over my shoulder. My face, when I wiped away the steam from the mirror, was fresh and pink and shiny, as if I'd just had a facial. I didn't have any of my cosmetics to arm myself with, but that seemed right for this evening. Most men didn't get to see me looking anything close to innocent; Steffen was in for a treat.

In my bare feet I padded out into the hallway. My nose wriggled at the heavenly aromas of tomato, basil and garlic. Laced through those smells were scents from the vineyard, scents from the sea. I followed their sensual trail to Steffen's kitchen, where he was stirring something in a large copper pot. Plump, translucent scallops were sautéing in garlic and butter in a saucepan nearby. Two long-stemmed wine glasses sat waiting to be filled with merlot from an open bottle.

I inhaled deeply. This beat the hell out of Lunar bars.

'I didn't know if you liked seafood,' Steffen said, 'but I took a chance.'

'I love seafood. Sea scallops are my favorite. And I'm starting to think that you know more about me than you're willing to let on.'

Steffen half-turned from the pot to smile at me. The steam had brought out a wave in his neatly combed hair, and he'd taken off his glasses. Seeing him without his specs gave me a shiver of intimacy. He wore his usual Oxford shirt – the pale blue one again, matching his eyes – but the top buttons were undone, and the sleeves were rolled up for cooking. Instead of the pressed slacks that he'd worn at the library, he wore jeans.

'Or maybe I'm just more perceptive than your average date. It doesn't take much to know what a woman wants, if you take some time to observe her.'

The terracotta tiles on Steffen's kitchen floor were cool against my feet. I could have stayed there, wriggling my toes against the chilly stone, but he pulled out a tall stool from the butcher-block counter and invited me to sit down. I let the forest-green robe fall open over my hips as I sat down; I even gave him a flash of the auburn swathe of curls at the pale spot where my thighs met. Another perceptive move on his part: he'd chosen the perfect shade of fabric for a redhead.

If it weren't for a slight tremor in his hand when he picked up a slotted spoon to stir the pasta, I wouldn't have known if Steffen had noticed my ten-cent peep show. Where had he learned composure like that? Maybe it came naturally to him, or maybe it was the result of hours of manning the reference desk at a downtown library. It had to feel like a battle zone back there at times.

'I didn't know you'd been observing me,' I said.

Though my host hadn't offered me any wine yet, I couldn't resist pouring myself a glass of the merlot. With all I'd been through in the past few days, he was lucky I didn't grab the bottle and chug it.

'Does that make you uncomfortable?' he asked.

I sipped and thought, then sipped again. 'No. And yes.'

'You strike me as the kind of woman who'd enjoy being watched.'

'That's true. But, when men watch me, it's usually just a physical thing – getting off on watching me undress, shower, have sex. I love putting on a show for a man, especially when he thinks I don't know he's watching.'

'So how is my observing you any different?'

Steffen put down the spoon. He walked over to the counter and stood near me, but not too near, leaning against the butcher block. He was far too subtle to gawk at my cleavage, but I knew he noticed. You'd have to be a near-sighted eunuch not to want to plunge face first into a pair of creamy-white mounds like mine.

I twisted one of my damp ringlets around my finger. 'Well, for one thing, I was never aware that you had your eye on me. For another, I get the feeling that you'd be the type who'd be gathering information, not just getting off. So what do you want to know about me?'

'Everything,' he said, in a tone that made me shiver. 'Where you're from, where you've been, what your favorite flavour of ice cream is. I want to know what books you love, what music you listen to before you go to sleep at night. Your first memory. What you majored in at college. Whether you wear panties trimmed with lace, or simple G-strings.'

'Now that's more typical,' I said dryly. 'And now that you've washed my clothes, you have an answer to that question. I love lacy, silky, creamy lingerie. By the way, I hope you didn't wash my undies on the permanent press cycle.'

'Of course not,' he said. 'I'd never do such a thing! I've been well trained by the women in my past.'

'Really? Anything serious?'

He sighed. 'Let's just say I was deeply in love once. All of my relationships after that have been pleasant, or convenient, or satisfying, or all of the above, but nothing's ever come close to that one special attachment.'

'What was she like? Tell me!' I wiggled on my seat. 'I love a doomed love story.'

'It wasn't "doomed",' he winced. 'It just never came to fruition.'

'Well, why not? Did she dump you?'

(Do you ever get the feeling, Dear Deviant, that your heroine sometimes has the sensitivity of a bull elephant?)

'She disappeared,' he said curtly, turning back to the stove. 'Damn, the scallops are overcooked. They're going to have the texture of pencil erasers, but they should taste OK.'

'I like chewy scallops. And I'm sorry,' I blurted. 'That was a stupid, cruel thing to say. I have a big mouth. It's big enough for both my feet, my dad used to tell me.'

'It's all right. You couldn't have known.' He poured the saucepan of buttery scallops onto a huge oval serving dish, then dumped the pasta into a colander in the sink. Steam billowed up, veiling his face. 'It wasn't the typical end to a romance.'

'Can you tell me what happened?' I asked, more gently this time. 'I'd really like to know.'

'We got engaged after we graduated from college, and we were living together in Denver. She was a daddy's girl, always running home to her father's house whenever we had the slightest disagreement. Her family lived in Kansas; I used to tease her about going home to Oz.'

'That wasn't very sensitive of you. A father's love can't be replaced.'

I suddenly wondered what my dad was doing. Stoking the fire in the cabin, stirring a hot toddy, draping his arm around Chastity's tanned shoulder ... or maybe he was thinking about me, and wondering what *I* was doing.

'I know. I was jealous. It was the one thing I couldn't tolerate about her. In every other respect, she was perfect. Sensitive, creative, smart. Sexy too, a curvy redhead. She looked a bit like you.'

'So what happened to her?'

'We had an argument one weekend. It started out as something trivial, then took a serious turn. Her father wanted her to come home for some kind of family occasion; I wanted her to stay. There wasn't any good reason for me wanting to keep her at home. I'd just gotten tired of her dropping everything at his beck and call. As soon as he wanted her for any reason, our lives together stopped mattering. I was incredibly stupid about it – I gave her an ultimatum. As if any daughter should have to choose between her father and her fiancé. She got in her car and drove away. Long story short: I never saw her again. None of us did.'

Steffen was staring into space, his hands braced against the countertop. His face was a study in pain. Normally I love a man in torment, but this was too serious, even for me.

'They never found her, did they?'

'No. It was as if she'd flown off the face of the earth. Her car was never found. Her credit cards were never used. No sign of her anywhere. At first the police didn't want to get involved. She was an adult, a grown woman, had the right to disappear, the usual spiel. But her father had a certain amount of influence in Kansas, and he put his foot down. It started out as a typical manhunt, then blew up into a huge local mystery. The bottom line, from my point of view, was that I never saw her or touched her again.'

I shuddered and pulled the robe tightly around me. 'What did you do?' I asked in a small voice.

He smiled again, this time without humor. 'All the wrong things. I kept all her belongings in the house, exactly the way she'd left them. I wouldn't let her go. I refused to move on. I didn't date for years after she left. I went crazy for a while and pretended she was still living with me. I wrote letters to myself that I pretended were from her, explaining where she'd gone and why she'd left. Finally, one day, I packed up everything and moved. Gave all her things away. I couldn't live with the illusion of her anymore.'

A clock on the wall ticked loudly in the silence that followed. I hadn't even seen that clock before, but its sad staccato suddenly filled the room.

'You had to move on,' I said, because I had to say somthing.

'That's right. And I did. Shall we eat?'

Briskly he began to pull dishes out of the cupboard. I hopped off the stool to help him. We made ourselves very busy carrying things back and forth to the dining table, and, after a few minutes, the ghost of Steffen's missing fiancée quietly slipped away.

I couldn't stop inhaling Steffen's food. The scallops, in spite of being singed at the edges, melted on my tongue. The pasta sauce was a rich tomato-and-basil broth. The wine flowed, one bottle after another. In between bites and gulps I managed to mumble 'Thank you' and 'More please'. More, more, more – I couldn't imagine ever getting enough.

'I'm sorry,' I gasped, when my belly was finally too full to hold any more. 'You probably think I haven't eaten in days.'

'It's a pleasure to have a hungry guest. Nothing's more exciting to me than a woman with appetites,' Steffen said.

'Do you think our appetites match?' I asked, wiping my mouth lustily with a napkin (linen, he didn't mess around with paper). 'I mean, I'm a glutton. You seem like more of a gourmand.'

'True, but I'm more than happy to sit back and watch you enjoy yourself.'

'Watch me pig out, you mean.'

'I like a woman who's ravenous. The women who've meant the most to me have always been hungry for life.'

He gazed at me over the rim of his raised wine glass, his lips a blur behind the ruby liquid. There was still a shadow in his eyes, and it wasn't hard for me to picture him as a younger man, dining alone in his house, pretending that his fiancée was sitting across from him. I wondered if he'd set a place for her at the table every night after she vanished. I had enough tact, for once, not to ask.

But I'm ashamed to admit, Darling Deviant, that doubt flickered through my mind as I watched Steffen drink his wine. When his upper lip twisted wryly over the rim of the glass, a weird notion popped into my head: what if the missing fiancée was pure bullshit? What if she were a prop in some creepy seduction game, and I happened to be that night's prize? I've never been a cynical girl, but I'd been played a few times by less skillful gamers.

Or what if our mild-mannered librarian had, in fact, been responsible for his fiancée's disappearance, and his long spell of grieving had been a charade masking his guilt? A crime like that would make Steffen a true Bluebeard, and that thought, Darling Deviant, made the nerves in my lower body twinkle like strings of Christmas lights. There's a reason I chose the Bluebeard fairy tale as my romantic ideal. I'd fill you in on the details, but they've shocked even my therapists.

'What's for dessert?' I asked.

'Tiramisu, served with an apricot brandy.'

My stomach had the gall to rumble. For tiramisu and apricot brandy, I was willing to let my doubts about Steffen go their merry way. If I was going to be played, it might as well be by a master.

'But first, I thought we'd spend some time in the library. I'd like to show you my books before we dive into anything rich and creamy.'

'From the way you described your collection, it sounded pretty rich and creamy to me.'

Steffen rose from the table, came over to my chair, took my hand, and lifted it to his mouth for an old-fashioned courtly kiss. He stood over me for a moment. Eye-level with his crotch, I had a sudden urge to unzip his jeans, reach past his fly and pull out his cock. Well fed, I was feeling predatory again, and this time the game I was hunting was a species known as Mature Naked Male.

Before I'd made any rational decision to perform fellatio on my host in his kitchen, I was watching my claws – I mean, fingers – working at his belt buckle. I felt him swelling under the denim as I unbuckled the belt and attacked his zipper and, by the time I made my way through his blue boxers, he was ready to spring out, long and firm, into my hands.

(If you've noticed a theme here about the way I approach men, you're a very perceptive little deviant. I make no apologies for the fact that I'm an oral gal; Freud himself would have fallen over in a dead faint if he could see a written record of all the blow jobs I've given over the years. But every one of those acts was performed with affection, Dear Reader, and with respect for the individual penis that found its way between my lips.)

'Stop,' he said, just as I was about to kiss the rosy tip. Steffen had a lovely cock; the skin was the color of apricots, and had the same texture, velvety soft and slightly fuzzy over the stiffened shaft. He wasn't extremely long, but he was nice and thick. I couldn't wait to taste him, then I heard that strange directive: *stop*.

I glanced up into his face. He stared down at me over the rims of his glasses, and his lips were set in a stern line. That look of disapproval only upped the volume on my lust. I wondered if this was the part where he would put his hands around my throat, pull me out of my chair, and lead me off to the secret chamber in his town house, where he would perform all kinds of lewd and perverse acts on my naked body.

There was only one word for that vision: yum.

'Are you always so greedy?' he asked.

I nodded. 'With very few exceptions, yeah. I'm that greedy.'

'No impulse control?'

'I'm addicted,' I confessed.

'To what?'

'Well, to everything. Sex, love, chocolate, lingerie, feather comforters, French perfume, brand new paperback novels, bright shiny sports vehicles. But especially the first two.'

'You're a very sexy woman, Dana,' he said, 'but I'm not one to be gobbled. I prefer a much slower seduction. And I like to be the one who directs it.'

'How slow?' I asked, in a tiny voice. 'Are we talking hours here? Days? Years? You don't have to build me a Taj Mahal or anything; I'd settle for dessert.'

'You'll have to wait and see,' he said, in a maddeningly cryptic tone.

I love a mysterious man, but not when the mystery stands in the way of my sexual gratification. Meanwhile, I couldn't believe that gorgeous erection was slipping out of my hands, the peach skin shriveling over a rapidly shrinking organ. Even his cock seemed to peer at me in one-eyed disapproval as he tucked it back into his pants.

I'd never been so humiliated in my life. Well, no, that's not true. I'd been insanely humiliated when Ted Delaney hung my bra and panties from the flagpole one January morning in high school, and they froze there in full salute. From this the entire school learned two things: 1) Ted (a.k.a. Teeny Tiny Ted) and I had had sex the night before, which was embarrassing in and of itself, and 2) I wore the biggest panties in my class.

I'd also been humiliated at a production of *La Traviata*

when the city's mayor and his wife had wandered into the aisle where I was sitting back with my thighs parted, being pleasured by the most orally gifted attorney I'd ever met (I'm not referring to his debating skills).

But I don't think I'd ever had a man simply put the goods away and tell me to *wait*.

Delayed gratification was the pits. It was also an incredible turn-on. I'd never had to wait for sex; the novelty sent shivers across my skin.

'Don't worry. I won't be building any temples. I'm only human,' Steffen reassured me. 'Now, if you'll kindly follow me to my library, I have something to show you.'

His library. Steffen had already told me about his collection of erotic memoirs, but what if the room held something more? An array of scary bondage toys, fit for a BDSM Bluebeard? Or a flat-screen TV on which he'd subject me to a festival of porn, torturing me with scenes of things he had no intention of doing until we'd waited a few hundred years?

Darling Deviant, I followed him.

Chapter Ten

Jordi: Stalking the Great Elusive

Jordi sits shoulder to shoulder beside Nolan while he reads Dana's blog on the library's computer. Aside from a widening of his eyes, a frown, and a soft *wow* here and there, he refuses to give her any feedback.

'Did you read about how she seduced her dad's accountant at the party?' Jordi whispers.

'Unh,' Nolan grunts.

'Or what she did with the security guard the other night?'

'Humph.'

'Did that librarian really get tied up naked in the janitor's closet?'

'Uh, maybe.'

'Did you ever tie up one of your girlfriends, Nolan?' Jordi tugs his sleeve.

'Shhh . . . I'm getting to the important part.'

'Do you think Dana's going to have sex with the reference librarian? I met Steffen, you know. He's attractive, in a squirmy sort of way.'

'Jordi, I don't mean to be harsh, darling, but could you please shut up?'

When he's read the final paragraph, Nolan quits the

browser, logs off and stares at the blank monitor for a few silent moments.

'I've never seen this Dana chick,' Nolan finally says, 'but I'm going to find her, and the confrontation isn't going to be pretty. I can't believe she thinks that undoing my life's work is "making a small dent in the entropy of the universe". Who the hell does she think she is?'

'She seems like one of those OCD types who can't help putting things back in order,' Jordi says. 'She doesn't have a lot of control in most areas of her life; maybe that's the only way she feels like she's in charge.'

'Please spare me the compassionate psychoanalysis, Miss Oprah-Freud. She's a subversive. She has to be stopped. Come on. We have work to do.'

Nolan jumps off the stool and takes Jordi's hand. A disembodied voice announces that the library will be closing in half an hour.

'Work?' Jordi asks in dismay. 'I thought we were going to spend the night stalking her.'

'We are. But first, we have to put some of the books back. I can't focus when there's too much order in the library. It feels obscenely wrong.'

'I can't believe you've kept your job as long as you have,' Jordi grumbles. 'How did you even get through the interview?'

'Same way as any other slacker,' Nolan says with a shrug. 'I lied.'

He leads Jordi upstairs to the third floor and enters one of the stacks, seemingly at random. Then Nolan pulls hand-fuls of books from the shelves and piles them in Jordi's arms. His face is grim, mouth set in a straight line.

He looks cute when he's grim, Jordi thinks, as she accepts the stack.

'What am I supposed to do with these?'

'Don't ask. Just do.'

'When did you get so bossy?'

I'm a natural born leader,' Nolan declares. 'And I'm passionate about my mission. Now go forth and put those books somewhere else,' Nolan tells her.

'But where?'

'Anywhere but where they belong.'

'I don't get it,' Jordi whimpers. 'I don't understand how this misdirection stuff works. I *like* things to be in order. I'm a software designer. Systems exist for a reason.'

'Exactly!' Nolan's green eyes, when they light up, are almost gold. 'What I'm trying to show you here is that this is a system. It's systematic chaos, created for the purpose of illumination. Let your intuition be your guide.'

'Whatever,' Jordi sighs. She checks the spines on a couple of the books. Most of them seem to be personal chronicles of fishing and hunting expeditions. She sets off toward Religion and Spirituality.

'When you're done with those, find more and keep going,' Nolan calls after her. 'We'll work till closing time, then we'll take a break till the place empties out. Wait, Jordi?'

She turns around. 'What?'

'Come here for a second.'

'Why? Don't I have enough books?' She drags her feet, her sneakers making static on the carpet.

'Just come closer, Jordi. Closer.'

Nolan waits, grinning, as she approaches, until there's nothing between himself and Jordi but a couple of armloads of books and a few layers of clothing. Then he leans over the books and kisses her. A few seconds of lip play, then the tip of his tongue slides across hers, back and forth, in a feathery motion that almost makes Jordi drop her books. Shifting his books to one arm, he touches Jordi's waist with his free hand, then moves up to the lower curve of her breast and strokes the soft flesh. His thumb rises to find her nipple, and when he starts to tweak the tight nub, she moans.

'I've always wanted to do this,' Nolan murmurs during a break in the action.

'Do what?' Jordi asks foggily.

'Snog in the stacks, with a beautiful girl who shares my mission. Makes me feel like a superhero. Now, let's wreak some havoc. We can get back to the make-out session later.'

He gives Jordi a gentle nudge, sending her off into the wilderness of the library. Still reeling from the kiss, her flesh warm where Nolan touched her, she wanders off in her quest to create disorder. Nolan's lips having scrambled her brain cells, his mission now makes more sense.

'Just be random, Jordi,' she says to herself. 'Be spontaneous, for once in your life. Take a chance on misdirection.'

She walks through the stacks, replacing the books in her arm with books on the shelves. The diary of a buffalo hunter replaces a yogini's guide to spiritual growth through pranayama. The yogini's book then travels over to a section on automechanics, where it spreads its mellow light among guides to the inner workings of car engines. One by one, the books that Jordi's carrying are spread in a hundred dissimilar directions, until she sees herself as a crazed star at the center of a misarranged galaxy of information. She gets so absorbed in her work that she doesn't hear the final 'last call' over the intercom. She lets out a gasp of surprise when she comes face to face with a towering male in uniform.

'Library's closed,' the guard says. 'You should have checked those books out fifteen minutes ago. 'Fraid you'll have to leave, Miss.'

This definitely isn't the fresh-faced, barely shaving Jimmy that Dana wrote about in her blog. This guy looks like he should be guarding a US president, not the Human Sexuality section of the public library. When his beefy mitt of a hand reaches out for Jordi's elbow, she feels like a vandal about to be hauled off to jail. She lets out a loud shriek. The guard jumps back.

'She's with me, Fred.' Nolan's voice is balm to Jordi's ears. 'Relax. We're just getting ready to head out.'

Nolan steps up and circles Jordi's shoulders with a protective arm. A grin splits the guard's wide face.

'Got yourself a girl, hey, kid?' he asks.

Nolan's grip on Jordi grows a little more snug. 'Yes. I do.'

'Don't know how you skinny guys end up with all the curvy ones,' Fred sighs. 'She's a cutie, Nolan. Don't let her go.'

He gives Nolan a lewd wink, then saunters off whistling, hands in his pockets.

'I don't intend to,' Nolan replies. Fred's out of earshot, but Jordi hears. Nolan is still holding on to her, and she wonders if he meant it literally.

'We'd better get back to work on the chaos thing,' Jordi says, moving away.

It still feels strange, to be touched by a boy, held, kissed. Suddenly it occurs to her that she hasn't missed LIRA once this afternoon. She hasn't even thought about Threading or Throbbing, much less Tingling, since Nolan showed her the real thing. She feels a twinge of guilt, and why shouldn't she? She's betraying her baby.

Not to mention her best friend.

'Tuan!' she cries. 'Oh, damn! I forgot all about him!'

'Who?'

'My friend Tuan. He flew out to see me this morning, to try to fix LIRA. He was working on her when I left the apartment, and I forgot all about him. How could I be such a bitch?'

'Is he someone you're dating?'

'Oh, no. No way,' Jordi says. She omits the fact that she's Threaded and Throbbed with Tuan more times than she could remember, but neither of those acts counts as 'dating', does it?

'He must know your computer pretty well.'

Nolan's tone is way too casual, which suggests to Jordi that he might be mildly envious. This is another mind-blowing novelty: arousing jealousy in a male.

'He does,' Jordi admits. 'He's one of the people who helped me develop the software. That's why he's out here. When LIRA crumped, it was kind of an emergency for all of us.'

'This is something that's really important to you, isn't it?' Nolan asks. 'It's not just your laptop. It's a huge project for you.'

'Yeah. She – I mean, it – *is* a huge project. If everything goes the way we've planned, LIRA's going to change a lot of things for everyone who uses it.'

'Such as?'

Jordi takes a deep breath. She could tell another white lie here, misleading Nolan for the sake of protecting her project. But is it really LIRA she's trying to protect? Or her secret suspicion that she's become addicted to the surges of erotic energy that come from Throbbing?

'Maybe we'd better go somewhere else,' Jordi says. 'Somewhere we can talk without being tossed out of here by one of the library bouncers.'

'Follow me. I know the perfect place.'

Nolan takes Jordi's books from her arms and sets them on a nearby cart. He leads her back down to the second floor, past the darkened bank of public access computers, through Periodicals, and down a hallway.

'These are the Administrative Offices,' Nolan explained. 'Command Central. We're in enemy territory. These people worship the LOC cataloging system. They wake up in the middle of the night moaning the name of Melvil Dewey. They live and breathe MARC records. If they ever caught me, I'd be executed at dawn. Or fired. None of these guys would trouble themselves to wake up at dawn just to shoot me.'

'So why are we here?' Jordi asks, scanning the hallway. 'Shouldn't we go somewhere safer?'

'We're heading for the administrative break room,' Nolan says. 'Commonly known as the Wipeout Room, or the Make-out Room, depending on your reason for being here. It's the safest place in the building; there's no security camera. You need a key to get in, and only the head librarians have one.'

'How did you get one, then?'

They stop in front of an unmarked door. Nolan pulls a ring of keys from his pocket, slips one of them into the lock. It opens effortlessly. He glances at Jordi and grins.

'I'd tell you, but then I'd have to kill you. Come on in.'

He opens the door with a flourish. Half-expecting to see a sultan's den, Jordi is disappointed to find herself in a drab little room furnished with a couch that's more threadbare and swaybacked than her own, an old Formica table surrounded by a few listless chairs, and a countertop equipped with a crusty microwave oven and a Mr Coffee.

Nolan closes the door, then throws himself onto the couch and pats the cushion beside him.

'Make yourself comfortable,' he says. 'The night is young, and we're not even thirty yet.'

Jordi eyes him warily. She moves toward one of the straight-backed chairs. 'I'm pretty comfortable over here.'

'Oh, come on. I'm not going to bite – not yet. I promise you, we'll have at least twenty-two minutes of conversation before I bust a move on you. Don't sit on those chairs; they're all sticky with stuff.'

'The couch doesn't look much better.'

'It's not, but at least it's soft. And I'm on it. How can you top that?' He cocks his head, green eyes darkening as his voice drops an octave.

Jordi walks over and sits down beside him, perching on the sofa's edge. She fights back a flashback to the grappling session with Samantha's boyfriend Kurt. As much as she likes Nolan, as hot as he looks with his nerdy glasses and rumpled dark hair, she doesn't know if she's ready for full-on flesh sex. Especially in a building dedicated to public literacy.

He does have pretty eyes, though. Now that she's closer, she can see that they're rimmed with long black lashes. There's a bump on the bridge of his nose that turns his whole face asymmetrical when you see him from the side, and his lips are soft pink under a layer of peeling skin. He could use some Chapstick, but then his mouth wouldn't look so sexy, and bitable.

'Twenty-two minutes,' he says, glancing at his digital watch. 'Then I'm going to ravish you. Better start giving up your secrets. What does LIRA do?'

'LIRA is a software application based on the neurological changes that occur in people during the stages of attraction, dating, and love,' Jordi says, in the rote tone that she's used to describe the project for possible investors. 'It has great potential to be used as a commercial matchmaking site or for recreational cyberdating.'

'Recreational cyberdating? Sounds about as much fun as a root canal,' Nolan remarks. 'Net geeks have been doing that since the Stone Age of the internet. Say I'm a horny lonely guy living in his mother's basement. Why should I use LIRA instead of just hitting up a camgirl on the web?'

'If all you're looking for is a cheap gawk, you might as well stick with the camgirls,' Jordi snaps. 'LIRA isn't just a way to meet dates, or find hot thrills with anonymous strangers. It's a highly nuanced replica of the neural exchanges that occur between humans at all levels of intimacy, from sparks to climax, without all the complications that come from dragging a body into the mix. In an ideal situation, you never have to meet the other person at all.'

'No flesh, no fuss. Is that how it goes?'

'Yes. As a matter of fact, it is.' Jordi draws herself into a prickly ball in a corner of the couch. Up until now, Nolan's grin has made her melt. At this point, it makes her want to pop him one in the mouth.

'Sounds like good ol' fashioned cybersex, to me.'

'Well, it's not. It's making the ultimate connection – mind to mind. When you Throb with someone on LIRA, it's more than an orgasm. It's like this long continuous wave of erotic energy. It's desire without all the bulk involved; it's fulfillment without any of the letdown. It's not like anything *you've* ever experienced, or probably ever will.'

'Jordi?'

'What!' she barks.

Nolan reaches over and takes both of her hands. 'You're

panting. Calm down. I was kidding, OK? I don't get what you're doing, or why you'd want to do it, but I respect your dedication. A woman with a higher purpose is a huge turn-on for me. But I have to say, in all seriousness, that I don't think you've been meeting the right men. Sex doesn't have to be a let-down, you know.'

Jordi stares down at her lap. 'Maybe it's not, for everyone else,' she mumbles.

'Hey. Can I ask you something really personal?' Nolan tips her chin so that she has to look at him.

'OK. As long as it's not too, *too* personal.'

'Have you ever had an orgasm? With someone else, I mean?'

Horrified, Jordi stares at him. 'I can't believe you just asked me that.'

He smiles. 'I can't believe I didn't ask you before. First time I met you, at Café Wifi, I knew you'd never had a lover who made you come before.'

'You couldn't possibly have known that,' she sputters.

Nolan nods, a huge smile slowly illuminating his face.

'How?'

'State secret. Know what else?'

Jordi buries her face in her hands and shakes her head. Whatever he's going to say, she prays, just don't let it be as embarrassing as what he just said.

'I swore to myself, right there at the table, that I was going to be the first one to do that for you. Or to you. Whatever. I wanted to be the first guy to look up or down or sideways into your face while you're having an orgasm, and watch your eyes change colors.'

'My eyes don't change colors,' Jordi mutters.

'How do you know? Do you watch your face in the mirror when you masturbate?'

'I don't – well, no,' Jordi stammers. The lounge feels way too warm. Though Nolan hasn't moved any closer to her, the intensity of his attention is making it hard for her to breathe. His crooked smile holds a twist of mockery, but his eyes are completely sincere. She wishes he would reach across the sofa for her; she prays he doesn't try. Why does desire in the flesh have to feel so awkward, so bumpy? You have to reach through all those walls of cloth, then skin, then flesh and muscle and bone, to touch the part of the other person that you wanted to reach all along.

'So you don't know,' he says. 'I bet you don't know a lot of things about your body. Like what makes you sigh, or smile, or moan.'

'I suppose you're a sex expert, too?' Jordi asks, sarcasm hardening the edges of her question.

'Nah. But I'm a serious student when I care about the subject. I like to ask a lot of questions, especially embarrassing ones. That's when you really get to know someone, deep down.'

'I don't see why you have to humiliate someone just to get to know them,' Jordi sniffs.

Nolan wags his index finger like a pedantic punk. 'I never said "humiliate"; I said "embarrass". There's a big difference. Humiliation brings people down, makes them feel like less than they are. Embarrassment just makes them drop their masks. It makes them more real.'

'You think I have a mask? Are you kidding?'

'No, you have one, big time. You wear the smart-girl mask. The "Don't even talk to me because you're not half as cool as my laptop" mask.'

Jordi draws back, stung. 'You're nuts, Nolan. For your information, the word "to embarrass" comes from a French verb that means to block or put up a barrier. If anything, you're only making things harder for me right now.'

'See what I mean?' Nolan laughs. 'Smart girl.'

This time Nolan does reach for her. He pulls Jordi close, and takes off her glasses, then he rubs his forehead against hers.

'I'm sorry,' he says. 'That's not what I meant to do. But I just don't get it – why is all this so hard for you? Even when we kiss, it's like you're getting to know your own lips, and you don't really like the way they feel. Or maybe you just don't like the way *my* lips feel. Is that it?'

'No. That's not it. I like kissing you. A lot.'

Something inside Jordi is melting and cracking at the same time, like a thin layer of ice. Underneath lies pure liquid, warm and turbulent. It flows through the core of her body, spreads up into her chest and along her limbs all the way to her fingers and toes.

'Then you'll like this even better,' Nolan whispers.

He cups her breasts in his hands and lets them rest there for a few moments, his palms cradling their weight. Then he lightly strokes the upper slopes, circling her nipples with his fingertips, until Jordi feels her areolae turn to tight rings. Teasing, taunting, never quite touching her nipples themselves, he coaxes tremors of pleasure from the ultra-sensitive flesh. While he's torturing her this way, Nolan never takes his eyes off Jordi's face. Without her glasses she can't see him all that clearly (huge relief), but she knows he's watching the transformations in her eyes, mouth, skin.

Jordi flashes back to an especially intense Throb that she shared with someone once, some stranger out in the ether. She wasn't even sure if the person was male or female; they Threaded by accident one day, just locked neural nets at random and, before she knew it, she'd been drawn with magnetic force into this stranger's sensual self. Their connection was more powerful than anything she'd experienced and, within minutes, she was soaring. They floated together in a state of low-level ecstasy, winging toward a shared cerebral orgasm, then turning to coast the currents again. Their rapport was incredible, unforgettable. All of a sudden, in a cruel act of Throbbus interruptus, the other had messaged out of the blue: *I wish I could see you.*

Jordi, in a fit of angry panic, had slammed her laptop shut and disconnected LIRA. Anyone who had worked on the project, or officially been allowed to participate in testing, took Rule Number 1 with deadly seriousness: never interrupt a Throb with a request for meat contact. Any reminder of flesh, or its cumbersome needs and demands, was totally *verboten* when you were basking in LIRA's radiant relational waters.

Jordi not only invented that rule, she was a hard-core enforcer. Now, with a live boy gazing at her as she shifts and sighs under his hands, she wonders if she's been insane. She never knew that meat contact could make you feel so supple, so succulent, so fully, achingly sexual. If Nolan gives her anymore pleasure, she'll swell to the point of bursting, like a ripe grape popping its skin.

'Would you take your clothes off for me?' Nolan asks huskily. Then he feels her muscles tense, and he adds, 'Never mind.'

'Later?' she says.

'OK. But not too much later. I'm patient, but not to any superhuman degree.'

'How about the day after tomorrow?' Jordi hears herself say. The words seem to drift up to her from a colorless planet, the one she used to inhabit.

'Day after tomorrow? Sure, I'll put it on my calendar – the one I keep in my pants.'

Nolan glides on top of her, easing her onto her back on the couch, then they're kissing again, lips grazing hungrily on each others' mouths and cheeks and foreheads. They kiss with an uninterruptible energy, as if someone has hit the 'resume' button on the make-out session they began earlier in the stacks. Jordi has never thought of sex as a continuum; for her, physical love has always been a series of isolated events, as random and rare as traffic accidents. To be with one guy more than once, to feel her attraction for him not only sustain itself, but grow – it is all so new, it makes her head spin.

'What are we doing?' she gasps, when Nolan lets her come up for air.

'Huh?' Without his glasses, Nolan's nearsighted eyes are soft with desire. 'I thought that was kinda obvious.'

'What are we doing here tonight? I need to know,' she insists.

'What does it feel like we're doing?' he laughs. Nolan rolls onto his side, propping his weight on his elbow and leaning his head on his hand. 'We're stalking the great elusive fill-in-the-blank, like everyone else. We're stalking Dana. We're pursuing erotic satisfaction. We're trying to find love. We're searching for the Great Mystery of Life. What else is there to understand?'

'But is it really that easy for you to figure out how you relate to another person?' Jordi asks. 'How do you know if you're really connecting with them, or if it's all in your own head?'

'Sometimes I think you're from another planet, Jordi. You really don't get this love-and-sex stuff, do you?'

'You mean I'm like some kind of alien?'

'Well ... yes,' Nolan admits. 'I mean, most girls don't need to analyse a kiss or touch or hug. It's unusual. What can I say?'

'You could say something a bit more romantic,' Jordi snaps.

Five seconds ago Jordi was soaring on the heights of passion. Now she wants to cry and eat Fritos. Being in love with a meat-boy, she decides, is a lot like PMS, only with sex replacing the crucial role of junk food.

'What would be the point?' Nolan laughs. 'If I said something romantic, you'd get that paranoid look on your face again.'

Jordi sits straight up. 'What paranoid look?'

'The one where you squinch up your mouth, and your eyes get big and round, then narrow, then huge again. It's cute. But it's still paranoid. I don't think you believe in all this, Jordi.'

'All what?'

Nolan makes a frustrated sweeping gesture with his hand. 'Everything we're doing here. The kissing, the making out. Me telling you that I'm falling in love with you.'

Jordi stares at him. Her mouth flops open, but no words come out. Nolan never said anything like that. Never. He's crazy. No wonder he makes her paranoid.

'You never said that,' she says in a mousy squeak.

'I was going to. You just won't give me a chance.'

A furious buzzing noise, accompanied by a red throbbing like the beating of a heart, bursts from Jordi's backpack, which is sitting on the opposite end of the couch. It's her top-secret pager, reserved for emergencies; only her co-developers have the number. Instinctively she dives for her backpack, her elbow landing in the middle of Nolan's abdomen.

'Ow! Give a dude some warning before you tackle him!' he shouts.

But Jordi doesn't notice. The text message on the pager display is the most beautiful thing she's seen in ages – more beautiful than the sun rising over the ocean, more beautiful than a brand new baby or a new fully loaded wireless notebook.

LIRA LIVES!!!!

'She's awake,' Jordi whispers. She blinks, just to make sure she's not hallucinating the words on the electronic display. Then her voice rises to a jubilant squeal. 'She's awake! Nolan, listen. LIRA's back. We're connected!'

Frantically Jordi texts back to Tuan: THREAD ME!!!

She closes her eyes and waits. One beat, two, three, then she feels the first tickle of a successful Thread – weaker than usual, but it's her friend, her dear friend, touching her from inside. Their connection is unmistakably real.

'I feel it. I feel it again!'

Nolan puts his glasses on again. He looks at Jordi with a small tight smile and sighs. 'That's nice.'

She wants to shake him. 'Nice? This is way beyond "nice", Nolan. This is the best thing that's happened to me since she crashed.'

'Great. I'm happy for you.'

'I gotta go,' Jordi says. She grabs her backpack and tumbles off the couch in her haste to get up, landing with a thud on the floor. She clambers to her feet and brushes off her jeans. She leans down to give Nolan a quick kiss on the cheek. He turns his head, and her mouth brushes his ear. His green eyes have gone dark, darker than the pools in the heart of a cave. Jordi's heart does something strange – it jumps, trips, then plummets to the floor of her chest. For a crazy moment, she wishes Tuan had never texted her, that she and Nolan could have kept kissing and kidding around on the couch, until the jokes and kisses melted into something wild, naked and wordless.

'Come with me, Nolan,' she begs. 'I'll show you how amazing LIRA is. Once you've Threaded and Throbbed, every other connection you've had in meat life will seem silly and lame by comparison. It'll be the deepest, most thrilling experience you've ever had with another person.'

'You really don't get it,' Nolan says. He's still not looking at her.

No, *you* don't get it. Jordi thinks the words, but doesn't say them.

'I'll call you later,' she says.

And then she's gone.

'I don't know what crack house you spent your day in,' Tuan calls out when he hears Jordi stampeding through the door, 'but I've been working my skinny butt to the bone, girlfriend!'

Jordi's never seen anything as sweet as the sight of her beloved LIRA, awake and glowing on the kitchen table. Tuan's face, beaming ecstatically under his magenta crest of hair, fades next to the vision of a working computer, with all its promises of restored connection.

'What did you do?' Jordi breathes. 'How did you get her working again?'

'Erm, I dropped her.'

'You did what?'

Tuan sheepishly kicks the table leg with the toe of his black Converse sneaker. 'I dropped her. By accident, of course. I was reaching across the table for something, and she fell on the floor. Next thing I knew, she was making that hummy noise, and her monitor lit up like the Fourth of July.'

'But Tuan, that means it could be a fluke. What if it doesn't last?' Jordi wails. Her arms itch to scoop up LIRA and cuddle her against her chest, but she's scared of breaking the spell.

'You guys blow my mind – getting all emo over your stupid computer. You'd think it was your baby or something.'

Samantha strolls into the room. Her slim toasty brown body sparkles with beads of her favorite post-shower oil, and she's rubbing her wet blonde hair with a terry-cloth towel that's only slightly smaller than the towel she's wearing around her bare torso. When she steps up behind Tuan and wraps both arms around his neck, the towel half-falls, revealing her perfect pert boobies with their gumdrop nipples.

'Oops!' Sam giggles, hitching the towel back into place. 'Free titty shot!'

Jordi gawks at her roommate. Then she shifts her stare to Tuan, whose face is a slightly more subtle shade of red than his hair. She points at Sam, then slowly moves her finger to point at Tuan, tracing a visual line between them. She takes her time to link one word, one image, to the next, but she can't avoid the final horrifying reality of what happened in her kitchen that afternoon.

'You two had sex today,' she says. 'On the kitchen table. You knocked my computer on the floor.'

Sam rolls her blue eyes. 'Oh, Jordi. Lighten up. It's a *computer*. Besides, it was dead till Tuan shoved it off the table. It's working now. You should be peeing your pants with joy.'

Pounded by pornographic visuals, Jordi closes her eyes

and clutches her head. She sees Samantha giggling as she seduces Tuan with her predictable striptease, peeling the tight clothes off her lithe body. Tuan rises from the chair to meet her, accepts her invitation to dance, touch and taste. Sam leads him to the nearest elevated surface, backing toward the kitchen table till her taut butt cheeks are pressed against the edge. Then she lowers herself, parting her thighs, drawing Tuan down towards her pussy: a soft pink shell rimmed with a golden thatch of fur. Tuan, with the awestruck lust of a Horny Net Geek who's finally found his Valhalla of the flesh, clears away every obstacle with a crazed arm. Chalk one up for the meat world.

'Did you even see LIRA fall?' Jordi asks accusingly.

'Well, no. But I knew she fell.'

'Because you heard her go crashing to the ground.'

'Yeah.'

'But you didn't save her?'

'Jordi,' Tuan says, his liquid brown eyes pleading for mercy, 'don't glare at me like I'm some kind of baby killer. I just wanted a chance to touch something beautiful. Is that so evil?'

'Yeah, Jordi, back off,' Sam pipes in. 'He's not evil. I really like him. And he gives the best head ever! I had so many orgasms, I lost count.'

'That's because he's had so much time to watch other guys performing oral sex on the internet,' Jordi says. 'All Tuan's ever done is fantasise about it.'

Samantha tightens her grip on Tuan, acting as a shield against her roommate's wrath. Then she has the audacity to bend down and nuzzle his neck with her cheek; even worse, Tuan is insensitive enough to nuzzle back.

'You don't care, do you? Either of you,' Jordi says. 'She's not just a computer. She's my life. Everything I worked for is in that machine. What if you'd smashed her to bits?'

'But we didn't,' Samantha shrugs. A puzzled look wrinkles her perfect little nose. 'Everything's cool now.'

'I don't know that for sure,' Jordi says. 'All I know is that she juices up now. Her neurological interfaces could be totally screwed.'

She feels fat hot tears welling in the corners of her eyes. The last thing she wants to do is break down like a baby in front of her roommate and best friend. They'd see that as proof that she really is dysfunctional, sobbing over her computer as if it were a living being. They'd feel sorry for her for a minute or two, then they'd excuse themselves so they could sneak off to the bedroom and bonk a few more times. Jordi can already see lust mingling with the guilt on their treacherous faces as Sam's nuzzling turns into feathery kisses.

Tuan gently extracts himself from Samantha's arms, stands up and walks over to Jordi. He reaches for his friend but stops short of touching her, his arms paralysed by the force field of her hostility.

'We'll test her, Jordi. I'll let all the others know she's back online. We'll stock up on Mountain Dew and microwave popcorn and stay all night Threading and Throbbing, just like the old days.'

Jordi's mouth begins to shake, and this time there's nothing she can do to stop the flood of saltwater. The 'old days', the halcyon early development phase of LIRA, will never come back. If LIRA ever gets out of Beta, she'll be a commercial product like any other. People will have to pay. Those joyous moments of pure connection, those moments that felt like the ascent of two white balloons rising toward each other in mid-air, won't happen again, not without an investment in hardware, a one-time installation charge and a monthly membership fee.

'Jordi? Are you *crying*?'

Sam's voice rises in alarm. She rushes over to her roommate, the towel taking another dangerous plunge as she engulfs Jordi in a hug. Unlike Tuan, Samantha is completely at ease in her skin; the gestures of the material world don't faze her at all.

'It's OK, it's OK, it's OK,' Sam chants in soothing repetition, stroking Jordi's curls. 'Your computer's going to be OK.'

'It's not the computer,' Jordi sniffles. 'It's . . . something else.'

'Like what?' Tuan asks.

'Not what. Who. It's a guy I met. I dissed him for a machine. I suck,' Jordi sobs. She gives herself over to the tears. Though she's fully aware that her face has swollen into a snot-slick tomato, Jordi can't believe how good it feels just to dissolve into big messy emotions.

'You met a guy? A real one?'

Sam pulls back in surprise. Jordi wipes her eyes to find both of her friends studying her warily, as if she were a ticking bomb.

'We kissed,' Jordi confesses. 'I kissed a meat-boy. It hasn't gone any farther than that.'

'But he's in love with you, isn't he?' Sam presses. 'He is! You're smirking!'

'Hey, I thought you two were just make-out buddies.' Tuan plants his fists on his hips as he scolds her. 'You never said love was involved. You can't get into a meat relationship, remember? Not till LIRA's out of development.'

'She can do whatever she wants,' Sam says loyally. 'Jordi's never been in love before. You two need to get a real life. You're turning into a couple of Cybergs.'

Jordi's giggle explodes into a snort. 'You mean Cyborgs, right?'

'Whatever. You know what I'm talking about: those things that are half machine, half human. Listen, I need to get out tonight and dance. I feel that salsa beat in my blood. Tuan, you're coming with me to the Bamba Room. Jordi, you're going out to get laid.'

Sam shakes damp hair and salsas out of the kitchen, her slim hips twitching to the rhythm in her head. As soon as she leaves, her fizzy joyful energy evaporates, leaving two sullen software developers to eye each other resentfully.

'You should have been more responsible,' Jordi mutters to Tuan.

'You started it all, with your snorkeling,' Tuan shoots back. 'You're the leader; you have to set a good example.'

Half machine, half human . . . Samantha's words echo in Jordi's mind. She goes back to the table and touches LIRA. The machine wakens, responsive as ever, with a purr and a burst of iridescent light. So why doesn't Jordi feel that familiar buzz of desire and anticipation?

Tuan shoves his hands in his pocket and drags his toe back and forth across the linoleum as he stares at the floor. 'I'd better head over to the Bamba Room with Sam. It's kinda dangerous for a girl out in the city alone at night.'

'Go ahead,' Jordi says. 'I'll stay here, put LIRA through the usual tests. If Fleek's online tonight, he'll help me. He doesn't have a life, either.'

Jordi's voice sounds as flat and lifeless to her ears as LIRA feels to her fingertips. She turns her head to catch Tuan's reaction to that little barb, but the spot where he was standing is already empty. He's off dancing, or kissing, or stalking the Great Elusive fill-in-the-blank, as Nolan would say.

Chapter Eleven

Dana: The Art of Penetration

Delightful Deviant,

By the time Steffen opened the door to his library, I'd worked myself into a lather of anticipation. I half expected to see a torture chamber worthy of the Marquis de Sade himself, and was actually a little disappointed to see a room filled with nothing more sinister than books. The only leather in sight was the battered burgundy upholstery on an old recliner, which took pride of place between a fireplace and a backgammon table. Across from the chair sat a flat-screen television. A decanter of brown liquid sat on the mantel above the fireplace. The stuff looked strictly ornamental, more like brackish root beer than booze. I scanned the room in vain for stray copies of Kahlil Gibran or Anaïs Nin lying around. All I saw were a few back issues of *National Geographic* and *TV Guide*, and the latest military thriller by Some Rightwing Guy. I hadn't inspected the books on Steffen's shelves, but his current reading material wasn't too promising.

'What do you think?' he asked, as he ushered me in.

'Charming,' I lied.

'My library bores you, doesn't it?' he laughed.

'No, not really.'

'It's a bachelor's hideout. Women never come here.'

My libido growled, telling me it was time to shift this exchange to a higher gear. 'Well, if I'm never going to "come" here, I'd just as soon leave now,' I said suggestively.

Steffen didn't miss a beat. He turned to me, and once again I noticed the sensual potential in his smile. His lips weren't thin, they were just ... economical. A mouth didn't have to be a succulent wedge of Mick Jagger flesh to be sexy.

'Don't worry, Dana. You'll get everything you could possibly want here,' Steffen said, in a shiver-making baritone that made me forget the military thriller and the brackish liquor. When I saw the tip of his tongue, neat as a cat's, flick across his lower lip, I felt deeply reassured.

Deeply. Way down in the molten core of my body, I knew I was going to get royally laid that night. A purr was already forming in my larynx, and I felt the telltale thump in my pussy that always alerts me to the presence of a man who knows what he's doing in bed. Or on an armchair, or a threadbare oriental rug, or the top of a backgammon table, as the case might be tonight.

Being the bold wench-without-boundaries that I am, I strolled right over to Steffen's recliner and curled up in it. I've always gotten a charge out of grabbing the symbolic source of male power in any situation, whether it be a cock or an armchair. My campaign to take over Steffen's recliner was more successful than the move I'd made on his cock earlier. He smiled at me indulgently and patted my hair as he crossed the room, heading for the bookshelf.

'Why don't you read something to me? Something erotic,' I suggested, doing my best Kathleen Turner imitation. I sounded more like a female bullfrog with a few glasses of wine under her belt, but, what the hell – I was the sexiest thing in the room right now.

'Oh, there'll be plenty of time for that,' Steffen replied. His fingertips, grazing the spines of his books, looked so sensually attentive that I felt a pang of envy.

'Like when?'

'When we're both ready, Dana.'

'When do you think that will be?' I asked, with sharp-edged sweetness.

'Not before dessert.'

'Well, I'm ready for more than tiramisu,' I grumbled.

His cool, calm and collected routine was starting to get to me. I do love a man with composure, but not when it knocks me off my game. I hadn't felt the thrum of lust in hours, the thrill of love in days. I wanted to be swept off my feet tonight, not plunked down on my behind. Sulking, I yanked the wooden lever on the old leather recliner. I expected the chair to fall back obediently, but it lurched, heaved and shot me out like a catapult. I landed in a graceless heap on Steffen's oriental rug, my legs tangled in his long dressing gown.

'Ouch.' The syllable was muffled by the rug's fringe; my mouth was full of it.

'Damn it! Fucking useless chair. Are you all right, darling?'

The 'darling' made me prick up my ears. Steffen knelt beside me, suddenly attentive. I usually didn't have to injure myself to bring a man to his knees, but, what the hell. Desperate times, desperate measures, all that stuff.

'Something hurts,' I said. I reached under the robe to palpate a few sore places on my body, mostly for effect.

'Tell me what hurts. I'm a librarian, not a doctor.'

'My pride. My dignity's been wounded too.'

I sat up, moaning piteously. My eyes met Steffen's. I was surprised to find him gazing at me with something much warmer than concern in his gray-blue eyes. Maybe he really did get into pain and humiliation. If so, he was with the wrong girl. I'll wear handcuffs and a satin blindfold and let a man torture my nude body with cat toys, but I'm no masochist.

'I'm so sorry, Dana.' His tone held more tenderness now. He petted the valley between my shoulder blades until I really wanted to purr.

'No need to be. I shouldn't have been diddling with your furniture. Furniture-diddling isn't one of my favorite kinks, anyway; I don't know why I bothered.'

'I should've had that recliner fixed ages ago. It's a grumpy old thing, not used to having eager voluptuous women sit down on it, much less flip its levers.

'Eager?' I repeated. It was a bitter, wounded little echo. 'Don't you mean "desperate"? Or did you have something more like "horny" in mind? Maybe I should just haul my "voluptuous" butt out of here. It's been a lovely evening, Steffen.'

I'd had enough. Whatever Steffen had learned in his Library Science education, it wasn't how to charm the fair sex. I struggled to my feet, feeling every extra pound on my body. After a few days of what I considered starvation, my clothes weren't as snug, but I was still too plump. OK, under all my vanity and enlightened self-awareness, I knew I was fat. I was the kind of woman who waltzed into men's libraries and broke things with her body, clearly too big and hungry for a man of Steffen's patience and genteel appetites.

I was almost upright when Steffen pulled me back down onto the floor. His grip was surprisingly strong and firm; before I knew what was happening, he had manipulated me into his lap and into his arms. He cuddled me, rocked me, wrapped his arms around me and murmured soothing nonsense into my ear. For the first time since I left home, I felt safe.

'You aren't going anywhere,' he said. 'You're going to stay here while I read to you, and then we're going upstairs to make love. You'll spend the night in my bed, and in the morning I'll make you breakfast.'

'But I have to get back to the li – I mean, I have to get home,' I sputtered. I'd hoped for dessert and sex; I hadn't expected a real bed and a hot breakfast, or a firm male body spooning me through the night. I glanced up at the ceiling, as if the Hand of Fate might reach through the plaster and snatch those delicious promises away from me.

'No objections allowed. My plans are unchangeable,' he said. 'They've been written in stone since the first day I saw you.'

Dear Deviant, I'm sorry to interrupt here, just when the Subtly Sexy Librarian was making his declaration of desire, but my intuition was nudging me in the ribs. Everything felt right – Steffen's hard chest, the warm book-lined room, the visions of bed and sex and food – but this notch in the nape of my neck was glowing. That only happens when something's out of whack in Dana's world. I'd never questioned a stranger's generosity before; I'd always happily assumed that life had endless gifts to offer me, and that those gifts would come from a variety of hands. Some of those hands would belong to kind people, some to not-so-kind people, and most of them, ideally, would be attached to hot rich guys with a taste for juicy redheads.

I wasn't sure which category Steffen fit into. I couldn't figure him out, and that bugged the hell out of me.

'Why are you doing all this for me?' I asked, looking at

him over my shoulder. 'What do you want? Besides the obvious, I mean.'

'How do you know I want the obvious?' Steffen asked, with an elliptical smile. 'Maybe I want something entirely different.'

'Like what?'

Now he was really making me nervous. My curvy body, my high-octane libido, and my erotic imagination had always been my selling points. Sure, I was smart, but I had the attention span of a gnat, and was intellectually lazy. I could be generous and affectionate, but I was no Mother Teresa. I'd been rich a few days ago, but I was currently penniless. If Steffen intended to hold me hostage, he'd be severely disappointed; Daddy Dearest wouldn't be paying any ransoms anytime soon.

Steffen let me go and got to his feet. 'Let's go get dessert and take it upstairs.' His voice was brisk and practical, and, as I looked up into his blue eyes with their sexy creases at the corners, I wondered why I'd doubted he was anything but a lonely mature male with a longing for booty.

'I thought you were going to show me your erotica collection,' I pointed out. 'Fanny Hill's fanny is getting cold over there on the bookshelf.'

'I've got something I think you'll like even better,' Steffen said.

I gave him my balls-to-the-wall, flirt-to-the-death smile, the one that's steamrolled a hundred men into my arms.

'I certainly hope so,' I said.

I let the implications of that remark simmer in the air for a second or two, then I scrambled up and let him take me back to the kitchen. He cut two tremulous slices of creamy tiramisu, and plopped them into porcelain bowls, which he placed on an antique pewter tray. I followed him up a narrow flight of stairs to a room with a four-poster bed. Mellow light from a pair of bedside lamps spilled across a blue-and-white wedding ring quilt. I couldn't help it: I let out a whoop of joy and threw myself onto the mattress.

'A bed, a bed, a real bed,' I repeated ecstatically, rolling back and forth. You'd think I'd been sleeping under a bridge for six months.

'Calm down, Dana,' he laughed. 'It's just a mattress.'

'No such thing as just a mattress. Or just a dessert, for that matter.'

I snatched my tiramisu off the tray and proceeded to gobble it, filling my mouth with heavenly, liqueur-laced, chocolaty creaminess. I cleaned my plate, then snatched Steffen's off the tray before he could touch it, and finished that too. I didn't care if my host thought I was a greedy slut; every orifice in my body was crying out for some sort of fulfillment, and I was going to take everything I could get. My heart, which still craved love, would have to wait.

'Had enough?' Steffen chuckled. He didn't seem to mind that I'd polished off his tiramisu.

'For the moment, yes,' I announced.

Sated, I flopped onto my back and bounced a few times on the mattress, reveling in its firmness. I gazed up at the beamed ceiling and realised that, for the moment, I was fulfilled, with or without a lover. If my life hadn't been such a never-ending flood of pleasure and affection, maybe I'd have found it easier to be content. Food was wonderful. Shelter was wonderful. Sex after a meal, under a roof, would be bliss.

'Read to me now,' I said. 'I want to hear a story.'

I felt perfectly safe making my demands. Cozy and

protected, I could ask for what I wanted, secure in the knowledge that if I was a good girl, I'd get it. If I wasn't a good girl, I might get a spanking, which wasn't a bad alternative.

'Would you think I was terribly kinky if I blindfolded you first?'

'No doubt,' I replied.

Even as he asked, Steffen was opening a wooden box at the foot of his bed and pulling out a white satin blindfold. It looked harmless enough, like one of those sleeping masks my granny used to wear. It's not as if he were asking me to wear studded black leather. Besides, the thought of a kinky reference librarian was already making me feel flushed.

'So what do you think?' he held up the blindfold. His blue eyes held a dare, a promise, and something more.

'Why not?'

I sat up and let Steffen place the blindfold over my eyes, then tie it at the back of my head. Suddenly in darkness, I was acutely aware that, under the robe I'd borrowed from Steffen, I was naked as the day I was born. I curled up on the bed, my head nestled in one of his sumptuous feather pillows, and waited for Steffen to join me.

I heard him undressing, then opening the closet and slipping something on, probably a robe very much like the one he'd loaned me. I felt his weight sink onto the bed beside me; I smelled his spicy aftershave as he leaned over to kiss me lightly on the lips.

'My beautiful princess,' he said, 'I have the perfect story for you.'

Then he read to me from Frances Hodgson Burnett's classic novel, about a little rich girl who finds herself destitute in the cruel, materialistic world of a Victorian boarding school. I'd loved that book when I was a child, but I'd never in a million years thought I'd end up like Sara Crewe. Of course, in the end, she finds another rich man to replace her dear dead daddy, but, in the meantime, she suffers all kinds of horrible deprivation and is teased mercilessly by the mini-bitches at her stuffy school.

I could definitely relate to Sara's story, probably a bit too much. I thought about suggesting something else – maybe he had a few Judith Krantz or Jackie Collins novels under his bed – but Steffen's rich voice hypnotised me. The guy had really missed his calling; he shouldn't have been sitting behind a reference desk, but behind a microphone, reading for National Public Radio. What a rare luxury to find a man whose voice melted over me like warm butterscotch sauce as the sentences spilled flawlessly from his lips! He could have read to me from the back of a shampoo bottle; I just didn't want the words to end.

But they did end when he set the book down and reached for me instead.

'Why did you choose that story?' I asked.

'Because the princess reminded me of you. You're a princess, aren't you, Dana? But you've lost your castle. Am I right?'

'Yes,' I whispered.

The novel still held me in thrall. I wanted to tell Steffen that I'd never been like brave little Sara; I wouldn't put up with a cold attic room for more than five minutes without pitching a fit and calling the management. But I was floating on a spell of words, and I couldn't do anything but agree.

'I'm going to touch you now,' he said, 'just like I promised. Are you ready?'

I nodded. Goosebumps broke out in strips along my belly

and inner thighs even before his cool hands slipped under the robe. I rolled over to give him full access to my body. He loosened the sash, then pulled open the robe's lapels slowly. He unwrapped me as if I were a gift, one he wanted so desperately that it made his hands shake with desire.

I love a man who shakes for me. I love a man who turns to Jell-O when he gazes at my curves and watches the changes in my flesh as I open for him. I love a man who thinks I'm beautiful and isn't afraid to tell me so as soon as the thought crosses his mind. I love a man who falls for me as soon as his hands meet my satin body, but who waits to tell me he loves me until he's also in love with my soul.

Of course, I mostly meet these guys in my daydreams. Most of my lovers are as greedy and impatient as I am. We tell ourselves we crave pleasure and affection, but what we're really searching for is a quick fix to calm our existential jitters. If I'm not the focus of someone's adoration, even if it only lasts as long as the Jack Daniel's in the pint we're sharing, who the hell am I? We dive headfirst into the sex to avoid questions like that, and when we burst back to the surface, gulping for air, we hope we never see each other again.

Steffen was different. He didn't devour me; he *savored* me. His mouth was as gifted at creating pleasure as it was at reading prose. When he moved from one erogenous zone to the next, he orchestrated the motions of his lips and tongue to pay court to a new constellation of nerves. He set off a small series of rippling orgasms with the torture he inflicted on my nipples: painting the areolae with his tonguetip in teasing circles before nipping at the hard inner buds. I howled when he bit my nipples hard, but I loved the sharp taste of pain in the sweet stew of all that sensual delight.

'What are you doing?' I moaned, when he left for a moment to dig through his toy-box again.

'Getting something new for us to play with,' he said. There was a sly tone in his voice. 'This should bring back a few memories.'

It didn't take long for me to figure out what Steffen had in mind; as soon as I heard that telltale battery-operated whirr, I knew he was wielding a vibrator. He held the device over me, letting me listen, before I felt its tangible purr at the notch between my thighs. I loved the fact that he wasn't plunging the wand into my pussy, but was using it to coax me open. Not that I needed much coaxing; within seconds, I was splayed for him like an oyster on the half-shell.

'That *was* you in the library that day! I knew you were a pervert from the moment we met,' I gloated. 'You were watching me from behind the bookshelf. Shame on you! Who was minding the reference desk while you were on your spy mission?'

'The public survived without me somehow,' Steffen said. 'How could I have missed out on your little show? You were spectacular.'

'How long had you been playing Peeping Tom when I started to masturbate?'

'Longer than you might think. Watching you read and eat candy bars was a delight in itself. I love watching women read. It's a secret fetish of mine. There's something about seeing a woman lost in a book, unconscious of her day-to-day surroundings, that turns me on.'

'Sounds like you need a more active sex life,' I remarked, but my sarcasm dissolved as Steffen began to ply my moist inner folds with the vibrator's humming head. The buzzing sensation gradually moved through my outer lips, then spilled through my loins. He rolled the device around and around my clit, then brought it into contact with the very tip of the tiny bud. I tumbled headfirst into a waterfall of climaxes – swift and tumultuous. When the last of the ripples died off, he slid the wand into my pussy and brought me to orgasm in an entirely different way. These spasms were so intense they were almost brutal. Behind the smooth darkness of the blindfold, I came and came and came, until I had to beg Steffen to stop.

'Let me take this off,' I whined, reaching for the blindfold. 'I want to see what's going on.'

'No. Not yet. My sensory deprivation experiment is just beginning.'

I felt him leaning over me to pull something out from behind the bed. It turned out to be a pair of silk ties, which he used to bind my wrists. Somehow it didn't surprise me that Steffen was into bondage. I wondered if the library administration knew about this. If I'd known librarians were so kinky, I would have enrolled in a Master of Library Science program straight out of college.

With my hands secured over my head, I had no choice but to submit to this particular librarian's search for information. He subjected my nude body to an amazing range of textures and sensations: from feathers to fur, deerskin to candle wax, with tongue and fingers intervening to provide their own stimulation. One of his toys made me yelp for mercy, another made me beg him not to stop. There were sharp pricks interspersed with tender strokes, and velvet was applied to my skin with the same gusto as leather. Because I never knew what kind of object he would apply to me next, I was suspended in uncertainty; I finally gave in and surrendered to a state of lush passivity.

'How does this make you feel?' he would ask me every so often.

'Exquisite,' I said. Or, 'tense'. Or 'ecstatic', or 'agonised'. My vocabulary dwindled, though, as the pleasures multiplied. I eventually gave up trying to find words to describe every sensation, and responded with inarticulate moans, grunts and sighs. I sensed that Steffen approved. Though I couldn't see his face, I felt that he wanted to turn me into a mound of melting butter, incapable of speech. He was doing a damn good job; I was about ready to be spread over pancakes.

Once he was done with the stroking, tickling, prodding and prickling, Steffen moved on to more serious business.

'The art of penetration is more than physical,' he said, with all the didactic flair you'd expect from a man who spent his life providing information to others. 'It carries a huge psychological freight. I want to see how you respond to a variety of insertable objects.'

'If that includes your cock, it should also include a condom,' I said, as sternly as possible in my orgasm-fogged state.

Steffen assured me that he believed as strongly in latex as I did, and then he began what I would later think of as The Great Penetration Experiment. I don't think I've ever been so deeply explored as I was that night, not even by my gynecologist; certainly my OB-GYN had never felt my inner walls with such passionate curiosity. His fingers whirled inside me, stroked the spongy recesses, inspiring muscular contractions that made me writhe and squeal. He never did use his penis, but he used a variety of penis-shaped objects. Some of them were almost as warm and yielding as flesh, while others felt hard and severe, like swords. He plunged, he parried, and, as before, Steffen asked me to describe my reactions. After making a few lame attempts at verbalising my feelings, I lapsed into mush-mind once again.

I did do some thinking, though, about what it really means to have another person inside you. When it comes to describing sexual intercourse, I've always been partial to the good old Anglo-Saxon term 'fucking'. No beating around the bush, so to speak; I've always been a straight-forward kind of tart. But the act of sliding one sex organ into another, and moving back and forth until one or both parties hits the erotic jackpot, had little to do with the way Steffen was penetrating me. His experiment left me utterly vulnerable. At times, this openness was bliss. At other times, it made me feel so exposed that I wanted to run away, run back home to the same bed I'd slept in since I was a teenager.

When I was a virgin, I used to fantasise about having someone inside me who truly, deeply loved me. I knew that sex could be fun, but I'd always imagined that the 'fun' part involved only the peripheral zones: lips, nipples, clit. As soon as the penis entered the vagina, all the giggly enter-tainment would come to a screeching halt, and the lovers would gaze into each other's eyes with all the gravity of pure devotion as the fucking took place. Like many wide-eyed virgins weaned on Disney movies, I equated fucking with love until I had intercourse for the first time. Then it dawned on me that fucking was also fun. Fucking was so fun, in fact, that it soon became my sexual *raison d'être*, and the visions of undying love were filed in the same mental rubbish can as my memories of my first *NSync concert.

'What are you thinking about?' Steffen asked, breaking into my reverie.

'Fucking,' I said.

'Excellent,' he replied.

I didn't care if my answer pleased him or not at this point; I just wanted more. He was giving me what I'd always wanted: to be filled in more ways than I could imagine. I stopped thinking, lay back, and let him have his way with me.

After I'd come to the syncopated rhythms of Steffen's tongue on my clit and the vibrator in my pussy, Steffen rolled me over on my belly and propped a pillow under my hips. I went from soft-as-butter to stiff-as-wood within seconds.

'I don't do anal,' I warned, clenching my uplifted cheeks with all my might.

Call me a tight-ass if you want, Darling Deviant; your heroine doesn't put foreign bodies up her rectum. It wasn't as if I'd never tried anal sex – I'd just never tried it without excruciating pain. I explained all this to Steffen. He pleaded with me to reconsider. If I couldn't enjoy anal penetration as an erotic experience, could I at least endure it as an intellectual exercise?

'I don't see any direct correlation between my bum and my intellect,' I objected. 'Can't you try another hole? I have others, you know.'

'But your bum is so perfect,' he said. 'Entering you there will give me access to another doorway to your being.'

'I don't know, Steffen. It sounds like you're asking me to donate my bottom to a hopelessly abstract cause. Is sex always so academic for you?'

'If you hate it, I'll stop. I promise. I'd be willing to bet that your previous lovers never used enough lube.'

'They used enough lube for a luge slide,' I sighed, 'but go ahead. Give it your best shot.'

I was grateful that I couldn't see what Steffen was using

for this phase of his experiment. He parted my cheeks, slicked the cleft and the tight opening with KY Jelly, then inserted what felt like a row of small beads. One after another, they entered me. They weren't big enough to cause any serious pain; in fact, after the first few, I relaxed enough to enjoy the way the ridges rubbed against my inner sphincter. When he felt me go limp, Steffen began to pull the row of beads back and forth. It still felt alien, but I didn't hate it, and as their nubbly friction continued, my body relaxed and accepted the sensation. I pressed my hips into the pillow, grinding my mound against its smooth surface to stimulate my oh-so-swollen clit. To my total amazement, I found myself climaxing, the muscles in my bottom and pussy clenching in tandem as the spasms rolled through me from loins to belly.

'What did you just do to me?' I panted. 'What did you put inside me?'

'A string of pearls,' Steffen said. I didn't need to see his face to know that he was smirking with satisfaction. 'Not cultured ones, either. Those were the real deal. Quite expensive too.'

'Couldn't you have just put them around my neck, like other guys?'

'You're welcome to wear them, if you want.'

'Um, no thanks. Not after where they've just been. What did you learn from this experiment, anyway?'

Steffen didn't answer right away. He untied me first, rolled me over, then pulled up my blindfold. I blinked at him in the lamplight. His professorial face gazed down at me with something close to awe.

'I learned you inside and out,' he said.

'Was I what you thought I'd be?'

He thought for a moment. Damn, he looked sexy when

he was thinking. I've always loved cerebral men, but I don't think I'd ever fully appreciated the erotic appeal of a male in full cogitation.

'No,' he said. 'You were much more. More than I ever dreamed.'

Totally spent, I drifted off to sleep wrapped in Steffen's fine hand-stitched quilts. My sleep was peacefully dream free, pure relief for my exhausted mind and body. When I opened my eyes to sun streaking across the sheets, I saw Steffen's silhouette bending over the night table, leaving a mug of coffee, before he slipped back into the hallway. It wasn't until that moment that a strange thought flashed through my mind.

He never came. Throughout that whole carnal funfest that we shared last night, Steffen had never had an orgasm. I felt a twinge of guilt (just a twinge, mind you) for my selfishness. I'd come over and over again, but I'd never returned the favor to my host.

'Hey, Steffen?' I shouted, sitting out in bed. 'Are you still here?'

There was no answer from downstairs. A note propped up against the blue-and-white coffee mug informed me that he'd left for work, but that I should feel free to stay as long as I liked.

'Does that mean I can stay all day, or all week?' I said to myself.

Maybe my host would let me camp out at his house until I could find a job and rent my own apartment. Since I'd never been employed by anyone but my father for more than two weeks, landing a source of income might prove difficult. Did Steffen need a full-time French maid/erotic guinea pig, I wondered?

Realistically, my employment options were limited. I had a degree in English, I loved to read, and I liked to tell people what to do. I could be a teacher, but I didn't have the patience. I loved to paint my face and stare at myself in the mirror, but I was so *not* service-oriented so I could never sell cosmetics. My primary ambition, before Dad kicked me out, was to shop and screw my way through life until I met a man who was willing to fulfill both needs within the bonds of holy matrimony.

I heaved an angst-heavy sigh and wriggled across the mattress to the night stand. Steffen's coffee was rich and strong, an aromatic Italian roast laced heavily with cream and sugar, exactly the way I liked it. Apparently he'd learned a lot more about me last night than I realised, I thought as I sipped. There wasn't any rush for me to find a job this morning. I could hang out here, finish the pot of coffee, take another shower, raid his kitchen for something to eat.

I looked around Steffen's bedroom. There's something else I dearly love to do, a vice so shameful that I don't even confess it to my closest friends. I'll tell you, though, Dear Loyal Deviant, since you've stayed with me through public masturbation, a blow job on city property and anal sex with pearls: I have a weakness for snooping.

I don't think it's jealousy that drives me to ferret out my lovers' secrets, though I've identified more than a few chronic cheaters by rifling pockets and underwear drawers. I think my ultimate, unspoken goal is very much like Steffen's: I want full penetration. I want to know what's in my lovers' heads and hearts, as well as in their coats and closets. Even after a one-night stand, I've been known to sneak through bathroom cabinets and kitchen cupboards in search of clues to a man's hidden identity.

To tell you the truth, most guys I've been intimate with don't have much of a hidden identity. They're just guys, equipped with the predictable stash of condoms, mouthwash, postcards from old girlfriends, and holey socks. But every now and then I'll strike gold and discover something staggeringly strange about a man I've slept with. I had a sneaking suspicion that my mild-mannered reference librarian was going to be a gold mine.

After polishing off the rest of the coffee and helping myself to three slices of toast slathered with butter and marmalade down in the kitchen, I set to work investigating Steffen. I wonder if it's that old Bluebeard archetype that draws me to men with secrets. I felt a lot like Bluebeard's bride as I rummaged through the drawers in his kitchen, before moving on to his sacred library. Oddly enough, I didn't find anything more sordid than a small stack of bondage mags tucked behind an assortment of sado-masochistic paperbacks, all authored by Anonymous. I briefly admired his 'official' collection of erotic literature before heading back upstairs to ransack his bedroom.

Sometimes the truth is well concealed, and you have to sniff it out before carefully unearthing it. Other times, the truth is so obvious that it smacks you right between the eyes. I shouldn't have bothered to leave Steffen's bed that morning. The secret I craved was tucked right in the drawer of his night stand, inches away from the coaster where he'd set my coffee. He hadn't even bothered to bury his little bomb under the packets of tissue and condoms; it was almost as if he'd meant me to find the black leather-bound notebook.

I wasn't the only woman whose erotic life was sketched in miniature in Steffen's little black book. Apparently the reference desk at the public library was quite the hot spot for middle-aged voyeurs. I had to give Steffen credit for craving more than a glimpse of tit or leg here and there; he longed to peer into the psyches of the women he watched, and he'd peered mercilessly into mine.

D's promiscuity reflects a profound insecurity. Her bottomless need for affirmation reflects an effort to forestall a serious identity crisis. D is reluctant to take responsibility for her emotional growth; in spite of her overt display of sexual bravado, she remains a child at heart, with a child's compulsive need for immediate gratification. Winning D's affection was not difficult. She gave herself up without resistance and proved to be an enthusiastic but somewhat lazy sex partner. As she matures, her beauty will no longer be sufficient to fulfill her hunger for attention. She will need to develop an integrated self and acquire emotional maturity before she can sustain a successful adult relationship. Truthfully, I believe her chances of finding a deep and lasting love are almost nil.

I sat there, numb, with the notebook in my lap and read Steffen's vicious thumbnail portrait over and over again until the phrases lost some of their sting. His analysis wasn't even all that sharp, I realised. Any idiot could see that I was promiscuous (no shit!), I was a child at heart (what was wrong with that?), and that I gave myself up without resistance (OK, I'm a slut and proud of it). I knew that I was lazy and selfish; up until now, those defects had been working for me just fine.

The one barb that stuck in my heart, the only jab that truly wounded me, was Steffen's final line: I believe her chances of finding a deep and lasting love are almost nil.

Why did people always preface cruel statements with the word 'truthfully'? Did truth always have to be so painful? And was it painful only because in the shallow pit of my pampered soul, I knew he was probably right?

Steffen had not only achieved full penetration with me; he'd pulled off a major mind-fuck. He'd invited me to his home, where he'd cooked me a heavenly meal and given me a cozy bed to sleep in. He'd made love to me in ways that even my freaky imagination couldn't have invented. He'd made me feel like a precious, fascinating, gorgeous princess. He'd stuffed deep sea pearls up my ass, for crying out loud! And after that long and complicated seduction, he'd dissected me like a lab rat in some bizarre psychological experiment.

I don't recall much about the rest of that day, Dear Deviant. I know that I went downstairs after a while and found my jeans, sweatshirt and lingerie lying in a neatly folded stack on Steffen's dryer. I took another shower and got dressed. Before I left, I shredded every page of that ugly little black book, and shoved the fragments down the toilet. I threw in the leather cover, too, just in case the paper wasn't enough to clog his plumbing. All of this happened in a fog. My vision was blurred, not by tears, but by a red haze of rage and confusion.

One thing I do remember clearly is finding a payphone at a convenience store near Steffen's house, walking inside to beg the cashier for a quarter, and making a phone call to my father.

Chapter Twelve

Jordi: Throb Rocket

Jordi has called Nolan's cellphone 27 times. She's sent him six text messages, all of them asking him to meet her at Café Wifi at 12.30, during his lunch break. Now she's at the café, sitting at the same table where she met him the first time, praying he hasn't tossed his phone under a bus out of sheer irritation.

Jordi stares glumly into her cappuccino. She draws a hieroglyphic in the foam with her swizzle stick, then lifts the wide cup to take a sip. Her drink has gone cold. She checks her watch. It's 1.45. Nolan's lunch hour has been over for fifteen minutes. She flips open her cellphone for the thousandth time, checking to see if he's sent her a text message.

He just did. Her heart leaps into her throat.

It's a two-character message: NO.

Her heart plunges to her sneakers.

Why does love feel like a form of mental illness? Jordi wonders. You're either too high or too low, at the pinnacle of ecstasy or in the depths of despair. The middle ground isn't much better: an endless desert of routinised affection. Watching your lover scratch the roll of flesh under the waistband of his boxers while he eats potato chips and watches football on TV has never been Jordi's romantic ideal, yet millions of women seem to long for that kind of familiarity. Maybe that's because the alternative requires mood-stabilising medication, or large quantities of alcohol, or both.

Jordi looks over at the adjacent table. A woman about her age is staring intently at the monitor of a notebook computer, her fingers arched above the keyboard. Lucky girl. She probably doesn't have a boyfriend. Probably doesn't even date. Jordi's life was so clear, so streamlined, before Nolan swaggered into it, with his kisses and massages, his ravioli and his theory of misdirection.

Misdirection. That's what this has all been about. Jordi's next sip of cappuccino is not only cold, it tastes of cynicism. Nolan jumbled Jordi's emotions on purpose, as some kind of cruel experiment, just to see where she'd end up. Well, now she's here, with no potential boyfriend and no computer, either. To all outward appearances, LIRA is still working, but no one is Threading or Throbbing the way they used to. The connections sparkle a bit, fizzle, then fall flat. None of the developers has had anything close to a Throb lately.

Tuan refuses to accept blame for the system failure. 'It's not the software *or* the hardware, Jordi,' he told her this morning, when LIRA still failed to Thread properly. 'It's you. LIRA's not working because you lost your faith.'

'Give me a break,' Jordi protested, rolling her eyes. 'This is a software application, not an act of God.'

But she has a queasy suspicion that Tuan's right. If LIRA's code emulates neural responses to emotional states, how does Jordi know what the effect of disillusionment might be? No one's ever tested the unpleasant emotions, like disappointment or anger. In the alpha version they've all been blissfully floating on the high of communal desire, lofting among fluffy clouds of good will.

A guy pulls out a chair next to the girl at the next table. Jordi watches her glance up from her computer. Her pinched features, focused in concentration, turn soft and radiant as she recognises him. He leans over to kiss her, and his elbow almost knocks the notebook computer into the girl's lap. She laughs.

'You're such a geek,' he says, tweaking a strand of her hair. 'That's why I love you so much.'

'Oh, make me *puke*!' Jordi shoves back her chair and gives the happy soulmates a meaningful glare before stomping off the café's patio. They probably met and fell in love on one of those lame online matchmaking services. Now they're undoubtedly engaged to be married; they've signed up with one of the online bridal registries and are booking their honeymoon through WebVoyage.

She finds her feet leading her to the public library. Though Jordi has no desire to go there, or to see Nolan after his rude non-message, there's something she needs that only the library can provide. Once she reaches the building, she hurries through the front doors and heads straight up to the public computers to get a fix of Dana. After the usual wait, Jordi finally sits down in front of an unoccupied computer and logs on. She feels some of the bitterness seeping out of her as she types in the URL of Dana's blog, her username and password. Dana would never put up with the self-pity that Jordi's been wallowing in, and she'd never, absolutely never, accept NO as a text message from a man.

'Darling, the word "no" is our prerogative, not theirs.' Jordi imagines Dana standing behind her, whispering wisdom into her ear. 'Don't let that little punk treat you like this. Men are like viruses: just because you catch one doesn't mean you're stuck with him. And there are new ones popping up all the time!'

Jordi hits the Enter key, expecting the browser window to fill with Dana's words. Fresh, bold, colorful words . . . nothing like the flat pale vocabulary that defines Jordi's world.

BLOG NOT FOUND. NO SUCH USER OR USERNAME INCORRECT.

Stunned, Jordi leans into the monitor, as if she might be misreading the error message. No such user? Impossible. She retypes the URL, hits Enter again. Then she goes back to the URL window and types furiously: IS ANYONE OUT THERE? All these electronic devices, with their cryptic, truncated messages, are driving her insane.

'It's never the application's fault,' her very first computer science lecture had told her back in her freshman year of college, 'it's the programmer's. The code only does what you instruct it to do. If your instructions are faulty, your code will not execute properly.'

'You look upset.'

A concerned male voice floats into Jordi's consciousness, stilling the chatter in her head.

'I *am* upset,' she says. 'I can't find the blog I was looking for.'

'You mean Dana's blog?'

'How did you know?'

Jordi turns, startled. Someone is standing beside her, someone caring and competent. It's Steffen the reference librarian, the older guy who was attractive in a squirmy sort of way. He's making her squirm now, the way he's standing so close, his forearm lightly touching hers. He's watching her so kindly, like a teacher who cares about how her life turns out, that she leans against his tweed lapel before she's aware of what she's doing. His arm automatically surrounds her, strong and reassuring. He smells of something spicy and soapy, like Jordi's dad, but he's breathing against her cheek in a way that her father never would in a million years.

'I thought you'd be looking for Dana. She's all you talked about the other day,' Steffen says with a laugh. 'I couldn't seem to interest you in anything else at the library. I'd love to get to know you better, Jordi. Maybe someday you'll even tell me your full name, the one you dislike so much.'

'I don't think so. I never tell anyone.'

'Not even the men you're intimate with?'

Ferociously embarrassed, Jordi chews the end of her thumb and tries to avoid eye contact with Steffen.

'What are you thinking?' he asks.

'I'm thinking that reference librarians aren't supposed to ask questions. They're supposed to answer them.'

Steffen laughs again. It's a cozy, lying-in-the-sheets-after-sex laugh. 'It's impossible to answer a question properly if you haven't laid the groundwork with a few questions of your own. It would be a pleasure to lay that ground with you, Jordi.'

He's even closer now, the pressure of his shoulder firm against Jordi's arm. She knows that he wants to kiss her. From the drumbeat deep in her chest, she also knows that she's thinking about kissing him back. It must be Dana, weaving her way into Jordi's consciousness, spreading bizarre sexual impulses through her nervous system. Jordi actually considers turning her face to the reference librarian, rotating her head like a sunflower to meet his mouth. He'd be the third meat male she'd kissed in the past week. First Kurt, then Nolan, then Steffen . . . was Jordi in heat? With Steffen, it's not so much raw lust that draws her, but a simple longing to be held. Held, comforted, understood. Why does that often seem like too much to ask from her fellow meat folk?

'The website says Dana's blog doesn't exist anymore,' Jordi says sadly.

'Do you think she might have deleted it?'

'I don't think so. That blog was too important to her. It was all she had; her life was falling apart.'

'Maybe she found a more effective way to solve her problems than by sharing them with strangers,' Steffen suggests. 'Why don't we go back to my desk and talk about it.'

His slate blue eyes are fixed on hers with flattering intensity. His breath sifts lightly through his mouth.

'Do you have time?' Jordi asks.

'I'll always have time for you,' he says, his deep voice dropping to a whisper. His words brush across Jordi's ear like the strokes of a feather. She tries to visualise how this 'talk' will evolve. At the reference desk, Steffen will listen to her outpouring of problems, then he'll propose that they move their discussion to the Make-out Room, where he'll hold Jordi on his lap and rock her a little before their talking turns into passionate kissing. And she's thinking that it might not be a bad idea to let a man like Steffen show her the true art of love making, since none of the other meat males in her life has come close to giving her anything like an orgasm.

I wanted to be the first guy to look up or down or sideways into your face while you're having an orgasm, and watch your eyes change colors, Nolan had said. The thought of Nolan gives Jordi a pang of longing. When she turns back to Steffen, he suddenly seems alien – not tender and affectionate anymore, but subtly manipulative. His arm, now heavy and possessive, has shifted to her waist, and his hand has come to rest on the upper slope of her bottom. She doesn't remember saying or doing anything that implied he could touch her rear end.

'Leave her alone, freakazoid.'

Nolan slices between them, his forearm coming down like a Samurai sword to detach Steffen from Jordi. Jordi gives a small grunt of surprise and almost falls off her stool. Steffen steps back, cool and suave.

'What do you think you're doing?' he asks Nolan. 'Shouldn't you be working, or doing some semblance thereof?'

Nolan's asymmetrical features, under his shock of black hair, are a vision of beauty to Jordi, not because she was afraid Steffen was going to ravish her, but because she never thought Nolan would forgive her. Even if he still hasn't forgiven her, just seeing him in the flesh again makes Jordi want to split open like a piñata, spilling confessions of lust and love.

'Don't believe anything this creep says, Jordi,' says Nolan. 'He's twisted. He gets all romantic with the cute girls, then he worms his way into their heads and does all kinds of kinky things with the secrets he finds.'

'Wow,' Jordi says. She glances at Steffen again, newly impressed. 'So you did know Dana, didn't you? I bet you read her blog.' She pauses, not sure if she dares to say what she's really thinking. 'Maybe you even *wrote* her blog. Maybe she was a pornographic fantasy you created.'

Steffen's lips form a condescending crescent as he shakes his head. 'I'm afraid that would take too much erotic imagination, even for a lonely librarian,' he says.

'Lonely, my ass,' Nolan snorts. 'This guy gets laid more than all the rest of the staff combined. He's got his routine down to a science. He asks them over to his place for dinner, then he gives them this sob story about how his fiancée left him a hundred years ago. That softens them up so he can lure them into his library and pull out his erotica collection. At the end of the night, he takes them up to his bedroom, where he shows them his toy-box. When I say "toys", I'm not talking about Lego. Know what I'm saying? I've heard the same story from at least five different women. You would've been next if I hadn't stepped in.'

'Please, Nolan,' Steffen says with a pained grimace, 'I'll admit to being a bit of a libertine, but you're making me out to be much more of a cad than I am.'

'I don't think so, *cad*.' The square toe of Nolan's boot lands centimetres from the toe of Steffen's wingtip loafer as Nolan stands off with librarian: disorder facing down the supremacy of order right in front of Jordi.

'You're out of line, Nolan.'

'I know I am. I live out of line.'

'Step back, or I'll call security.'

'Yeah, like that'll help. Those guys are on the side of justice.'

'Jordi, I hope this punk isn't the best you think you can do,' Steffen says out of the side of his mouth.

'I'm falling in love with her. That's the best anyone can do.'

The two men stand nose to nose. Jordi's eyes dart back and forth between them. A week ago today she couldn't have gotten a meat date if she tried. Now two men are locking horns over her like rams. It's all way too surreal.

Especially the part where Nolan said he was falling in love with her.

A small crowd has gathered at the computers, drawn by the raised voices. The librarian who oversees the public access computers is tugging at the elbow patch on Steffen's tweed jacket, while a security guard steps in to back up his opponent. Jordi wishes she could hit a keyboard combination that would force-quit this whole confrontation, so she could be alone with Nolan.

Had Nolan meant what he said, about falling in love with her? He couldn't have meant it. No doubt he just threw in that declaration of love for dramatic effect, because it fit the moment so perfectly. In movies, any revelation of romantic love always signals to Jordi that it's time to go out and buy popcorn. In meat life, the experience is so unheard-of for her that she doesn't know what to do. The basics of respiration are about all she can handle right now.

'Steffen,' begs the gray-haired librarian, yanking Steffen's sleeve again, 'please stop this. Please!' Her plea rises to a tremulous falsetto; she sounds like Glenda the Good Witch being tortured.

'Stop what?' Steffen asks. 'That delinquent is the one who needs to be stopped. He's deliberately undermining the whole cataloging system here. He doesn't think anyone knows about his activities, but I've seen him at it. When I was that age, I rebelled by protesting the Vietnam War and writing poetry. This loser rebels by shelving library books in the wrong places. *Pathetic*.'

Steffen spits the last three syllables out of the corner of his thin lips. Jordi can't believe she ever considered kissing that mean slit of a mouth. She wouldn't have, if Dana hadn't planted the idea in her subconscious. It dawns on Jordi that Dana, even in her absence, is the heart of this ugly little scene. She's what brought Jordi to the library alone, what drew Steffen to her side. If she and Steffen hadn't been standing so close, Nolan might never have come over. It was Dana's energy – the lusty attention-hungry vortex of her being – that pulled all these people together in a stew of desire and conflict.

A faint thrumming in her temple, like the rhythmic clack of a distant train, distracts Jordi from the Nolan/Steffen standoff. The two men, and the cluster of people around them, seem to be outlined in a milky haze. The thrumming in her head intensifies. Her right eye begins to twitch. She leans over the table and rests her head in her hands. Jordi closes her eyes, but the haze continues to swim behind her eyelids. She hears voices far away, a staccato of anxious chatter. One of the voices separates itself from the rest and stretches towards her consciousness, deep and soothing.

'Hey, Jordi. Are you all right?'

Nolan's standing at her side, rubbing the valley between Jordi's shoulder blades.

'I think I have a migraine.' Each word she speaks cuts her ears like a stainless steel blade. 'Or else . . .'

'Or else what? Tell me. You're scaring me here. You're as white as a ghost.'

Jordi glances up out of the cavern she's created with her fingers. Nolan is gazing down at her. There's a sharp groove between his eyebrows that Jordi's never seen before, and his lips are pale. Her heart reaches up to him with both hands, longing for everything she sees in those multi-colored green eyes of his. She loves him for being scared. She loves him for admitting it. She loves him for finding the exact spot on her spine where all her worries and doubts live, and for caressing them momentarily away. The milky light that fills Jordi's head is creeping around Nolan, engulfing him in swirling waves. The movements of the waves make Jordi seasick. She grips the edge of the table and catches herself before she topples off the stool.

'It could be someone doing something on the network, something through LIRA. Sabotaging me, maybe.'

Nolan's hand stops rubbing. One heavy black eyebrow

rises, and that infinitesimal motion changes the concern on his face to skepticism.

'I think you're getting a little paranoid, Jordi. Let me take you home. Security's about to ask us to leave, anyway. Might as well go with our dignity intact.'

Jordi nods weakly. She lets Nolan help her off the tall stool and lead her away. Funny how everything seems to be dissolving all around her, not only Steffen and the librarians and security guards, but all the solid fixtures of the library. Everything with mass or height or color seems to be melding into one giant pulsation of light.

How could Nolan brush off something like this as simple paranoia? None of the developers knows what kind of long-term effects LIRA could have. The connections they made are embedded in the group psyche. If one of them has some kind of crisis, who knows what could happen to the rest of the team? Or what if one of them, even one, were to lose faith?

Nolan's arm is wrapped around Jordi, but she still has a crazy sense that she could lose her balance at any moment. If this is a migraine, it's a doozy – but it can't be a headache if there's no 'ache' involved. Jordi doesn't feel the slightest twinge of pain, just a sense of disorientation that's making her world increasingly surreal.

'Nolan, let's not wait for the bus,' Jordi says, when they've escaped the evaporating library. She leads him to the curb, where a yellow cab happens to be slowing down for the traffic light.

'Rich girl, huh?' Nolan teases. 'We can take the taxi, but only if you pay. Ten to one I won't have a job tomorrow. Gonna have to take my anarchy elsewhere.'

'Can I go with you?' Jordi says, worried all of a sudden that this hazy glow might be more than a hallucination, and everything familiar might really be in the process of vanishing.

Nolan does a double take. Then he takes her in his arms and holds her tight, squeezing till she almost loses her breath as he buries his face in her hair. 'You have to ask?' he whispers into her ear.

The cab honks. Nolan opens the door and helps Jordi get in, then he climbs in after her.

'Where we going, kids?' the driver asks through a wad of chewing gum.

Nolan slings his arm across Jordi's shoulders. 'To my girl's place. I'm taking her home.'

'Home to bed,' Jordi adds. She sees a smarmy grin twist the driver's profile. Then she turns nine shades of hot pink, one for each circle of Hell.

'Good idea. You need to lie down in a dark room,' Nolan says. 'When my mom used to get headaches, she'd make us turn out every light on the block.'

'Who said I have a headache?' Jordi asks. 'Just a little glitch in my perception, I think.'

Jordi smiles. The light around Nolan's head illuminates the ends of his hair, making it look like he's wearing a jagged halo. Nolan grasps her hand. His palm feels warm and clammy. A pulse in his wrist beats light and fast. His face is so sweetly serious; traces of worry still crease the corners of his mouth. If it weren't for the pervy cab driver, she'd kiss Nolan until all signs of gravity were gone. Instead, she takes the hand that's holding hers and leads it down the length of her thigh, to the notch between her legs. She presses their intertwined fingers against the mound of her pussy. The movements of the cab through traffic increases the pressure every few seconds, and the cloth of her jeans and panties creates a friction that makes her bite her lip.

Nolan's breathing grows husky as he leans against her, partly to hide them both from the cab driver's rear-view mirror voyeurism, and partly so that he can subtly stroke the side of her hidden breast with his free hand.

At that moment it's clear to Jordi that though Dana's blog has vanished into cyberspace, Dana herself never disappeared. She's right there with them, urging Jordi on: Go ahead, grab his crotch! Knead his hard-on with your fingernails while you kiss him and suck on his tongue. If he doesn't clue in to what you're offering, check his pulse.

Jordi doesn't have to check. The whole taxi-cab is filled with the drumbeat of Nolan's heart. Or her own. Or both, in syncopation, moving one city block at a time toward the thing they want more than anything else in the world.

Arms wrapped around each other's waists, Jordi and Nolan climb the stairs to her apartment. Nolan can't stop kissing her cheek, ear, and throat, even as she's digging for her keys and begging him to stop. Before she can turn the key in the lock, he backs her against the door, her wrists pinned on either side of her head, and nips at her neck. He growls into the hollow where her throat and shoulder meet; he grates her soft skin with his stubbled cheek till her laughter coasts into moans.

'Don't do that anymore,' she pleads. 'Why didn't you shave this morning?'

'Too busy thinking about you.'

'Thinking about me? If you were "thinking" about me, you could have at least returned my messages.'

Nolan stops playing. 'I was hurt, Jordi. You dumped me for a laptop computer.'

'She's not just any computer –' Jordi starts to argue. Nolan holds up his hand.

'Listen for a second. I know she's a special computer, but she's not a person. She won't tell you you're beautiful, and mean it in a hundred different ways. She isn't going to know when there's something wrong that you can't put your finger on, and she won't hold you when that "something" makes you cry. She won't protect you from mosh pits, or feed you ravioli, or take you to bed and give you multiple orgasms. She won't show you the coolness of misdirection, because creative chaos is a uniquely human phenomenon.'

'Hey, that's not necessarily true,' Jordi butts in.

'Wait, Jordi. I'm not done. I didn't call yesterday because I didn't know whether I wanted to see you ever again. I mean, I knew I *wanted* to see you, but I didn't think I should.'

Fear, an icy fist, socks Jordi in the belly. 'You wouldn't have ever kissed me again?'

Nolan shakes his head solemnly. 'Not if I'd decided that we weren't meant for each other.'

'What changed your mind?' Jordi is almost afraid to ask that question, but she has to know what's keeping Nolan here. Otherwise, how will she know how to make him stay?

'I remembered how you looked the other day at the library, when I put that pile of books in your arms. You were staring at me like I was crazy – which is true, by the way – but I knew you believed in me anyway. You didn't understand why I'm passionate about screwing up LOC and Dewey, but you respect my dedication. On top of that, your lips do this cute puckery thing when you're thinking that I'm full of shit. I've never seen a girl's lips do that before. It made me want to suck your mouth like a mango.'

He demonstrates by proceeding to suck her mouth like a mango, fixing his teeth on her plump lower lip. He interlaces his fingers with hers to keep her hands restrained. She yowls and wriggles in his grip, but not with any serious hope of breaking free. This is exactly where Jordi wants to be right now. He surges against her, his pelvis nudging hers in a clear invitation.

'Maybe it's time to go in,' she whispers.

'It's definitely time to go in.'

He lets go of Jordi long enough for her to open the door, and they half-fall into her apartment. Jordi looks around, embarrassed, expecting to find Tuan waiting for her, tapping his foot, his face a study in reproach and lewd curiosity. The living room is deserted.

'Samantha? Tuan?' Jordi calls. 'Anyone here?'

As if in response, a melodic chime goes off in the next room. The chime makes the hairs on the back of Jordi's neck stand up and wave. She's only heard that sound once in her life.

'Good. We have the place to ourselves,' Nolan says. 'Where's your bed anyway? I think I'm over that whole "let's wait to have sex" thing.'

'Shhh. Did you hear that?'

'Hear what?'

The chime rings again, like a call to prayer. Leading an impatient Nolan by the hand, Jordi tiptoes towards the kitchen. But the kitchen, as she remembers it, is gone. The sink, counters, and cupboards are faint outlines of what they used to be. Everything has been swallowed by the shimmering, iridescent vortex of light in the center of the kitchen table.

'Is that your computer?' Nolan breaks away from Jordi and approaches the table. 'Can I touch her?'

'Not yet. Let me try her first,' Jordi says. She sinks carefully onto a chair and taps a few keys on the keyboard. A luminous swell of pink fills the monitor, tapering off to lavender, then blue, and finally the palest lemon yellow.

'What are you doing?' Nolan asks.

Jordi turns to him. She's seen other people's faces light up in the past; now she actually *feels* her own face light up.

'I'm Threading. Someone's out there, reaching for me. It hasn't felt this good in ages, Nolan, not since the very first time it worked. That was the first and only time I've ever heard LIRA make that sound.'

'So what's going to happen next?'

'We're going to connect in ways we've never dreamed.'

'Couldn't we do that in your bedroom?'

'Wait. Just try her. Once.'

They're both speaking in hushed tones, as if they were standing at the bedside of a friend who'd been comatose for years and was just beginning to stir.

'If we're really going to connect in ways we've never dreamed,' Nolan says, 'aren't we wearing too many clothes?'

A prickly heat floods Jordi's face. Nolan peels off his T-shirt as if this were a strip poker tournament, not a demonstration of her software design genius. He scoots his chair closer to hers and leans in to look at the monitor. Other than her co-developers, he's the first person who's seen LIRA, her first genuine demo with a person who was aware that he was being Threaded. Jordi hasn't felt so nerve-wracked since the first time she tried to do a striptease for a boy she loved madly in her freshman year of college, and the clasp on her bra got stuck.

ANNE TOURNEY

'You too,' he says, nudging Jordi with his elbow. 'Take something off.'

Jordi squirms as the reality of imminent nudity hits her. 'You don't have to be naked to Thread. That's the whole point. With LIRA, you never have to show skin.'

'I guess I'm archaic, then. I still love skin.' Nolan stands up and moves behind Jordi, wrapping his arms around her, bending over to let his lips whisk her collarbone as he unbuttons her blouse. He starts with the top button and moves down, till she feels a cool draft tickling her cleavage. 'Especially yours.'

His hands slip down over the mounds of her breasts. Jordi wishes she'd worn a prettier, cleaner bra, but then, she doesn't really own any pretty, clean bras. Her underwear exists in varying states of disintegration. Sex changes so many things, she thinks, gripped by sudden panic. She'll need new underwear. Birth control. Probably a therapist. What if she has sex with this man she really likes, maybe loves, and she hates it? What if she can't get enough of the whole mess – the passion, the cuddling, the screwing – and she turns into a love junkie?

The glow emanating from LIRA's monitor lingers at a mellow shade of gold. It's a tender peaceful hue, warmly sensual, utterly human. It's the gold that falls over the face of a quiet maiden in an old Dutch painting. It's the gold of Jordi's grandmother's wedding ring. Under the surface of the light, a steady pulse is beating, strong and reliable as Jordi's heart – but not permanent. That Throb of desire is never permanent enough to take for granted.

'Let's go,' she says.

This time Jordi's the urgent one as she pushes back her chair. She leads a startled but happy Nolan to the cluttered nest where she's been hiding since she graduated from college. With one arm, she shoves three weeks' worth of dirty laundry and a couple of cyberpunk paperbacks off of her bed, then strips off the bedspread. A clear mattress stretches ahead of Jordi and Nolan, an expanse of sheer possibility.

They glance at each other. The air around them sings with the promises of a thousand afternoons like this, but this one moment, before it all begins, will never be repeated again.

'Ready?' Nolan asks with a grin.

Jordi doesn't bother to answer. She just reaches for him, and he reaches back, and they land together on taut trampoline of her bed, bouncing with laughter and desire and all the other juicy things that Jordi's always wanted to share with someone in the flesh. She rolls on top of Nolan, bracing his hips between her knees as she focuses on his body. Seeing all that skin, smooth and hairless, exposed makes her catch her breath. Nolan gasps as she bends over to lick his nipples; she's delighted to find that they get as hard as hers when she teases the pink discs with her tongue. Sucking, nipping, biting her way down Nolan's half-naked body, she leaves her mark on his skin in a dozen different ways: Jordi was here, and here, and here . . .

'You're mine,' she growls. 'I just wrote my name all over you.'

'I don't have a problem with that,' he laughs. 'You can leave your graffiti all over me. Just don't be surprised if I bite you back later.'

Nolan groans as she unbuckles his belt. He lifts his pelvis to let her drag his jeans and boxer shorts down his hips. As his hard cock springs away from his belly, she catches the shaft in the palm of her hand. Long, firm, flushed and quivering with currents of blood, his penis seems to hold everything about him that's both strong and vulnerable.

Taking the velvety head into her mouth, Jordi realises that she's never wanted so much to taste or see a lover's cock. She's never liked fellatio, period. The few times she agreed to try it, she always squeezed her eyes shut and tried to imagine that the guy's dick was a banana smothered in whipped cream. With Nolan she doesn't need the fantasy, or any fantasy; for once, meat life is so delicious that she wouldn't trade it for the wildest Throb imaginable. As she feels his erection nudge its way down her throat, she takes his balls in her hand and rolls them in her palm.

'Better not do that for too long,' he whispers, tugging at her hair.

She looks up in surprise. His face is strained with desire. 'What's wrong?'

'Nothing. Nothing at all. You're doing a great job . . . too great. I just don't want to come yet.'

'Why?'

'Because I want you to be first.'

'What if I can't?' Jordi asks.

He smiles. 'You can. You will. And when you do, I'm going to be watching. You have to get naked first, though.'

With some regret, Jordi leaves Nolan's hard-on and gets up to peel off her blouse and jeans. Standing in her bra and panties, she finds herself frozen with self-consciousness. Now she remembers one of the major drawbacks of meat sex – the terror of being naked in front of a thinking, seeing, judging human being. She'd even considered using that as a selling point to market LIRA: *When you're Throbbing, you never have to show skin.*

But the human being sitting on Jordi's bed is too busy

stripping off the rest of his clothes to examine Jordi's skin at any length, or consider her awkwardness. When he finishes, and watches her stepping out of her panties, there's no judgment on his face at all.

'This is sex, not a burlesque show, Jordi,' Nolan reminds her. 'Could you hurry it up a bit?'

Jordi sticks out her tongue at him, kicks her panties into a corner, and dives at him before he can make any comments about her figure. They wrestle, laughing and shoving and tickling each other, until Nolan pushes Jordi onto her back. His hardness against her belly makes her giggles die away. His touch isn't playful any more; his hands are skillful and sensual on her flesh. His fingers stroke her breasts, her waist, the cleft between her thighs and, as they do their blissful work, he watches Jordi's face as if his caresses had no purpose but to make her eyes and mouth change expressions.

To think that, at one time, she hoped to go the rest of her life without being touched ...

Jordi's never been the object of such prolonged attention before, not from anyone without a row of medical diplomas and a script pad at the ready. Not even her psychiatrist had been this focused on her, come to think of it. The intensity of Nolan's green eyes makes her stomach do funny things, but she doesn't let herself look away. She wants to remember all of this – the warm length of Nolan's body against hers, the firm pressure of his cock against her hipbone, the gentle interrogation in his eyes – just in case it never happens again. Not that it *won't* happen again, but Jordi's never been one to take erotic ecstasy for granted.

'You know what?' Nolan asks.

'What?'

'I've wanted to do this since the first day I met you.'

'Do what?'

'Get you so hot and wet that you forget about your computer.'

'Who says I'm hot and wet?'

Nolan reaches between her thighs and touches the slick folds of her pussy. He pets her fur, fondles her lower lips. He finds the button at the heart of her sex and ever-so-lightly strokes it. Her eyelids flutter and her hips begin to move in a private dance all their own.

'I rest my case,' he says, with a smug grin. 'You haven't talked about LIRA since we got in bed. Now I know the secret to making you pay attention to reality.'

'LIRA *is* reality,' Jordi argues faintly, with only ghost of her old rabid conviction.

'Yeah, maybe. But this reality is much, much better.'

He settles his weight on top of Jordi and kisses her – a deep and serious kiss this time, with no room for counter-argument. She reaches up to clutch the soft spikes of his hair, eagerly kissing him back. His tongue swirls along the tender inner surfaces of her lips, and when he penetrates her mouth with a sweet French kiss, he slides into her pussy. She yelps, feeling him enter her so suddenly, but after a few strokes she loosens and opens for him, and his cock feels like it's always belonged there. Kissing and fucking, joined in two places, their bodies feel like a continuum. Their fingers are intertwined, wrists pressed together, hearts thumping in tandem till the layers of bone and muscle seem to disappear. Soon Jordi can't tell where her skin ends and Nolan's begins, where her pulse starts and Nolan's takes over.

Then he pulls back a little and starts thrusting in earnest. Jordi spreads her thighs as wide as she can; he hooks her knees under his forearms and lifts her bottom. He's buried to the hilt now, the head of his cock angling against a deep hidden spot that makes her whimper with pleasure.

'Perfect,' Nolan whispers.

Jordi has no clue what he's talking about, until he tilts his pelvis to one side and slides his hand down to her pussy again. When the pressure of his fingers against her clit begins to match the friction against her inner walls, Jordi knows exactly what he's talking about. It's not just perfect, it's something else, some other adjective that Jordi can't think of at the moment, because she's rising away from the place where words make sense. She's soaring, swelling, all of her softest places tingling and tightening in a way that feels like the start of a sneeze. She hangs there for a few beats, coasting in silence, looking up into Nolan's face and wondering what the hell is going to happen next.

Then it happens. The orgasm unfurls from the core of her body and rolls outward, sweeping down her nerves, curling her toes and fingers. The tightness between her thighs bursts into sweet stinging spasms as the outer edges of her body seems to dissolve and float away. Her back arches, pushing her even closer to Nolan; he drives himself into her and fills her so completely that he sets off another cascade of waves. The waves gradually ebb, leaving her floating in a semi-conscious haze.

'That was better than a Throb,' Jordi murmurs in amazement. 'It felt like going up to heaven in a rocket.'

Jordi smiles up at Nolan. He doesn't smile back; he's too intent on finding his own groove. It doesn't take long before he's climbing to the peak she just left. He comes hard and fast, calling out her name, and, even though she's already had her orgasm (a real one – with another person!), she's still there with him, feeling the reverb of his climax.

'Did my eyes change colors when I came?' Jordi asks,

when Nolan collapses on her shoulder. He lies there, moist and panting, his half-erect penis still throbbing lightly as it glides along her thigh.

He turns his head. A grin spreads slowly across his face, making that adorable slash-that's-not-really-a-dimple come out in full force.

'Oh, yeah.'

'Really?'

'You'd better believe it. Like a sunrise.'

'You know what?'

'Hhnnnh?' Nolan asks sleepily. Jordi tugs on his earlobe, but he's already slipping into a post-orgasmic nap.

'Your eyes changed colors, too,' Jordi whispers.

Chapter Thirteen

Coming Together

Darling Deviant,

He saved me. I hate admitting this, especially in writing, but he inspired me to change my life.

No, not my father, though Daddy did agree to meet me at a coffee shop near the library when I told him that I was ready to set off in a new direction. I'm talking about Steffen, the Pervy Librarian. Steffen the Ten-Cent Psychoanalyst, Steffen the Freudian Voyeur. Once I'd stopped licking the wounds that his scathing little sketch had caused, I actually gave the dude's character assassination some thought.

That thought kept leading me to one conclusion: everything he said about me was true. I was an insecure, selfish, immature attention whore (please feel free to break in and reassure me, Dear Deviant, that none of this is true) who would never find true love unless she 'developed an integrated self', whatever that meant.

I knew what it meant; the truth was simply too ugly to look at for very long. To ease the pain a bit, I sat down in the Children's Section of the library and made a list. With my knees rising over the edges of a low round table, and a copy of *A Little Princess* sitting by my side for moral support, I wrote down what it meant to be incomplete. It meant that I was unfinished (in my own defense, I think of myself as a work in progress), that I was emotionally needy (read: passionate), and that I didn't have a clue who I really was or what I wanted (hey, who does?).

By the time I'd finished my list, it was time to meet my father. We'd made plans to get together at Café Wifi at three o'clock. As I strolled down the sidewalk, I could already see him sitting at a table. His round, ski-tanned face looked older than it had only a few days ago; I couldn't recall those sharp parentheses around his mouth, or the shadowed half moons under his eyes. His hair, a late-middle-aged version of my own, straggled in gray-red curls around his collar. The plaid shirt he wore under his ski vest was rumpled. A paperback novel sat on the table next to a cup of coffee (I noted with ironic amusement that it was the same military thriller that I'd seen in Steffen's library), but the spine was still uncreased. His fingers, instead of being occupied with his book or his drink, were shredding a paper napkin.

He looked like a tired, aging, anxious man who wasn't taking care of himself very well. I had to look twice to make sure that this man was the same one who'd thrown the ill-fated cocktail party that had landed me on the streets.

'Dad?'

He looked up sharply. When he saw me, his broad face rose in the shaky beginning of a smile, then fell. His mouth drooped. He got up from the table and pulled me into his arms, knocking over his mug and spilling coffee all over Some Rightwing Guy's novel. A red bear of a man, my father has never had much grace.

'You look so different, Dana.'

'So do you, Dad.'

He seemed oblivious to the coffee spill. I mopped up the liquid with what little was left of his torn napkin.

The clean-up kept me busy while I tried not to cry. I managed to choke down the messy, humiliating sobs, but I couldn't stop the tears that prickled my eyelids before coursing down my cheeks.

'Has it really been less than a week?' he asked.

'Yep.' I dragged my forearm across my nose, wiping it with my sleeve.

With a shaking hand, he pulled a handkerchief out of his pocket and wiped my nose properly for me.

'Come home,' he blurted.

'I can't,' I said.

'Why?' He gave me the anguished stare of a crestfallen basset hound. I couldn't believe I'd reduced this powerful, jovial, articulate man to grief-stricken monosyllables.

'Because you're right, Dad. I'm different.'

'You mean you're not a –'

'That's right. I'm not a slut any more. Or I'm seriously trying not to be, for once. That's why I can't go home with you. Besides, it's time I got my life, my own apartment. I have lots of plans.'

'Let's sit down. Tell me.'

We lowered ourselves into our seats. A barista belatedly popped up at our table to swab the rest of my father's coffee. She asked me if I wanted anything. I ordered a small cup of the Brew of the Day – black. Plain and simple were my new buzzwords.

'Get her a sandwich, too,' my father added. 'Club sandwich on sourdough bread, cut into eight triangles, with three pickle spears and two bags of potato chips. That's what you like, isn't it, darling?'

'Make that a turkey on wheat, hold the mayo. One pickle will do, and I don't need any potato chips,' I corrected him.

'So tell me your plans. Tell me everything,' he said, when the barista had sauntered away.

I doubted he wanted to know *everything*, but I did tell him about the brilliant idea that had struck me that morning, as I sat in the Children's Section of the library making an inventory of everything that was missing from my life.

'I'm going back to school,' I announced. 'I'm getting a Master's Degree in Library Science.'

A full-on sunrise dawned across my father's face. His eyes widened, and he began to beam as if I'd told him I'd won the Pulitzer Prize. He reached across the table and covered my hands with his bearlike paws.

'Darling! You aren't serious. You're going to be a *librarian*?'

I could see the word 'librarian' giving birth to a hundred hopes in my father's mind: Daddy's little tart would be a professional, a dignified member of her community, a *good girl*. All the old stereotypes of the prim strait-laced librarian were coming into play in his paternal fantasy, but I let them stand. He'd discover the truth soon enough.

'Calm down, Dad. I'm not joining a convent,' I said dryly. 'But, yes, I'm going to be a librarian. I want to work in a public library.'

'How did you... when... you never, ever showed any interest in a career like that,' he sputtered.

'You know I've always loved books.'

'Yes, but in a library?'

'I love books in libraries, and periodicals and multimedia. Especially when they're shelved correctly. I just see it as a good way to be surrounded by the books I love, while performing a public service.'

'Did you say "public service"?'

'Yes, Dad. I did. For once in my pitifully self-absorbed life, I want to help others.'

Poor Dad. The revelation of my new-found altruism, on top of the news of my career choice, was going to do him in. He pressed his beefy hand against his heart, as if to contain a joy that was too wild to bear. I wasn't about to tell him about my less-pristine motives for wanting to spend more time at the library, like my interest in exploring bondage with Christopher the Multimedia guru.

'Let me help you, darling. Tell me how much you need.'

As usual, when stranded on a peak of emotion, my father reached for his check book to salvage his image. For once in my life, I didn't pounce on the blank check he handed me. I let the slip of blue paper lie on the table between us for a moment, then I picked it up and folded it carefully.

'I won't take much,' I said. 'Just enough to put down a deposit on an apartment. I'll be paying my own way soon.'

'I want you to have as much as you need. I don't want you going without, Dana. I love you. You're my precious little girl.'

Hah. If he'd only seen me performing my daily toilette in the library bathroom, or exchanging sex with a security guard for a secure place to put my duffel bag! An evil impulse almost made me spill everything – where I'd been staying, what I'd been doing, *whom* I'd been doing.

'I don't want to lose you, Dana. You're the only child I have.'

I smiled. The evil impulse went away.

'And you're my only Dad,' I said.

My Sweet, Attentive Deviant, I drew the curtain over that last scene just before it erupted into full-blown tenderness.

Suffice it to say, that reunion with my father – which ended with the waitress bringing us a whole dispenser of napkins to sop up our tears – was the most embarrassing moment of both our lives, at least since the night I got caught doing the naked tango with his accountant.

We finally parted, with weepy hugs and one more blank check tucked in my pocket. He wanted me to come back to the penthouse till I could get settled in an apartment, but I didn't want to risk it. The allure of a life of pure hedonism was still too strong. Purified by tears and virtuous resolutions, I walked back to my temporary home. When the public library rose to greet me, in all its surreal splendor, I felt as happy as a duck.

Wiped out by the father/daughter catharsis, I decided to find my favorite purple chair and doze off over a trashy novel. But first I had a score to settle. My heart began to pound as I headed upstairs. By the time I reached the reference desk, my mouth felt like cotton, and a faint buzzing noise filled my ears. I didn't know what I was going to say to the man who'd penetrated every hole in my being and recorded the whole experience for posterity, but it wasn't going to be pretty.

Steffen sat in his usual post behind the reference desk. He looked no different from the first time I'd seen him: capable, self-possessed, sane. He was impeccably shaven and subtly handsome in a tweed jacket over a white Oxford shirt with an open collar. Sitting down with his hands folded, he gazed up into the heart-shaped face of a pretty blonde, probably sizing her up for one of his psychological dissections.

I stood back and watched him as I considered what to say. A few possibilities jumped to my mind:

'Steffen! How splendid to see you! You look disgustingly

well rested, for a man who stayed up all night playing kinky sex games.'

Or how about this:

'Why, Steffen, is this your new protégée?' (Glancing at blonde.) 'Really, you must show her your toy-box. I'm sure she'll look divine in a blindfold and pearls.'

No, too catty. A direct approach was best:

'Hey, asshole, who do you think you are, talking smack about me in your secret notebook – which is somewhere in the sewer by now, incidentally – after I let you do obscene things to my body all night?'

Steffen glanced away from his latest groupie for a second and saw me. I must have looked like Lady Macbeth, sans bloody spot, because he actually had the decency to lose color in his face. I stepped up to the desk. His new little friend turned and saw me too. Her cheerleader's ponytail twitched as she tilted her head to give me a twinkly smile.

I stared at her, wondering what character defects Steffen would unearth behind that fresh young face.

Then I stared at Steffen.

'Thank you,' I heard myself say.

He cleared his throat. His sandy eyebrows rose above the rims of his glasses. 'For what?'

'For being my host last night. For the lovely dinner, and the even lovelier dessert. Mostly, thank you for showing me who I was. *Was*,' I repeated, for emphasis.

Then I spun around on the heel of my sneaker and walked away. I have no idea who inspired me to thank that man for slashing my character to ribbons. Maybe it was you, Dear Deviant; you are much wiser and more compassionate than me.

Before I could retire to my purple chair, I had one more

task on my agenda. I hoped the line at the check-in desk for the public computers wouldn't be too long. All these reunions and confrontations and clearing of my karma were wiping me out. I wasn't looking forward to the last item on my list. Releasing this tender piece of myself was going to be painful, and as you know by now, I'm no masochist.

'OW! Watch out!'

Speaking of pain, I'd just collided with a cartload of books, steered by a shelver who'd come hurtling out of one of the aisles as I passed by.

'God, I'm sorry. Are you OK?'

'Barely. I'm going to have a bruise on my hip the size of Brazil.'

The crazed driver looked worried. He was probably more concerned about his job than about me, but his face was still sweetly sincere. I felt that old switch in the pit of my belly flip on as I looked into his swirly hazel eyes. Cute. Punky. Iconoclastic. I'd guess he had a few tattoos in strategic places under those black jeans. He was the kind of misfit who used to fascinate me in high school, the type who hung out behind the gym smoking, and played in a garage band on weekends. He'd be cruelly aloof when you first approached, but once you admitted that you'd always gotten wet for Joey Ramone, you'd have his heart forever.

'What's your name?' he asked, squinting at me through his Buddy Holly glasses. The shelver was holding a copy of *A Confederacy of Dunces.* He saw me take note of the novel, and, from the guilty shadow that flickered across his green eyes, I guessed he'd been reading it as he shoved his cart down the aisle. I couldn't blame him. I love that book too. It glorifies the rebellious loser, the creatively destructive outcast. In my heart, I've always known I was part of that tribe.

I took a few seconds to think about how to respond to his question. Then I said, 'Jordana.'

'Jordana,' he repeated. He rolled the syllables around on his tongue, as if he were tasting them, then he smiled. I guessed my name tasted good. 'Never heard that name before. I like it. It's got a certain ... I don't know what.'

'Integrity?' I asked hopefully.

'Maybe. But I was thinking something more like dignity. It's dignified. And sexy, at the same time.'

'I've always hated it. I've tried shortening it in different ways. Most recently I was going by "Dana", but that doesn't fit me anymore.'

'No,' he said thoughtfully. 'It doesn't. Jordana is much better.'

I was starting to like this guy. From the way he cocked his head and met my eyes without blinking, I guessed he liked me too. We stood there in the 800s, just hanging around enjoying that starting-to-like-each-other buzz.

'Turnabout's fair play. What's your name?' I asked.

'It's Jack. Jack Nolan,' he said. 'Hey, what do you like to do for fun?'

A hundred lush images from the Kama Sutra cascaded through my mind. I could picture Jack in most of those positions; he looked like a flexible guy. But I was a new woman, I reminded myself sternly. The new Dana – no, Jordana – didn't flash straight to sex as the answer to every conceivable question.

'I hang out at the library,' I said. 'I love to read. And I play around on the computer whenever I get the chance.'

'Really? You don't seem like a computer geek, to me.'

'What does a computer geek look like?'

He tapped his toe, in its bulky combat boot. 'Well, geeky. Sweet, but a little defensive, like she'd kick your ass if you made fun of her. She's quiet, doesn't have much of a sex life.'

'Whereas I look like I have the sex life of a concubine?'

His neck flushed red, from his jawline all the way down to the top of his sternum. I would have liked to follow that flush, just to see how far down the red went, but I wasn't that type of woman anymore.

'That's not what I meant,' he said. 'I just meant that you look like you could have any guy you wanted.'

'I don't know. I think there's a hidden geek in me somewhere,' I said. 'Which reminds me, I have to go and take care of something. Will you be around later? I'd like to keep talking. That is, if you want to.'

'Do I want to? Are you kidding?'

Jack laughed. I liked his laugh; it was scratchy and wild and rough around the edges. After he got off work, I'd guess he hung out at punk clubs in the Warehouse District. I wouldn't mind mixing it up with Jack in a mosh pit . . . or in a bed, or a bathtub, or a public library.

I left Jack with his cartload of books and went to the public access computers. Luckily there wasn't much of a line; I waited less than five minutes before I was assigned a log-in code by the godmotherly Guardian of the Computers. I logged in and found the blog where I'd been writing the story of the girl I had wanted to be. She was too smart for her own mental health, too much of a geek to date, far too inhibited for casual sex. In other words, she was condemned to get to know herself before she would ever be brave enough to risk falling in love. When she did fall in love, it would be deep and wild, but it would also be comfortable and real. She'd love another geek, someone intense and sincere, who would love her back. He'd give her the first orgasm she'd ever had with a real live lover, and, while she came, he'd watch her eyes change colors.

'Bye, Jordi,' I said. Then I crossed my fingers and added in a whisper, 'Love is really accessible.' That was the spell we shared.

I chose 'Delete Blog' from a drop-down menu. A pop-up box asked me if I was sure I wanted to permanently and irrevocably wipe Jordi from the face of the earth.

I clicked 'Yes'. I knew she hadn't been deleted. Jordi and I were just coming into our own.